喚醒你的英文語感！

Get a Feel for English !

喚醒你的英文語感！

Get a Feel for English!

數位英文履歷寫作指南

外商企業
全球人脈
跨國團隊

寫作指南

*Job Application Writing
for Success in the Digital Age*

作者 **Nigel P. Daly**

連結社群創新自我行銷力

- 求職寫作逐步完成
- 個人化的履歷健診
- LinkedIn再晉級

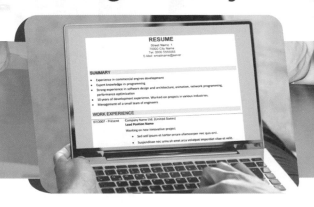

貝塔語言出版
Beta Multimedia Publishing

高點 美語系列

CONTENTS

PART 3 LETTERS and EMAILS

緒論
INTRODUCTION

數位履歷躍升求職利器

Writing to find a job

關鍵

Key point

在現今數位時代，想在國際商務領域謀得一份工作，最重要的語言技能就是寫作。企業招募人員在決定是否致電安排面試之前，對求職者的第一印象完全僅來自於其所書寫的內容。求職者需要知道如何：寫一份客製化履歷、職缺詢問信和求職信、與招募人員電子郵件通信、建立一個有說服力的 LinkedIn 個人檔案、在 LinkedIn 上發布交友邀請和評論來拓展人脈（networking）、請求寫推薦信，以及擬出自我介紹影片的腳本。

本書旨在協助你運用書寫的表達技巧，讓招募人員產生最深的印象，進而大幅度地提高你參加面試的機會。

學習藍圖

Plan

- 正在尋找跨國企業的職位？
- 了解自己，找到適合自己的工作。
- 數位時代的求職現況
- 數位招聘流程
- 現實生活中的你與網路上的你都在為你謀職
- 善用 "KISSES" 守則編寫數位履歷

正在尋找跨國企業的職位？

　　根據調查，一間大型國際公司的每一個招募職位約有 250 名求職者爭相應徵，而平均只有 5 名求職者會被邀請參加面試，最後只有 1 名被錄用。（Glassdoor，2015 [1]）這些企業職缺的競爭正是如此激烈。

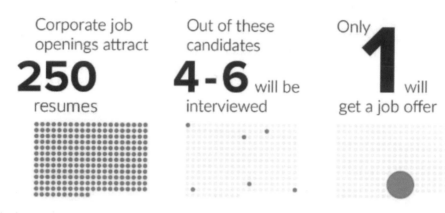

Figure [2] from Reference [9]

　　歡迎來到銷售世界！

　　你說什麼？你不想找銷售工作？

　　沒關係。一旦你開始找工作──任何工作──你就是在賣東西。你能猜出你是在賣什麼嗎？

　　沒錯──就是你自己！

　　當你找工作時，你需要吸引招募人員的注意力（以好的理由！）並展現出你就是該公司所需要的人才。這意味著你需要確保該公司正在招募的（如徵才廣告中所述）與你所能夠提供的（呈現於履歷和 LinkedIn 個人檔案）之間存在良好的媒合。而此過程的第一階段成敗全憑寫作見真章。從公司的角度來看，「你是誰」100% 是由你的寫作定義：你所表達的內容以及如何表達。

　　如果你的目標是從事國際商務或研究工作，你需要能夠用英語能力證明你的可信度。如果你的英文寫作足夠有說服力，你就會得到面試的機會。

求職過程中首先需要的寫作類型就是履歷。根據最近一項求職網站 CareerBuilder.com [2] 委託民調機構哈里斯民調（Harris Poll）所做的調查（2019），以下是招募人員剔除履歷的一些重要原因：

- 沒有溫度的應徵信函（未使用招聘經理的名字）—— 84%
- 面試後沒有感謝信—— 57%
- 不是量身訂製的履歷（未客製化）—— 54%
- 沒有求職信—— 45%
- 面試後未再主動聯繫應徵公司—— 37%

本書的目標在於確保你的英文寫作是專業的且具說服力，足以讓你獲得面試機會，並幫助你避免因上述原因被淘汰。讀完這本書，你將了解如何用專業的、有說服力的英文寫出：

- 履歷（Resumes）
- 求職信（Cover Letters）和其他應徵工作的電子郵件（Emails）
- 推薦信（Reference Letters）

並且由於約 87% 大型跨國公司的招募人員使用 LinkedIn 來搜尋或查看求職者的訊息（Jobvite，2016 [3]），因此本書還將協助你：

- 建立 LinkedIn 個人檔案
- 洞悉社群媒體研究和人脈拓展策略

簡而言之，你將擁有所有語言工具和數位寫作策略以最大化獲邀面試的機會，進而成為 250 名應徵者中的 4 到 6 名雀屏中選者之一。

了解自己，找到適合自己的工作。

如果你是應屆畢業生或打算轉換跑道到另一個職業，通常不太確定自己有什麼選擇，以及那些工作是否適合自己？但是不用擔心，現在有許多網路資源可助你一臂之力——也就是職業適性測驗（career aptitude test），這些測試會詢問你有關你的個性、技能和工作偏好等問題。

在 CareerExplorer.com 上可找到最全方位的免費職業適性測驗。這次測試我個人花了 30 多分鐘，所以對非英文母語人士可能需要 45 分鐘或更長時間。

確實很耗時，但這是非常有用的時間投資，因為你不僅可因此更了解自己，還能得知許多關於你的人格特質、技能和工作偏好的相關實用詞彙。該職業適性測驗會詢問有關人格特質的問題以測定你的獨特性格，詢問有關工作偏好的問題以媒合職業，並詢問有關你的教育背景或取得學位等問題，以提出更進一步鎖定的職涯建議。

此測驗的測試結果相當具有啟發性，對我的描述非常地準確。我是一個天生好奇的人，我熱愛學習、研究和教學。我對教育和商業都充滿熱情，我認為我蠻有創意且具革新精神。因此，從我的 CareerExplorer.com [4] 適性測驗報告（見下圖）中看到關於我的概述：

- 興趣取向是企業型（Enterprising）
- 性格取向是友善親切（Agreeableness）
- 性格特質是創新（Innovation）
- 技能偏好是教學（Teaching）
- 因為分屬企業型和研究型，人格原型是策畫者（Mastermind）
- 推薦職業是產品經理（Product manager）和市場研究分析師（Market research analyst）

雖然我更像是一名教師、研究員和創業家，但如果我必須選擇非教學領域的職業，產品管理和市場研究分析肯定是我將會很喜歡的兩項工作。

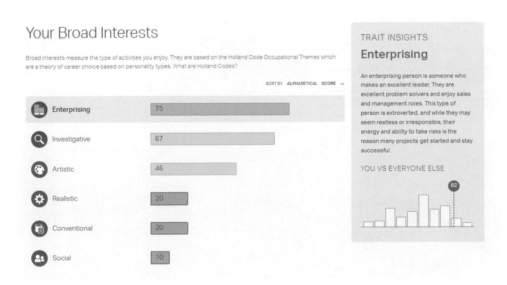

Figure [3] from CareerExplorer.com

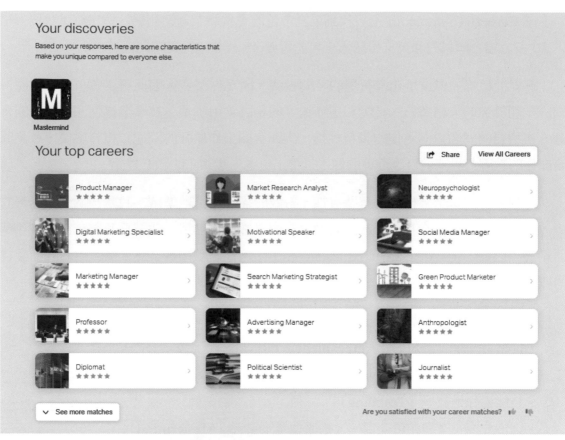

Your discoveries

Based on your responses, here are some characteristics that make you unique compared to everyone else.

M
Mastermind

Your top careers

Share | View All Careers

Product Manager ★★★★★	Market Research Analyst ★★★★★	Neuropsychologist ★★★★★
Digital Marketing Specialist ★★★★★	Motivational Speaker ★★★★★	Social Media Manager ★★★★★
Marketing Manager ★★★★★	Search Marketing Strategist ★★★★★	Green Product Marketer ★★★★★
Professor ★★★★★	Advertising Manager ★★★★★	Anthropologist ★★★★★
Diplomat ★★★★★	Political Scientist ★★★★★	Journalist ★★★★★

∨ See more matches

Are you satisfied with your career matches? 👍 👎

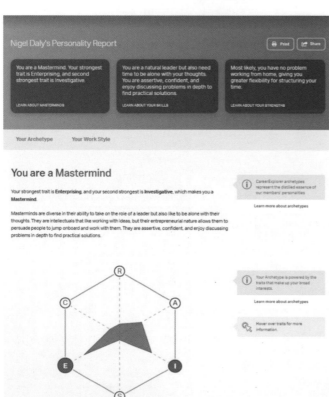

Nigel Daly's Personality Report

🖨 Print | ↪ Share

You are a Mastermind. Your strongest trait is Enterprising, and second strongest trait is Investigative.

LEARN ABOUT MASTERMINDS

You are a natural leader but also need time to be alone with your thoughts. You are assertive, confident, and enjoy discussing problems in depth to find practical solutions.

LEARN ABOUT YOUR SKILLS

Most likely, you have no problem working from home, giving you greater flexibility for structuring your time.

LEARN ABOUT YOUR STRENGTHS

Your Archetype | Your Work Style

You are a Mastermind

Your strongest trait is **Enterprising**, and your second strongest is **Investigative**, which makes you a **Mastermind**.

Masterminds are diverse in their ability to take on the role of a leader but also like to be alone with their thoughts. They are intellectuals that like working with ideas, but their entrepreneurial nature allows them to persuade people to jump onboard and work with them. They are assertive, confident, and enjoy discussing problems in depth to find practical solutions.

ⓘ CareerExplorer archetypes represent the distilled essence of our members' personalities

Learn more about archetypes

ⓘ Your Archetype is powered by the traits that make up your broad interests.

Learn more about archetypes

Hover over traits for more information.

Figure [4–5] from CareerExplorer.com

數位時代的求職現況

根據美國蓋洛普（Gallup）報告（2017 [5]），求職者經由以下這些地方尋找工作：

- 公司網站——77%
- 推薦轉介——71%
- 來自朋友或家人的建議——68%
- 網路求職網站（Monster.com、CareerBuilder.com）——58%
- 某個領域的出版品或網路資源——57%
- 綜合搜尋網站（Google、Bing、Yahoo）——55%
- 專業社群網站（LinkedIn）——47%
- 專業或校友會組織——41%
- 新聞媒體——39%

台灣的統計數據大抵是類似的，但這裡最受求職者歡迎的網路求職網站是「104 人力銀行」，它是台灣排行第 43 的最常被造訪網站，也是全球排行第 35 的最常被造訪之求職‧徵才網站。下表列出了求職者的其他常用資源：

台灣公司經常在以下網站發布職缺	大多數新創企業或外國公司在以下網站發布職缺
1. 104 人力銀行	1. LinkedIn
2. 1111 人力銀行	2. Meet.jobs
3. 518 熊班	3. Yourator 新創‧數位人才求職平台
4. yes 123 求職網	4. CakeResume

其他的職缺來源是特定的公司網站，這些網站經常發布工作機會。另外，像是每年三月在台大、台科大舉行的徵才活動也值得去探索。「台灣就業通」網站（https://www.taiwanjobs.gov.tw）也有線上就業博覽會。

問題是許多求職者將他們的求職活動限制在上述網路人力銀行。根據職涯顧問 Austin Belcak 的說法，「許多求職者通常將 80% 到 90% 的時間花費在投遞履歷應徵工作，剩餘的時間才花在拓展人脈，但這意味著你基本上把大部分時間都花在了勝算最低的地方。」（引自 Seaman，2020 [6]）。相反地，人們應將大部分時間花在拓展人脈，例如利用 LinkedIn 等專業社群網站（參閱第 6 章和第 7 章），其餘時間再丟履歷和進行其他部分。與你想應徵的公司之內部人員建立關係並向他們展示你能夠為該公司創造的價值可提高他們推薦轉介你的機會，同時亦可增加你從潛在雇主那裡得到回覆的可能性。

數位招聘流程

在大型跨國公司，你的工作申請可能會經由下列四個單位審閱：人工篩選者、人資專員、人資主管，以及一台求職者追蹤系統（Applicant Tracking System，ATS）裡的機器。

- ATS 機器（Machine ATS）：一種專門的電腦系統，用於分析履歷與申請函件的相關關鍵字。
- 人工篩選者（Human screener）：一般是人力資源部門的資淺職員，負責初步檢查是否符合基本資格。
- 人力資源招募人員（Human recruiter）：外部人資顧問或內部人力資源員工審查篩選出來的履歷，為招聘經理列出一個較短的名單。
- 招聘經理（Human hiring manager）：經常性監督新聘員工的決策者。

通常，這四個審閱者組成了一個三階段的篩選過程，如下圖所示。

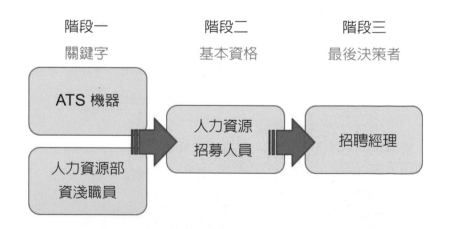

大約 90% 的「《財星雜誌》全球 500 大企業」使用求職者追蹤系統（ATS），大約 70% 的大公司和 20% 的中小企業（SME）（2022 [7]）也是如此。因此，了解 ATS 如何審閱履歷，並將系統分析之資訊如何傳達至 HR，可減少犯錯並降低被篩去的可能性。我們將在第 4 章和第 5 章對此進行更多討論。

現實生活中的你與網路上的你都在為你謀職

我們生活在一個資訊時代，大部分時間都花在網路上。因此，你應該意識到，招募人員審核的不僅僅是你的數位履歷，還包括你的線上自我或網路足跡——這對某些人來說可謂是雙面刃。

你的網路形象可能會導致你求職遭拒。根據 CareerBuilder.com 委託民調機構哈里斯民調所做的調查（2018 [8]），70% 的公司在社群媒體上查詢求職者，其中 57% 的公司因此發現了一些讓他們拒絕求職者的東西。以下是招募人員在經過搜尋後刷掉求職者的幾個主要原因：

- 搜尋挑釁或不當的照片、影片或資訊——40%
- 不實的資格證書——27%
- 不專業的網路暱稱——22%

即使你在網路上發布的內容可能會導致問題，但擁有網路形象也很重要。在同一份 CareerBuilder.com 報告中，47% 的招募人員表示「如果在網路上找不到某位求職者的資訊，他們就不太可能給予面試機會了」。

因此，你需要盡最大努力打造積極的網路形象。該如何做？根據上述 CareerBuilder.com 市調，招募人員透露了他們希望看到求職者的網路身分是具有專業形象的：

- 擁有支持其專業資格的背景資訊——37%
- 擁有傳達專業形象的網站——33%
- 展現出色的溝通技巧——28%
- 擁有優質的推薦背書——23%
  甚至
- 擁有大量關注者或訂閱者——18%

所有這些專業網路形象皆可在 LinkedIn 個人檔案中完整創建，且有助於在 Google 的搜索引擎中將你的名字排列在非常前面的位置。我們將在第 6 章詳細討論。

善用 "KISSES" 守則編寫數位履歷

無論是人類還是機器閱讀你的求職資料，你的所有文件都應該用 "KISSES" 來寫。這是基本的 "KISS" 溝通術的進階版，尤其適用於數位時代的任何寫作：

KISSES = Keep It Simple, Specific, Engaging, and Scannable
簡單明瞭、具體、引人入勝以及可供 ATS 機器掃描辨識

一般而言，商務寫作的用語和文法——尤其是求職文件——應該簡單明瞭（Simple），以使閱讀變得快速、容易；內容應該是具體的（Specific），包括數字和舉例，盡可能支持和闡明你的想法；內容也應該引人入勝（Engaging），能夠快速吸引讀者的注意力。俗話說，數位時代的讀者「注意力短、選擇性多」（short on attention and long on options），就找工作這檔事，翻譯成白話文就是「求職者比比皆是，所以你最好盡快把招聘單位的目光吸引到你身上」。

不分履歷、電子郵件或社群媒體貼文，寫作的格式都應該是可透過 ATS 機器解讀的（Scannable），以便閱讀和獲取主要資訊。空白、項目符號、短段落和章節標題皆有助於提升機器判讀性，非常重要。

本書介紹和章節概述

本書涵蓋了求職過程中的所有寫作需求，分為三個 parts：1. 履歷、2. LinkedIn、3. 信件和電子郵件。

在 Part 1，你將學習展示自己的優勢、創建個人品牌以及設計求職中最重要的文件——履歷所需之策略和用語。尤其是第 1 章，將幫助你打造涵括專長技能、工作經驗和個性的專業詞彙庫，以創建你最需要的令人印象深刻的個人品牌。這些將會是你在幾乎所有的求職寫作和口語（面談和電話面試）中會反覆使用的詞彙。

在 Part 2，你將會探索數位時代的求職寫作技巧，並使用 LinkedIn 建立無遠弗屆的個人線上形象。你還能夠利用 LinkedIn 來研究你感興趣的公司，甚至主動聯繫他們的員工。當你正在尋找工作時，這種網絡非常強大好用。其中還包含一個關於製作自我介紹影片的章節，你可將影片放在 LinkedIn 上，進一步讓你從其他求職者中脫穎而出。

在 Part 3，你將學習如何在面試之前和之後編寫所有需要發送的信件和電子郵件。

各章節包含筆者的見解、策略、範本／模板和關鍵語言技巧，有助於創造專業的求職作品集，從而大大提升獲得面試的機會。此外，還有增加理解和手感的實作單元：「Assignment」與「Exercise」，其中練習題的答案統一收錄於書末，幫助確實驗收學習成效。最後則是附錄，網羅了書中介紹的求職寫作範例，方便快速查找。

這本書的性質是一本指南。在每一章節讀者都將與一位名叫婕拉比（Jellabie）、正將展開求職的女孩對話，過程中她的每一步都從經驗豐富的人資招募人員那裡獲得建議：從寫履歷到在 LinkedIn 的網絡上開啟個人檔案，再到面試前後編寫信件和 email。這些對話是特別為求職經驗尚不足者所編寫的，而如果你已經有這方面的經驗，亦可略過對話部分，專注在筆者為各位精心彙整的求職寫作技巧、例子與文法練習。

希望本書內容對你發揮令人驚艷的功效。真誠地祝你好運，以及求職路上獲得許多青睞（KISSES）！

ocabulary 求職詞彙庫

名詞

career occupation vocation	職業	job opening vacancy vacant position	職缺
employment agency job fair job bank	職業介紹所 就業博覽會 人力銀行	job security	就業保障
headhunter human resources recruiter	獵才顧問 人力資源 招募人員	online job sites	求職網站
		probation / trial period	試用期
job full employment	工作 全職工作	promotion	晉升
job advertisement / job ad	徵才廣告	term contract work contract	定期合約 工作合約
job offer	工作機會		

動詞

apply for a job (to a company)	應徵工作	make a career	開創事業
appoint sb. manager appoint sb. to a post	任命某人為經理 任命某人某職位	promote sb. to ... upgrade sb. to ...	升遷某人至……
be in work have a job	在工作 在職中	recruit sb.	聘用某人
be job-hunting look for a job	找工作	sign a contract with sb.	與某人簽訂合約
demote sb. downgrade sb.	將某人降職 將某人降級	submit a job application	提交應徵申請
employ sb. as ... hire sb. as ...	僱用某人為……	take sb. on	僱用某人
fill a post	擔任某職位	transfer sb. to ...	將某人調任……

其他詞彙

agreeableness	友善親切
alumni organization	校友會組織
applicant tracking system (ATS)	求職者追蹤系統（ATS）
aptitude tests	適性測驗
digital online self	數位線上自我
enterprising	有進取心的
entrepreneur	企業家
Fortune 500 companies	《財星雜誌》全球 500 大企業
give/receive a referral	給予／接受推薦
hiring manager	招聘經理
HR recruiter	人力資源招募人員
human screener	人工篩選者
innovation	創新
Internet footprint	網路足跡

investigative	探究性的
lies about credentials	不實的資格證書
market research analyst	市場研究分析師
mastermind	策畫者
networking	人脈拓展
online job sites	求職網站
personal brand	個人品牌
personality archetype	人格原型
positive online presence	積極的線上形象
product manager	產品經理
professional impression/image	專業印象／形象
professional network site	專業社群網站
professional online self	專業的線上自我
professional portfolio	專業作品集
provocative or inappropriate photographs	挑釁或不恰當的照片
screen (v.)	篩選
self-brand	個人品牌
short on attention and long on options	注意力短、選擇性多
small and medium-sized enterprises (SMEs)	中小企業
strong online presence	強大的線上形象
teaching	教學
trade	貿易
unprofessional screen name	不專業的網路暱稱

📝 Assignment ➡ 關於應徵工作的筆記

寫一些關於本章關鍵點的筆記，比方說數位求職·招聘流程、KISSES 等，可以的話，也請記錄下你的職業適性測驗結果（從 CareerExplorer.com 等網站）。

_____

_____

_____

_____

_____

_____

_____

_____

_____

_____

_____

_____

_____

_____

_____

_____

_____

PART 1

RESUMES

1

Figure [6]: Successful man photo by jcomp – Freepik.com

自我行銷 Self-branding

在找到工作之前,你需要先了解你自己。

You need to find yourself before you find a job.

Key point

反思你的優勢以及讓你與眾不同的特質,尋找合適的詞彙來描述你的工作經驗、技能和個性。請注意千萬別造假,因為招募人員通常在面試前或面試途中就能夠察覺到。

Plan

· 你的名字
· 你的優勢與成就
· 你的成功事蹟
· 創造成功的技能和人格特質
· 是什麼促成了你的成功?

─────── Insight 洞見 ▶

你與他人的履歷競爭是非常激烈的。平均而言,一個公司職缺會吸引 250 份履歷,而這些候選人中只有 4 到 6 人會被邀請參加面試。[1] 這意味著你的履歷必須完美無缺,或至少沒有任何語言錯誤。

同時，根據人力資源專家的說法，68.7% 的履歷問題與缺乏成就描述有關。（TheLadders）成就描述在履歷當中是相當重要的元素，可使求職者從競爭同一工作的其他 249 份履歷中突出重圍。

然而，描述工作經歷與技能的方式須特別留意：80.4% 的履歷錯誤來自對過往工作經驗的描述，71.6% 則來自在技能描述上的詞不達意。（TheLadders）此外，這份研究還發現，75% 的雇主在履歷上發現了不實內容。（CareerBuilder，2018）別忘了，招募人員在履歷和審查求職者方面經驗豐富，往往能夠察覺或發現謊言。（以上數據引自 Turczynski，2022 [9]）

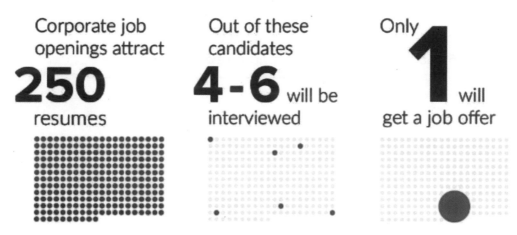

Source: Glassdoor

Figure [7] from Reference [9]

💬 Dialog

Jellabie (A) 是一名準備謀職的大學生，她正在向一位名叫 Jackson (B) 的職涯顧問諮詢她的履歷。

Dai Yi Ran

tel. 0955-5555   email: jellabie@school.edu   age: 21

Education

Jingmei Girls High School   2016-2019

Banciao University, New Taipei City   2019-2023

Bachelor of Arts

High scores; debate club

Experience

   Server at Bartissa Coffee Shop, intern at Epoch

戴怡然

電話：0955-5555   電子郵件：jellabie@school.edu   年齡：21

教育背景

臺北市立景美女子高級中學   2016-2019

新北市板橋大學   2019-2023

文學學士學位

成績優秀；辯論社

工作經驗

   Bartissa 咖啡館服務生、Epoch 實習生

A: I will graduate soon and I want to send out my resume to some companies. I think I would like to try working in sales. Can you look at my resume and give me some advice?

B: Sure. ... Well first of all, what is your name? Is your family name "Ran"?

A: No, you know it's Dai.

B: Yes, I know you, but the people reading your resume don't. What if they don't speak Chinese? They will assume your family name is Ran and your given name is Dai Yi.

A: So, I should write my name as Yi-ran Dai?

B: Yes. And if you're applying to an international company, it might be useful to use an English name if you have one. Yours is Jellabie, right?

A: Yes. I'll add it, too.

B: Back to the resume ... did you use this resume to get your server and intern jobs?

A: No. For those I just filled out an application form. Is the resume bad?

B: I'm afraid so. The recruiter will spend no more than two seconds on it before she throws it into the garbage.

A: No interview?

B: Nope.

A: That's not fair. She doesn't even know me.

B: Try to think about it from the recruiter's perspective. If it doesn't look neat, ... if it doesn't contain much information, ... and if it contains typos, it looks like you just don't care enough to put in the time to make a good impression. And no company wants to hire someone like that. Research shows that 61% of recruiters will reject a resume even if there is only one typo!

A: So, the recruiter will think that a sloppy and careless resume means that the applicant would be a sloppy and careless worker.

B: That's right.

> **A**：我馬上就要畢業了，我想投履歷給一些公司。我想嘗試從事銷售工作。你能不能幫我看看履歷，然後給我一些建議？
>
> **B**：沒問題……首先，妳叫什麼名字？妳的姓是「然」嗎？
>
> **A**：不是，你知道我姓戴。
>
> **B**：是啊，我認識妳，但看妳履歷的人並不認識妳。如果他們不懂中文怎麼辦？他們會假設妳的姓是然，妳的名字是戴怡。
>
> **A**：所以，我應該把我的名字寫成 Yi-ran Dai？
>
> **B**：沒錯。而且假如妳要應徵的是國際公司，有英文名字的話，使用英文名字可能會很有幫助。妳叫婕拉比（Jellabie），對吧？
>
> **A**：是的。我也會把它添加上去。
>
> **B**：回到履歷……妳是不是使用這份履歷去應徵妳之前的服務生和實習生工作？
>
> **A**：不是。之前我只有填寫了應徵申請表。這份履歷很不理想嗎？
>
> **B**：恐怕是這樣。招募人員應該會看不到兩秒就把它直接丟進垃圾桶裡。
>
> **A**：沒有面試機會？
>
> **B**：沒有。
>
> **A**：這太不公平了。她根本不認識我。
>
> **B**：妳試著從招聘者的角度來想想看。如果履歷看起來很亂，也沒有太多資訊……甚至還拼錯字，那會讓人覺得妳並不太願意去花時間給人留下好印象。沒有公司願意僱用這樣的員工。研究顯示，61% 的招募人員會淘汰打字錯誤的履歷，即便只有錯一個字！
>
> **A**：所以，招募人員會認為一份草率、不用心的履歷意味著該求職者也會是一個草率、不用心的員工囉。
>
> **B**：沒錯。

履歷範本：欠佳（Bad）

你發現到多少問題？

Dai Yi Ran

tel. 0955-5555   email: jellabie@school.edu   age: 21

Education

Jingmei Girls High School   2016-2019

Banciao University, New Taipei City   2019-2023

Bachelor of Arts

High scores; debate club

Experience

Server at Bartissa Coffee Shop, intern at Epoch

Interests

I like to watch movies, read books and magazines. I also like to travel.

Address

123 Chung Cheung Road, New Taipei City

References

Available upon request.

戴怡然

電話：0955-5555   電子郵件：jellabie@school.edu   年齡：21

教育背景

臺北市立景美女子高級中學   2016-2019

新北市板橋大學   2019-2023

文學學士學位

成績優秀；辯論社

工作經驗

Bartissa 咖啡館服務生、Epoch 實習生

興趣

我喜歡看電影、看書和雜誌，我也喜歡旅行。

地址

新北市中章路 123 號

參考

可依要求提供。

💬 Dialog

B: Apart from being a sloppy and incomplete resume, there is also another big problem: There is nothing that makes you stand out. I know you have some accomplishments, and you also have some skills and good personality traits. You need to add these.

A: I did win a model student award and I'm good at speeches.

B: You were on the debate team, right?

A: Yeah, I was the leader, and we even went to the national finals.

B: That's impressive. You need to put this on your resume!

A: But I don't want to show off.

B: It is not showing off. Tell the truth and show your strengths. Your resume highlights your self-brand. And all successful brands need to focus on what their strengths are.

A: Hmm ... a self-brand. OK.

B: So, write down all your successes and accomplishments. And then try to think what skill or personality trait helped you achieve these successes.

> **B**：除了草率、不完整之外，這份履歷還有另外一個大問題：沒有什麼能讓妳顯得突出。我知道妳有一些成功事蹟，並且有一些技能和良好的人格特質。妳需要把這些加上去。
>
> **A**：我確實有當選過模範生，而且我很擅長演講。
>
> **B**：妳以前是辯論隊的，對吧？
>
> **A**：是啊，我是隊長，我們還闖進了全國總決賽。
>
> **B**：那很令人印象深刻啊。妳要把它寫在妳的履歷上！
>
> **A**：但是我不想炫耀。
>
> **B**：那不是炫耀，而是說實話，展現妳的強項。妳的履歷會突顯妳的自我品牌。所有成功的品牌都需要聚焦它的優勢所在。
>
> **A**：嗯……自我品牌。OK。
>
> **B**：所以，寫下妳所有的成功經歷，然後試著想想是什麼技能或人格特質幫助妳取得了這些成功。

自我行銷：你的名字　▼

讓你與眾不同的最明顯的東西——至少在書面文件上——就是你的名字。

因為英語仍是商務的國際語言，所以如果你正在應徵國際公司的工作，尤其是跨國企業，書寫履歷姓名部分時最好遵循英文的慣例。

讓我們來看看 Jellabie 的英文名和中文名的不同寫法，以及這些不同的寫法意味著什麼。

名字的不同寫法	隱含意義
Yi-ran Dai (Jellabie) Yi-ran (Jellabie) Dai	我比較喜歡怡然，但是你可以叫我 Jellabie。
Jellabie (Yi-ran) Dai	叫我 Jellabie，不過我的中文名字是怡然。
Jellabie YR Dai	叫我 Jellabie，不過我的中文名字母縮寫是 YR。
YR Dai	怡然對非華語人士來說可能太難唸，所以叫我 YR 就好。

你的名字是你身分的關鍵，所以選擇你認為最合適的寫法。不過，假如你的名字對其他國家的人來說真的很難發音，你就應該考慮使用英文名字（如 Jellabie），或使用易於發音的名字縮寫（如 Yi），或甚至只用字母縮寫（如 YR）。

自我行銷：你的優勢與成就 ▼

在求職過程中，你需要推銷自己，並努力打造一個與眾不同的自我品牌（self-brand）。為此，請思考看看你的所有優勢和成就，例如：

- 工作經驗
- 技能
- 知識
- 人格特質

如果這方面你還不太清楚，請參閱緒論中的建議並做個職業適性測驗，如職涯探索網站 CareerExplorer.com [4] 所述。

現在我們來看 Jellabie 的履歷，我們首先注意到的是它很草率，這等於告訴招募人員 Jellabie 根本連檢查拼寫和格式的一致性都不在乎！

　　我們注意到的另一件事是，Jellabie 的優勢部分乏善可陳。招募人員的目光所及之處落在履歷中與職缺相匹配的工作經驗（Experiences）、技能（Skills）、教育背景（Education）和人格特質（Personality traits），同時他們也在徵才過程中密切關注任何有關你的個性和專業精神的蛛絲馬跡。

　　在準備履歷或其他求職資料時，選擇正確的詞彙和關鍵字方可使你展現專業度進而嶄露頭角。這類履歷關鍵字通常需要使用特定形式的文法來表達：

經驗（動詞）

例如：trained（訓練過）、managed（管理過）、organized（組織過）

技能（形容詞＋名詞）

例如：fluent English（流利的英語）、strong interpersonal skills（卓越的社交能力）、experienced negotiator（經驗豐富的談判者）

個性（形容詞）

例如：creative（有創意的）、dedicated（盡責的）、enthusiastic（富有熱忱的）

自我行銷：你的成功事蹟　　▼

　　你的成就是什麼？

　　我們都擁有一些成就。試想你的學校和校外經驗，你經歷過的比你想像的還要多。回想一下你以前在求學階段、住家社區、家庭或個人生活中取得的成功經驗，這些代表是你擅長並樂在其中的事情。比方說：

一次成功的學校活動	自己貢獻良多的成功專案
一次成功的社區活動	成功學會一項技能
成功克服具有挑戰性的狀況	一次成功的冒險經歷
引以自豪的財務成功	求學時期的獎項或成就
一個重要的團隊成功	創業成功

Vocabulary 描述成功經歷的動作動詞

找到正確的動作動詞（action verb）來描述成功經歷是很重要的。為此，你需要建立一個動詞詞彙庫，因為這些詞彙是在描述經歷，並且由於「經歷」發生在過去時間，因此務必使用過去時態（v-ed）。

—————— Insight 洞見 ▶

超過 2/3 的招募人員會在求職者的履歷中尋找相關的工作經驗 [3]，下列動詞詞彙對於描述經歷便可派上用場。

溝通技能 Communication Skills

negotiated	協商	interpreted	口譯
translated	翻譯	clarified	闡明
corresponded	通訊	encouraged	鼓勵
persuaded	說服	presented	發表

創作技能 Creative Skills

created	創造	presented	呈現
acted	表演	composed	作曲
established	建立	founded	創立
improvised	即興創作	introduced	引進
navigated	導引	originated	創始

數據 / 財務技能 Data / Financial Skills

computed	運算	documented	記錄
verified	驗證	allocated	分配
budgeted	編預算	compared	比較
estimated	估計	forecasted	預測
inventoried	盤點	invested	投資
predicted	預測	projected	預測
quantified	量化	recorded	記錄

支援技能 Helping Skills

assisted	協助	trained	培訓
volunteered	自願	aided	幫助
demonstrated	示範	facilitated	促進
helped	幫助	performed	執行
represented	代表	solved	解決
supported	支持		

管理／領導技能 Management / Leadership Skills

achieved	實現	attained	獲得
headed	領導	led	引導
managed	管理	oversaw	監督
delegated	委派	assigned	分配
supervised	監督	handled	處理
coordinated	協調	organized	組織
planned	計畫	established	建立
administered	管理	implemented	實施
recommended	推薦	executed	執行
launched	發動	initiated	發起
challenged	挑戰	incorporated	合併
intervened	調停	mediated	調解
motivated	激勵	prioritized	優先考慮
scheduled	計畫	united	使團結

效率技能 Efficiency Skills

eliminated	消除	downsized	縮小
lessened	減輕	edited	編輯
reduced	縮減	revised	修訂
simplified	簡化	streamlined	使有效率
maximized	最大化	heightened	提高
accelerated	加速	boosted	提升
enhanced	增強	expanded	擴展
leveraged	槓桿化	centralized	集中化
optimized	最佳化	prioritized	優先化

standardized	標準化	systematized	系統化
expedited	加速	merged	合併
outlined	概述	outsourced	外包
prevented	預防	reorganized	重組
synthesized	綜合	upgraded	升級

研究技能 Research Skills

analyzed	分析	wrote	書寫
detected	檢測	diagnosed	診斷
evaluated	評估	examined	檢查
investigated	調查	measured	測量
researched	研究	surveyed	調查
collected	收集	compared	比較
gathered	收集	reviewed	審查
searched	搜尋	identified	識別
located	定位	organized	組織
reported	報告	replicated	複製

教學技能 Teaching Skills

taught	教導	instructed	指導
trained	培訓	guided	引導
helped	幫助	lectured	講授
facilitated	促進	supported	支持
supervised	監督	encouraged	鼓勵
fostered	培養	aided	幫助
advised	建議	clarified	闡明
defined	定義	prepared	準備
communicated	溝通	evaluated	評估

技術能力 Technical Skills

programmed	【電腦】編程	built	建造
engineered	策畫	maintained	維護
operated	操作	reengineered	重新設計
remodeled	改造	calculated	計算

computed	運算	conducted	進行
analyzed	分析	assembled	組裝
designed	設計	devised	設計
transmitted	傳輸		

📝 **Exercise** ⇨ 寫下 3 ～ 5 個成功經驗

Experiences:

_____

_____

_____

_____

_____

_____

_____

履歷範本：描述 success

Jellabie 寫了三句話來描述她引以自豪的三項成功經歷：

- I led the university debate team to the national championships 2 times, and we came in second place.
- I won awards for excellent academic performance in high school and college.
- I achieved a TOEIC score of 790.

- 我曾帶領大學辯論隊參加過全國錦標賽 2 次，我們獲得了第二名。
- 我在高中和大學時期曾獲得書卷獎。
- 我的多益成績達到 790 分。

Exercise ⇨ 寫下 3 ～ 5 個句子描述你的成功經歷

請用上頁 Jellabie 的經歷作為範例。

My success: _____

_____

_____

My success: _____

_____

_____

My success: _____

_____

_____

My success: _____

_____

_____

My success: _____

_____

_____

創造成功的技能和人格特質 ▼

💬 Dialog

A: OK, so here are my three achievements:

- I led the university debate team to the national championships two times, and we came in second place.
- I won awards for excellent academic performance in high school and college.
- I achieved a TOEIC score of 790.

B: Wow. That is quite impressive. You see, you do have some interesting things to put on your resume. Now I'm starting to see how you are different from other people.

A: Is this self-branding?

B: Exactly. Now, before we go on to revise your resume, think about how you were able to achieve these successes.

A: What do you mean?

B: What were the skills or the personality traits you have that helped you achieve these successes? This can be difficult, so here is a list of words for personality and skills to help you figure it out.

> **A：** OK，以下是我的三項成就：
>
> - 我曾帶領大學辯論隊參加過全國錦標賽兩次，我們獲得了第二名。
> - 我在高中和大學時期曾獲得書卷獎。
> - 我的多益成績達到 790 分。
>
> **B：** 哇。這相當令人印象深刻。妳看，妳確實有一些很吸睛的東西可加在履歷上。現在我開始看到妳和其他人的不同之處了。
>
> **A：** 這就是自我行銷嗎？
>
> **B：** 沒錯。現在，在我們繼續修改妳的履歷之前，想想看妳是如何取得這些成功的。
>
> **A：** 什麼意思？
>
> **B：** 是什麼技能或人格特質幫助妳達成了這些成功事蹟？這可能很困難，所以這裡有一個關於個性和技能的單字表能助妳一臂之力。

adventurous	勇於冒險的	extroverted	外向的
ambitious	雄心勃勃的	flexible	靈活的
approachable	平易近人的	focused	專注的
articulate	口齒伶俐的	friendly	友好的
autonomous	自主的	honest	誠實的
calm	冷靜的	imaginative	有想像力的
charismatic	有領袖魅力的	independent	獨立的
cheerful	開朗的	inexperienced	初出茅廬的
clever	聰明的	inquisitive	好奇的
competitive	有競爭力的	insightful	有見解的
confident	有自信的	intuitive	有直覺力的
cooperative	合作的	meticulous	一絲不苟的
courteous	有禮貌的	open-minded	心胸開闊的
creative	有創意的	organized	有條理的
curious	好奇的	patient	有耐心的
determined	堅定的	perceptive	有洞察力的
devoted	專心致力的	persuasive	有說服力的
diligent	勤奮的	procedural	遵循程序的
easygoing	隨和的	punctual	準時的
educated	受過教育的	quiet	安靜的
efficient	效率高的	relaxed	放鬆的
eloquent	口才好的	resourceful	善用資源的
energetic	精力充沛的	responsible	負責的
enthusiastic	有熱忱的	technological	善用科技的

Exercise ➡ 寫下 3 ～ 5 個最能描述你個性的詞彙

Personality:

_____

_____

Pro Tip

如果你不太清楚自己的人格特質或優勢是什麼，建議利用網路資源來幫助你增加自我意識和英語詞彙量。你可以在線上進行一些免費的性格測試，如 www. high5test. com；或者職業適性測驗，如 www.careerexplorer.com，這裡也能推薦就業方向（參閱緒論）。

Vocabulary 描述硬技能・軟技能的名詞

除了工作經驗和個性之外，展示你的技能是讓人們知道你能提供什麼的重要方式。以下八項技能可能是招募人員最常尋求的類別 [4]：

- 溝通技巧 Communication skills
- 電腦技能 Computer skills
- 人際互動能力 People skills
- 領導能力 Leadership skills
- 組織能力 Organizational skills
- 時間管理技巧 Time-management skills
- 協作技巧 Collaboration skills
- 解決問題的能力 Problem-solving skills

── Insight 洞見 ▶

根據美國皮尤研究所（Pew Research Center）做的《美國就業狀況》（2016 [10]）調查報告，與 1980 年相比，工作必備條件當中：

- 社交能力增長了 83%
- 分析能力（電腦／批判性思考）提高了 77%
- 社交和分析能力提高了 94%

技能可分為專業／硬技能或社交／軟技能。有許多社交／軟技能可被視為人格特質並改用形容詞描述，例如「adaptability 適應力」→「adaptable 適應力強的」。

會計 / 簿記	Accounting/Bookkeeping
數據分析	Data analysis
數據隱私	Data privacy
企業資源規畫	Enterprise resource planning
外語能力	Foreign language ability
人力資源	Human resources
數學	Mathematics
使用多種語言的能力	Multilingualism
流程自動化	Process automation
產品設計	Product design
專案管理	Project management
研究技能	Research skills
精通軟體	Software proficiency
搜尋引擎優化	Search engine optimization
打字技巧	Typing skills
影片 / 照片編輯	Video/photo editing
網站設計	Website design
寫作和編輯	Writing and editing

社交 / 軟技能（名詞）

適應力	Adaptability	能夠應對不斷變化的職場與職責
注重細節	Attention to detail	細心、勤奮、認真
協作	Collaboration	能夠與團隊中和跨部門的其他人一起工作
溝通	Communication	口語表達、寫作與簡報技巧
創造力	Creativity	能夠跳脫框架思考並提供嶄新的解決方案
客戶服務	Customer service	致力於滿足公司和顧客的期望
決策	Decision-making	能夠獨立做出正確的決策
同理心	Empathy	能夠與同事、主管和客戶建立互相體諒的融洽關係
領導力	Leadership	能夠激勵團隊成員及鼓舞士氣，並以正直、公平和策略思維模式行事
多工處理	Multitasking	同時處理不同項目並清楚任務優先順序的能力
積極性	Positivity	樂觀、適應力強、願意接受新的挑戰
解決問題	Problem solving	能夠自己解決問題或尋找解決問題的方法

自我激勵	Self-motivation	能夠獨立工作且主動性強
時間管理	Time management	能夠妥善利用時間並安排任務的優先順序
職業道德	Work ethic	誠實、準時、負責、可靠、正直

 Exercise ⇨ 寫下 3 ～ 5 個最能描述你的軟 / 硬技能的詞彙

Person/Soft skills:

_____

_____

Technical/Hard skills:

_____

_____

是什麼促成了你的成功？ ▼

 Dialog

A: I think I identified the skills and personality traits that helped me achieve my accomplishments.

B: OK, what are they?

A: I have a strong passion for learning languages and learning about culture, and this pushed me to read a lot of English news and watch English movies and TV shows. That's why my English is quite good, even though I didn't study at cram schools.

B: This also means you are an independent, diligent, and quick learner.

A: Thank you. I'll add those words to my self-branding list. I guess that can also explain why I was given awards for excellent academic performance in high school and college.

B: And how about your skills and personality traits relating to your debate club achievements?

A: I think the reason I joined the debate club was my interest and skill in communicating with and persuading people. And also my strength in analyzing ideas. Perhaps that's why Professor Lin asked me to lead the debate club in university.

B: That's great. Now you can write your "success sentences," like

"I led the debate team to the national championships two times because of my skills in persuasive and interpersonal communication, analysis, and leadership."

> **A**：我覺得我已經找出幫助我取得成就的技能和人格特質了。
>
> **B**：OK，是什麼呢？
>
> **A**：我對語言學習和了解文化有著強烈的熱情，這促使我閱讀了很多英語新聞，還有看英語電影和電視節目。這就是為什麼我的英語還不錯，即使我沒有補習過。
>
> **B**：這也意味著妳很獨立、勤奮，而且學習能力很強。
>
> **A**：謝謝。我會將這些詞添加到我的自我行銷清單中。我想這也可解釋為什麼我在高中和大學時期曾獲得書卷獎。
>
> **B**：那妳的技能和人格特質與辯論社的成就有關嗎？
>
> **A**：我想我加入辯論社是因為與人溝通和說服人是我的興趣和技能，而且觀點分析是我的強項。或許這也就是大學時的林教授要求我領導辯論社的原因吧。
>
> **B**：很棒。現在妳可以寫下妳的「成功經歷」了，比方說：
>
> 「由於我在說服、人際溝通、分析和領導等方面的能力與技巧，我曾兩次帶領辯論隊闖進了全國錦標賽。」

履歷範本：進一步說明 success

- I led the university debate team to 2 national championships (winning second place both times) because of my skills in presentations, interpersonal communication, analysis, and leadership.
- I won awards for excellent academic performance in high school and college due to my independence, diligence and quick learning ability.
- I achieved a TOEIC score of 790 as a result of my passion for learning languages and cultures as well as years of effort reading English news and watching English movies and TV shows.

- 由於在發表、人際溝通、分析和領導等方面的技能，我曾帶領大學辯論隊闖進 2 次全國錦標賽（兩次都獲得亞軍）。
- 由於我的獨立、勤奮和快速的學習能力，我在高中和大學時期曾獲得書卷獎。
- 由於對學習語言和文化的熱情以及多年來閱讀英語新聞和觀看英語電影、電視節目的努力，讓我的多益成績達到了 790 分。

Assignment ➡ 寫下 3 ～ 5 個你之所以成功的原因

記住：

☑ 使用二～三個名詞、名詞片語或名詞子句 (S+V) 來書寫。

☑ 可以的話，請加入詳細細節和具體數字。

☑ S = Subject 主詞、V = Verb 動詞、n = noun 名詞

成功經歷	成功的原因 技能／技巧和人格特質
I _____ _____	... because of my ... (n) [or: ... because S+V] _____ 因為……
I _____ _____	... as a result of my ... (n) [or: ... since S+V] _____ 因為……
I _____ _____	... due to my ... (n) [or: ... as S+V] _____ 由於……
I _____ _____	... thanks to my ... (n) [or: ... because S+V] _____ 多虧了……
I _____ _____	... because of my ... (n) [or: ... since S+V] _____ 因為……

文法	例句
a) 因—果複雜句 **Because/As/Since** S+V, S+V	**Because/As/Since** she can type 100 words a minute, she got the job as secretary. 因為她一分鐘能打 100 個字,所以得到了秘書的工作。
b) 果—因複雜句 S+V **because/as/since** S+V	She got the job as secretary **because/as/since** she can type 100 words a minute. 她得到了秘書的工作因為她可以一分鐘打 100 個字。 注意:a 句中有逗號,b 句沒有逗號
因—果複合句 S+V, **so** S+V	She can type 100 words a minute, **so** she got the job as secretary. 她一分鐘能打 100 個字,因此得到了秘書的工作。 注意:逗號在 "so" 之前
a) 因—果簡單句 **Due to** + n, S+V (Because of + n / As a result of + n / Owing to + n / Thanks to + n)	**Due to** her ability to type 100 words a minute, she got the job as secretary. 由於她一分鐘能打 100 個字,她得到了秘書的工作。
b) 果—因簡單句 S+V **due to** + n	She got the job as secretary **due to** her ability to type 100 words per minute 她得到了秘書的工作因為她每分鐘能打 100 個字。 注意: (1) a 句中有逗號,b 句沒有逗號 (2) "Thanks to + n"(多虧了~)僅限用於正面含意之 　　子句 錯誤例子 Thanks to her irresponsible attitude, she was fired. 由於不負責任的態度,她被解雇了。

Exercise ➡ 選出錯誤的選項（答案見 **P.259**）

1. She didn't need to go to cram schools in high school _____ her self-disciplined study habits.

   a. because   b. due to

2. Many people don't emphasize their strengths on their resumes, _____ they don't get called for a job interview.

   a. because   b. so

3. He couldn't get promoted to international sales manager _____ his low TOEIC score of 650.

   a. as a result of   b. thanks to

4. _____ all the spelling mistakes and typos, the recruiter threw her resume into the garbage.

   a. As a result   b. Because of

5. _____ she has strong collaboration and leadership skills, her sales team always surpasses their quotas.

   a. Due to   b. Since

2

履歷個人簡介 Resume Profile

你的自我行銷告示牌

Your self-branding billboard

Figure [8]: Advertisement bill board photo by rawpixel.com (edited) – Freepik.com

Key point

為幫助招募人員快速了解你是否適合所開出的職缺，請在履歷最上方寫下個人簡介，以展示你的所有相關資格和優勢。此段簡介就像你的自我行銷告示牌。

Plan

· 自我品牌檔案：用 4 ～ 6 點闡述你的強項
· 量化成就事蹟：善用數據和 "CAR" 敘述法
· 個人簡介（Profile）和工作經驗（Experiences）

Your Profile

Insight 洞見 ▶

▪ 77% 的雇主特別注重軟技能。（CareerBuilder，2014 [11]）
▪ 93% 的雇主認為軟技能是在做招募決策時不可或缺或非常重要的因素。（Wonderlic 汪氏人事測驗，2016 [12]）
▪ 41% 的招募人員希望在履歷中首先看到求職者的技能敘述。（CareerBuilder，2016 [13]）
▪ 68.7% 的履歷失誤與缺乏成就的描寫有關。（引自 Lainez，TheLadders，2021 [14]）

自我品牌檔案：用 4 ～ 6 點闡述你的強項 ▼

💬 Dialog

B: Now that you have thought about your successes, you need to add them to your resume at the top, just below your name and contact information. This section is called your Profile. Sometimes people will call it "Summary of Qualifications" or just "Qualifications."

A: Why should this information go at the top of the resume?

B: Recruiters will scan your resume from top to bottom in an F or Z pattern. So, the most important information should go at the top to make a quick and positive impression on the recruiter.

A: That makes sense. ... OK, I added the information.

B: Well, I'm glad you made your family name clear, but you should still add your mailing address. And you don't need to say your age. But let's focus on your profile now.

> **B：** 既然妳已經思考過妳的成功經歷，妳要把它們加在履歷的最上方，就在姓名和聯絡資訊的下面。這個部分叫作個人簡介，有時也有人稱為「資歷摘要」或簡稱為「資格」。
>
> **A：** 為什麼這些資訊要放在履歷的頂部？
>
> **B：** 招募人員會以 F 或 Z 字形的視線走向從上到下掃視履歷，所以，最重要的資訊應該放在最上面，以便快速地給招募人員留下正面的印象。
>
> **A：** 有道理……OK，我加上去了。
>
> **B：** 嗯，我很高興妳把妳的姓氏清楚地列出來了，但妳還要加上妳的郵寄地址，而且不需要提及年齡。好，現在就讓我們來仔細看妳的個人簡介。

Jellabie Dai

tel. 0955-5555   email: jellabie@school.edu   age: 21

Profile

- I led our university team to 2 national debate championships (winning second place both times) because of my skills in interpersonal communication, analysis, and leadership.
- I won awards for excellent academic performance in high school and college due to my independence, diligence, and quick learning ability.
- I achieved a TOEIC score of 790 as a result of my passion for learning languages and years of effort reading English news and watching English movies and TV shows.

婕拉比・戴

電話：0955-5555   電子郵件：jellabie@school.edu   年齡：21

個人簡介

- 拜人際溝通、分析和領導方面的能力所賜，我曾帶領我們的大學團隊闖進 2 次全國辯論錦標賽（兩次都獲得亞軍）。
- 由於我的獨立、勤奮和快速的學習能力，我在高中和大學時期皆曾獲得書卷獎。
- 基於對學習語言的熱情，以及多年來閱讀英語新聞和觀看英語電影、電視節目的努力，我的多益成績達到了 790 分。

Pro Tip

履歷就是為你量身訂做的個人品牌廣告。你需要將你的獨特賣點（USP）傳達給潛在雇主，而個人簡介欄位絕對是最佳亮點。四～六行的簡介就是你的強項告示牌，並應回答下列問題：

- 如果你只能夠告訴潛在雇主三件關於你的知識、技能、能力、才能和背景的事，你會怎麼寫？
- 你的同儕、員工和合作夥伴如何形容你？
- 是什麼讓你從其他具有相似技能和背景的人嶄露頭角？
- 你最擅長解決什麼問題？

簡而言之，你希望雇主如何看待你？

量化成就事蹟：善用數據和 "CAR" 敘述法 ▼

招募人員往往需要閱讀數千份簡歷，且其中許多看起來都一樣。當他們看到「團隊合作者（team player）」、「強大的溝通能力（strong communication skills）」和「出色的時間管理能力（excellent time management skills）」時，他們只會翻白眼，心想著：「又來了」。

儘管這些技能非常重要，但沒有具體的例子來支持，它們就僅僅只是文字。

下面這份專案經理履歷量化了哪些職責和經驗？

Chong Yuan Precision Co., Ltd., Taipei, Taiwan　　　　　　May 2019–Oct 2020
Project Manager

a. Kept track of updates, solicited feedback, managed changing expectations, and assisted in external communications daily to ensure that the customers' needs were met, while improving cross-functional communications
b. Estimated costs of launching new models and identified risk levels in new projects
c. Executed 2 major projects that were completed on schedule and under budget by 6%
d. Guided and performed strategic analysis for the projects, and in 2020, the bidding cases increased from under 68% to 80.4%

崇源精密股份有限公司，台北，台灣　　　　　　2019 年 5 月至 2020 年 10 月
專案經理

a. 追蹤更新，徵求反饋，管理不斷變化的期望，每天協助外部溝通以確保滿足客戶的需求，同時改善跨部門溝通
b. 估計新型號產品之上市成本並鑑定新專案的風險等級
c. 曾執行 2 個大案子並使其按時且低於預算 6% 完成
d. 曾指導專案進行並給予策略分析，在 2020 年，使標案比例從 68% 以下提高到 80.4%

答案是 c 和 d。試比較量化敘述使履歷看起來如何更具效果：

Before and After：工作經驗（Experiences）

Before		After
• Executed 2 major projects that were completed on schedule • Guided and performed strategic analysis for the projects, and in 2020, the bidding cases increased		• Executed 2 major projects that were completed on schedule and under budget by 6% • Guided and performed strategic analysis for the projects, and in 2020, the bidding cases increased from under 68% to 80.4%
▪ 曾執行 2 個如期完成的大案子 ▪ 曾指導專案進行並給予策略分析，在 2020 年使得標案增加		▪ 曾執行 2 個大案子並使其按時且低於預算 6% 完成 ▪ 曾指導專案進行並給予策略分析，在 2020 年，使標案比例從 68% 以下提高到 80.4%

因此，如果你有很強的溝通技巧，請用具體的例子來證明這一點，例如所學的課程或曾經做過的專題演講，以上若能佐以數據則可使履歷顯得更有說服力。以「流利的英語能力（fluent English ability）」為例，若能加上多益成績（例如 800 分）或雅思成績（例如 7.5 分）則更佳。以下是證明「出色的時間管理技巧（excellent time management skills）」的量化成就範例：

> Excellent time management skills: maintained 3.5 GPA, worked 10 hours a week, and was an active player on department volleyball team by using a planner to organize my time and communicating with supervisors to prevent school, work, and volleyball conflicts
>
> 出色的時間管理技巧：透過利用計畫工具安排時間並與主管溝通以防止學校、工作和排球隊的事務有所衝突，達成了學期平均成績維持在 3.5，且每週工作 10 小時，同時也是系排球隊的活躍球員。

請注意，上例中的成就首先用數據表示：學期平均成績 3.5、每週工作 10 小時，接著才描述自己曾為一名活躍的排球隊員。

如果是求職信或 LinkedIn 個人檔案、工作經驗（參閱第 6 章）需要一個段落來介紹自己的技能，那麼上述時間管理成就範例，便可採取 "CAR"（Challenge–Action–Result）敘述法（挑戰→採取的行動→結果）寫成：

CAR function	Example: Time management
Challenge	Managing school, work, and volleyball schedules.
Action	Used a planner to keep on top of school assignments and set aside time for homework.
Action	Communicated with supervisor in advance to avoid conflicts between work and practice/game schedule.
Result	Maintained 3.5 GPA.
Result	Worked an average of 10 hours a week and had perfect attendance.
Result	Remained an active participant on my school volleyball team.

CAR 功能	範例：時間管理
挑戰	管理學校、工作和排球日程。
行動	利用計畫工具掌握學校作業，並預留時間做家庭功課。
行動	提前與主管溝通，避免工作、練習與比賽日程發生衝突。
結果	學期平均成績維持在 3.5。
結果	每週平均工作 10 小時，保持完美出勤率。
結果	持續積極參與學校排球隊。

綜上所述，若以 "CAR" 敘述法來完整說明時間管理能力便是：

To organize and manage my school, work, and volleyball schedules, I used a planner to schedule my school assignments, homework, and volleyball practices and games. I also communicated regularly with my supervisor to avoid conflicts between work and my volleyball practice and game schedule. As a result, I was able to maintain a 3.5 GPA in school, work 10 hours a week, and be a contributing member of my department volleyball team.

為妥善管理學校、工作和排球事務的行程，我使用了一個計畫工具來安排學校作業、家庭功課以及排球練習、比賽的時間。同時我也經常與主管溝通，以避免工作與排球日程發生衝突。因此，我能夠在學校維持學期平均成績 3.5，每週工作 10 小時，並成為系排球隊的一名積極貢獻的球員。

在編寫個人簡介・Profile（有時稱爲「資歷摘要・Summary of Qualifications」或簡稱「資格・Qualifications」）時，有些人會寫成包含完整句子的段落。不過，對招募人員而言，條列式更便於迅速閱讀，有鑑於此，筆者建議列出 4 ～ 6 點（項目）就好。

第一個項目請描述目前的職位。（假如你至今仍在職中）

我是一個：

Highly-skilled	技術很好的		
Highly-motivated	主動積極的	recruiter 招募人員	
Knowledgeable	有見識的		
Reliable	可靠的	marketer 行銷人員	with specific/broad experience in (n or v-ing) 在某方面有特定 / 廣泛的經驗
Creative	有創造力的		
Diligent	勤奮的	sales manager 業務經理	
Flexible	靈活的		who V+O （描述工作內容）
Confident	有自信的		
Competent	稱職的	researcher 研究員	
Enthusiastic	充滿熱忱的		
Effective	有效率的	programmer 程式設計員	
Qualified	合格的		
Energetic	精力充沛的		

其他項目

包括技能、能力和人格特質或個人素質等。（參閱緒論）

我是一個 / 我具備：

• A team player who enjoys challenges and working in groups to find solutions
  喜歡挑戰並在小組中尋找解決方案的團隊合作者

• Superior/Proven ability in ____(v-ing)____
  ____（動名詞）____ 方面卓越 / 經驗證的能力

- Excellent/First-class _____ (, _____ , and _____) skills
  優秀／一流的 _____ （、_____ 和 _____ ）技能

- A quick learner always trying to improve himself
  總是嘗試讓自己更進步、學習能力強的人

- Effective interpersonal and communication skills
  有效率的社交和溝通技巧

描述工作經驗的動作動詞：（參閱第 1 章）

例1 如果你曾經「創始」過某事物，例如小組、組織或專案等

created 創造	designed 設計	developed 發展	organized 組織
established 建立	founded 創立	introduced 引進	launched 推出
initiated 發起	installed 安裝		

例2 如果你曾經「領導」過某事物，例如小組或專案等

administered 管理	directed 指導	headed 率領	managed 管理
supervised 監督	conducted 引領	chaired 主持	guided 指導
instructed 指導	coached 訓練	planned 策畫	prepared 籌備
solved 解決			

💬 Dialog

B: Let's look at an example from one of my friends, Peter. Do you see what his current job is?

A: Yes. In the first line it says "science tutor."

B: Right. And the other lines describe his key experiences, skills, and personality traits. The details in Peter's profile are his USPs, the things that make him unique compared to other job applicants.

A: I see he's not using sentences.

B: Right. Do you know why?

A: To make it easier to read?

B: Right. Now you're learning.

B：我們來看一個我的朋友 Peter 的例子。妳有看到他現在的工作是什麼嗎？

A：有。第一行寫著「科學家教老師」。

B：對。其他幾行描述了他的主要經歷、技能和人格特質。Peter 個人簡介中的細節就是他的獨特賣點，讓他在與其他求職者相比之下超群脫凡。

A：我看他都沒有使用句子。

B：對。妳知道為什麼嗎？

A：讓履歷更容易閱讀？

B：沒錯。妳抓到訣竅了。

履歷範本：進階的個人簡介

Peter Chen

Profile
- High school science tutor with a Bachelor of Science
- Designed promotional posters and videos for student orientations
- Able to edit photos with Photoshop, make videos with Adobe Premier for social media, and livestream events with StreamYard
- Coordinated student orientations and trained group leaders
- Highly-motivated team leader and team player with excellent communication skills

陳彼得

個人簡介
- 擁有理學學士學位的高中科學家教老師
- 曾為學生迎新活動設計宣傳海報和影片
- 能夠使用 Photoshop 編輯照片，使用 Adobe Premier 製作社群媒體影片，以及使用 StreamYard 做直播活動
- 曾任學生迎新活動總召和小隊長訓練員
- 主動積極的團隊領導者和團隊合作者，具出色的溝通技巧

Grammar 片語和項目符號

　　為提高履歷的易讀性並減少字數，大多數人的履歷都會使用片語（phrase）搭配項目符號（bullet）逐條列出技能／能力、個性或經驗等資訊。以下練習有助於進一步分析這點並促進理解。

Exercise ➡ 查看 Peter 個人簡介中的文法並回答下列問題（答案見 **P.259**）

注意：

☑ 正確答案可能不只一個。

☑ S = Subject 主詞、V = Verb 動詞、v-ed ＝動詞過去式、adj = adjective 形容詞、
n ＝ noun 名詞

1. Why are there no sentences (S+V)?
   a. It is easier and faster to read
   b. The writer was lazy

2. What information can we see in the bullets?
   a. Skills and abilities
   b. Experiences
   c. Personality
   d. All of the above

3. The three types of bullet grammar are:
   a. (1) S+V   (2) v-ed   (3) adj+n
   b. (1) v-ed   (2) adj+n   (3) Able to+v

4. What two grammar types are used to describe Peter's skills and abilities?
   a. S+V   b. v-ed
   c. adj+n   d. Able to+v

5. What grammar is used for Experiences?
   a. S+V   b. v-ed
   c. adj+n   d. Able to+v

6. What grammar is used for the personality bullet?
   a. S+V   b. v-ed
   c. adj (or adj+n)   d. Able to+v

Peter Chen

Profile

- High school science tutor with a Bachelor of Science
- Designed promotional posters and videos for student orientations
- Able to edit photos with Photoshop, make videos with Adobe Premier for social media, and livestream events with StreamYard
- Coordinated student orientations and trained group leaders
- Highly-motivated team leader and team player with excellent communication skills

🗨 Dialog

B: Basically, all the information about you that the recruiter wants to see is experiences, skills, and personality. Did you notice the grammar used for each of these?

A: Not really.

B: Because experiences are actions, we use verbs. And since the experiences relevant for the job you are applying for happened in the past, the verb should be in the past tense, v-ed, like "Designed promotional posters."

A: That makes sense. And now I can see that skills are described with noun phrases like "excellent communication skills" or with "able to" like "Able to edit photos with Photoshop." And personality words are adjectives or adjective-noun combinations like "Highly-motivated team leader."

B: Right. And ideally, the profile section should contain examples of each type of USP: experiences, skills, and personality traits. OK. Now do the same with your profile.

> **B**：基本上，招募人員所關心的資訊不外乎就是工作經驗、技能和個性。妳有沒有注意到這裡所使用的每一個文法？
>
> **A**：沒有。
>
> **B**：經驗是指一個人的所作所為，所以我們使用動詞。而且由於與妳申請的工作相關的經驗發生在過去，因此動詞應該是過去式，也就是 v-ed，比如「設計了宣傳海報」。
>
> **A**：有道理。我現在發現技能部分是用名詞片語來描述的，比如「出色的溝通技巧」或使用 able to，比方說「懂用 Photoshop 編輯照片」。描述個性則使用形容詞或形容詞加名詞的組合，比方說「主動積極的團隊領導者」。
>
> **B**：對。然後最好個人簡介部分應包含各賣點的例子：經驗、技能和人格特質。OK。現在就這樣來調整妳的個人簡介吧。

Before and After：個人簡介（Profile）

Before	After
Jellabie Dai tel. 0955-5555 email: jellabie@school.edu age: 21	**Jellabie Dai** 0955-5555 jellabie@school.edu 123 Chung Cheung Road, New Taipei City

Before:

Profile

- I led the team to 2 national debate championships (winning second place both times) because of my skills in interpersonal communication, analysis, and leadership.
- I won awards for excellent academic performance in high school and college due to my independence, diligence, and quick learning ability.
- I achieved a TOEIC score of 790 as a result of my passion for learning languages and years of effort reading English news and watching English movies and TV shows.

After:

PROFILE

- Led university debate team to 2 national championships
- Strong interpersonal communication, analysis, and leadership skills
- Won awards for excellent academic performance in high school and college
- Responsible, independent, diligent, and a quick learner
- Achieved a 790 TOEIC score with passion for learning languages and cultures

---

Before:

婕拉比・戴
電話：0955-5555
電子郵件：jellabie@school.edu   年齡：21

個人簡介
- 拜人際溝通、分析和領導方面的能力所賜，我曾帶領團隊闖進 2 次全國辯論錦標賽（兩次都獲得亞軍）。
- 由於我的獨立、勤奮和快速的學習能力，我在高中和大學時期皆曾獲得書卷獎。
- 基於對學習語言的熱情，以及多年來閱讀英語新聞和觀看英語電影、電視節目的努力，我的多益成績達到了 790 分。

After:

婕拉比・戴
0955-5555
jellabie@school.edu
新北市中章路 123 號

個人簡介
- 曾帶領大學辯論隊闖進 2 次全國錦標賽
- 具強大的人際溝通、分析和領導能力
- 高中和大學時期曾獲書卷獎
- 負責、獨立、勤奮、學習能力強
- 對學習語言和文化充滿熱情，多益成績達 790 分

Exercise ➡ 在下列個人簡介中填入正確的詞彙（答案見 **P.259**）

a. passionate	b. who	c. strong interest in
d. presentations	e. serve clients and solve	f. fluent

PROFILE

- University graduated with Certificate in International Trade

- **1.** _____ business management and analysis

- Able to **2.** _____ their problems

- Aggressive, **3.** _____ , and fast-learning, team player **4.** _____ works well under pressure

- **5.** _____ business English for email communication and **6.** _____

Assignment ➡ 寫下你的個人簡介（**Profile**）

記住：

☑ 維持 4 ～ 6 點即可。

☑ 第一點最重要。

☑ 列出你獨特的人格特質、技能、工作經驗或教育背景等詳細訊息。

☑ 盡量使用 "CAR" 敘述法會令人更印象深刻。

_____

_____

_____

_____

_____

_____

_____

Chapter

3

履歷（基本版）Resume (general)

應載項目與文法

Resume sections and grammar

Figure [9]: White puzzle photo by Racool_studio – Freepik.com

關鍵

Key point

履歷就像是在講述一個故事，通常按時間倒序排列，最近的以及與職缺相關的訊息要往上方呈現。除了將姓名和聯絡資訊置頂外，技能（**Skills**）、工作經驗（**Experiences**）和教育背景（**Education**）也應放在頂部。有些人喜歡添加應徵職務（**Objective**）此標題以描述他們所申請的工作。除此之外，成就（**Achievements**）和推薦人（**References**）亦可填入。請注意，為使招募人員更容易閱讀，請使用前後一致的片語加條列式文法。（見左圖）

Figure [10] from Reference [7]

學習
藍圖

Plan

· 履歷應載項目

· 使用動作動詞提升文字說服力

· 教育背景（Education）

Insight 洞見 ▶

招募人員和人資經理是從上到下、從左到右閱讀履歷，因此請確保將關鍵訊息置於左側頂部。如果你有很多工作經驗，請將你的經驗部分放在教育背景之上；如果你才剛畢業且經驗不足，請將教育背景資料放在經驗之前。

🗨 Dialog

A: I made changes to the profile and cleaned up some of the sloppy mistakes.

B: Good. The resume is looking more complete and less sloppy, but it still needs a lot of work.

> **A**：我修改了我的簡介，並清除了一些粗心的錯誤。
>
> **B**：很好。履歷看起來更完整也比較不草率了，但仍需要花很多工夫去調整。

履歷範本：稍佳但仍有待加強（**Better**）

Jellabie (Yi-ran) Dai

0955-5555   jellabie@school.edu   123 Chung Cheung Road, New Taipei City

PROFILE
- Led university debate team to 2 national championships
- Strong interpersonal communication, analysis, and leadership skills
- Won awards for excellent academic performance in high school and college
- Responsible, independent, diligent and a quick learner
- Achieved a 790 TOEIC score with passion for learning languages and cultures

EDUCATION
Jingmei Girls High School   2016-2019
Banciao University, New Taipei City   2019-2023
Bachelor of Arts
High scores; debate club leader

EXPERIENCE
Server at Bartissa Coffee Shop, intern at Epoch

INTERESTS
I like to watch movies, read books and magazines. I also like to travel.

REFERENCES
Available upon request.

婕拉比（怡然）· 戴

0955-5555　　　　　jellabie@school.edu　　　　　新北市中章路 123 號

個人簡介

- 曾帶領大學辯論隊闖進 2 次全國錦標賽
- 具強大的人際溝通、分析和領導能力
- 高中和大學時期曾獲書卷獎
- 負責、獨立、勤奮、學習能力強
- 對學習語言和文化充滿熱情，多益成績達 790 分

教育背景

臺北市立景美女子高級中學　2016-2019

新北市板橋大學　2019-2023

文學學士

成績優秀；辯論社社長

工作經驗

　　　Bartissa 咖啡館服務生、Epoch 實習生

興趣

　　　我喜歡看電影、看書和雜誌，我也喜歡旅行。

推薦人

　　　可依要求提供。

🗨 Dialog

A: OK, so where do we start?

B: Let's start with the sections of a resume and where they go. We need to make your resume look a bit more like Peter's.

A: OK, I admit that his really does look more professional and easier to read.

B: Yes. You might have noticed that the key information in each section is dated and starts from the most recent experience. Your resume is like a life story and recruiters pay close attention to the times in your story.

A: Peter put his dates on the far-right side. Does everyone do that?

B: No, but many do. Just make sure it is easy to find that information. Did you notice Peter has a lot of white space on his resume?

A: Yes, and also more details about his experiences.

B: Absolutely. The recruiter wants to see your experiences first, then your skills and relevant achievements, and then education.

A: But I don't have much experience.

B: Of course not—you just graduated. You should still describe your experiences, but you will emphasize your education, skills and achievements, as well as your personality.

A：OK，那我們從哪裡開始呢？

B：我們從履歷的各個項目以及應記載於何處開始吧。我們要讓妳的履歷看起來更像 Peter 的。

A：好吧，我承認他的確實看起來更專業，也更容易閱讀。

B：是的。妳可能已經注意到，每個項目中的主要資訊都有標示時間，並且是從最近的經驗開始記載。妳的履歷就像一個人生故事，招募人員會很注意看故事中的時間。

A：Peter 把他的日期都放在最右邊。每個人都會這樣做嗎？

B：不是，但很多人都這樣做。只要確保資訊很容易被找到就好。妳有注意到 Peter 的履歷上有很多空白嗎？

A：有，並且還有更多關於工作經驗的細節。

B：沒錯。招募人員會希望首先映入眼簾的是求職者的工作經驗，接著是技能和相關成就，然後是教育背景。

A：但我沒有太多工作經驗。

B：當然沒有——畢竟妳才剛畢業。不過，妳仍然應該描述一下妳的經歷，但更應強調的是妳的教育背景、技能和成就，同時包括妳的個性。

Exercise ⇨ 將下列八個履歷應載項目添加到 **Peter** 的履歷中（答案見 **P.260**）

a. Interests	b. Skills and achievements	c. Objective
d. Work experience	e. Education	f. References
g. Volunteer experience	h. Profile	

Peter Chen

123 University Street, Taoyuan, Taiwan   0934 987 654   peterchen@gmail.com

1. _____

Marketing assistant position in a pharmaceutical company

2. _____

- High school science tutor with a Bachelor of Science
- Designed promotional posters and videos for student orientations
- Able to edit photos with Photoshop, make videos with Adobe Premier for social media, and livestream events with StreamYard
- Coordinated student orientations and trained group leaders
- Highly-motivated team leader and team player with excellent communication skills

3. _____

University of Taoyuan, Taoyuan City   _2015–2019_
Bachelor of Science, Biology

4. _____

College Housing Resident Advisor, University of Taoyuan   _Mar 2018–Present_
- Currently provide academic and personal counseling for residents
- Participated in diversity awareness and leadership training

5. _____

City High School, Taoyuan   _2016–Present_
- Tutored science and math to 10-11th graders and helped develop a study program for struggling urban students
- New Student Orientation (3 years)   _Aug 2015, 2016, 2017_
- Selected to participate in peer-leadership, team-building, and multicultural-conscientiousness workshops; trained group leaders
- Coordinated and promoted new student orientation events
- Designed flyers and posters with Photoshop

6. _____

Adobe Premier and Da Vinci Resolve video editing, Photoshop,
MS Excel and PowerPoint certifications (highly proficient)
Strong English proficiency (TOEIC 820)

7. _____

Professor Li Chi-Ming (University of Taichung, Biology Department), Licc@ut.edu.tw

便利模板：履歷基本格式

為使履歷更具可讀性和可掃描性，請保持字形簡單（如 Arial）且一致，並為不同的部分使用不同的字體大小，比方說，名字 20–24 pt、段落標題 14 pt、內容 12 pt。

社會新鮮人版本	有工作經驗者版本

YOUR NAME
Address:
Tel: , Mobile: , Email:

OBJECTIVE

PROFILE
- Key skills, knowledge, training, experience, personal qualities, etc.
- Fill with key words

EDUCATION AND TRAINING
Name of School, Location
Qualification Achieved, Date
- **Key Subjects**: subject, subject, subject
- List any skills, knowledge, experience, training, etc.
- Also add any special honors received or activities involved in

Name of School, Location
Qualification Achieved, Date
- **Key Subjects**: subject, subject, subject
- List any skills, knowledge, experience, training, etc.
- Also add any special honors received or activities involved in

WORK EXPERIENCE
Name of Company, Location
Job Title, Dates
- Skills, responsibilities, achievements, etc.
- Use action verbs and key words

Name of Company, Location
Job Title, Dates
- Skills, responsibilities, achievements. etc
- Use action verbs + key words

SPECIAL SKILLS, ABILITIES, EXPERIENCE, ETC.
Skill, Skill, Skill

LANGUAGE SKILLS
Language, Language, Language

REFERENCES
Name, title, company/school, email

YOUR NAME
Address:
Tel: , Mobile: , Email:

OBJECTIVE

PROFILE
- Key skills, knowledge, training, experience, personal qualities, etc.
- Fill with key words

PROFESSIONAL EXPERIENCE
Name of Company, Location
Job Title, Dates
- Skills, responsibilities, achievements, etc.
- Use action verbs and key words

Name of Company, Location
Job Title, Dates
- Skills, responsibilities, achievements, etc.
- Use action verbs + key words

SPECIAL SKILLS, ABILITIES, EXPERIENCE, ETC.
Skill, Skill, Skill

LANGUAGE SKILLS
Language, Language, Language

EDUCATION AND TRAINING
Name of School, Location
Qualification Achieved, Date

Name of School, Location
Qualification Achieved, Date

REFERENCES
Name, title, company/school, email

你的名字

地址：
電話： 手機： 電子郵件：

應徵職務

個人簡介
- 關鍵技能、知識、培訓、經驗、個人素質等
- 填入關鍵字

教育和培訓
學校名稱，地點
取得資格，日期
- **重點科目**：主題、主題、主題
- 列出任何技能、知識、經驗、培訓等
- 添加任何獲得過的特殊榮譽或參與的活動

學校名稱，地點
取得資格，日期
- **重點科目**：主題、主題、主題
- 列出任何技能、知識、經驗、培訓等
- 添加任何獲得過的特殊榮譽或參與的活動

工作經驗
公司名稱，地點
職稱，日期
- 技能、職責、成就等
- 使用動作動詞＋關鍵字

公司名稱，地點
職稱，日期
- 技能、職責、成就等
- 使用動作動詞＋關鍵字

特殊技能、能力、經驗等
技能、技能、技能

語言能力
語言、語言、語言

推薦人
姓名，職稱，公司／學校，電子郵件

你的名字

地址：
電話： 手機： 電子郵件：

應徵職務

個人簡介
- 關鍵技能、知識、培訓、經驗、個人素質等
- 填入關鍵字

專業經驗
公司名稱，地點
職稱，日期
- 技能、職責、成就等
- 使用動作動詞＋關鍵字

公司名稱，地點
職稱，日期
- 技能、職責、成就等
- 使用動作動詞＋關鍵字

特殊技能、能力、經驗等
技能、技能、技能

語言能力
語言、語言、語言

教育和培訓
學校名稱，地點
取得資格，日期

學校名稱，地點
取得資格，日期

推薦人
姓名，職稱，公司／學校，電子郵件

　　看了 Peter 的履歷後，Jellabie 重新整理了她的履歷並添加了應徵職務和更多細節。她打算應徵業務類的職位。

履歷範本：稍佳但仍有待加強（**Better**）

Jellabie (Yi-ran) Dai

0955-5555   jellabie@school.edu   123 Chung Cheung Road, New Taipei City

Objective: Sales specialist

Profile
- Led university debate team to 2 national championships
- Strong interpersonal communication, analysis, and leadership skills
- Won awards for excellent academic performance in high school and college
- Responsible, independent, diligent and quick learner
- Achieved a 790 TOEIC score with passion for learning languages and cultures

Education
Banciao University, New Taipei City   *2019–2023*
Bachelor of Arts, Economics
- I received award for excellent academic performance.
- I was the leader on the university debate team, trained new members and taught classes on debate procedures and skills; we won second place at the national championships.

Jingmei Girls High School, Taipei   *2016–2019*
- I received award for excellent academic performance.

Experience
Intern, Epoch Foundation in Taiwan, Taipei, Taiwan   *Mar. 2022–present*
- I help communication between the governmental, schools and businesses.
- I help manage cases, welcome guests, and do some research.

Server, Bartissa Coffee Shop, Banciao, Taiwan   *2020–2022*
- I opened and closed the store, counted the cash and talked to customers.

Skills and Achievements
I am a native speaker of Chinese and Taiwanese and have strong English ability.

Interests
Movies, reading, advertising books and magazines

References
Mr. Chien-Ming Tsao, Bartissa Store Manager, cmtsao@gmail.com
Dr. Mei-hua Wang, Banciao University, Economics

婕拉比（怡然）‧戴

0955-5555　　　　jellabie@school.edu　　　　新北市中章路 123 號

應徵職務：業務專員

個人簡介

- 曾帶領大學辯論隊闖進 2 次全國錦標賽
- 具強大的人際溝通、分析和領導能力
- 高中和大學時期曾獲書卷獎
- 負責、獨立、勤奮、學習能力強
- 對學習語言和文化充滿熱情，多益成績達 790 分

教育背景

新北市板橋大學　　　　　　　　　　　　　　　　　*2019–2023*

文學士，經濟學

- 我曾因成績優異獲書卷獎。
- 我曾擔任大學辯論隊的隊長，負責訓練新成員並教授辯論程序和技巧的課程；我們曾在全國錦標賽中獲得第二名。

臺北市立景美女子高級中學　　　　　　　　　　　　*2016–2019*

- 我曾因成績優異獲書卷獎。

工作經驗

實習生，台灣大紀元基金會，台北，台灣　　　　　　*2022 年 3 月至今*

- 我負責協助政府、學校與企業之間的溝通。
- 我負責協助管理案件、接待訪客以及做一些研究。

服務生，Bartissa 咖啡館，板橋，台灣　　　　　　　*2020–2022*

- 我負責開店和關店、清點現金以及與顧客交談。

技能與成就

我的母語是中文和台語，英語能力佳。

興趣

看電影、閱讀廣告書籍和雜誌

推薦人

曹建明先生，Bartissa 店經理，cmtsao@gmail.com

王美華博士，板橋大學，經濟系

B: That is looking much better. But we can improve it even more.

A: But I've already spent hours on this resume.

B: I'm sure you did. It takes a long time to write a good resume. You have to think a lot about your experiences, skills, and personality and then use words to describe them clearly.

A: ... and make it easy to read!

B: That's right. You know, I think you can still add more details to make you sound more professional. But before you do that, you need to correct your grammar.

A: But I did—I even asked my friend to look for grammar mistakes and he didn't find any!

B: That's not what I mean. Resumes have their own grammar, just like I showed you for the Profile section. Did you notice Peter did not use any sentences anywhere?

A: How did I miss that!

> **B**：看起來好多了。但我們可以讓它更好。
>
> **A**：我已經在這份履歷上花費了好幾個小時。
>
> **B**：我相信。寫一份好的履歷很花時間。妳必須對自己的工作經驗、技能和個性好好地思考一番，然後用文字清楚地加以描述。
>
> **A**：……而且還要讓它易於閱讀！
>
> **B**：沒錯。我認為妳還可以添加更多細節，讓妳看起來更專業。但在這樣做之前，妳需要修正一下妳的文法。
>
> **A**：我有啊——我甚至還請我的朋友幫忙查找文法錯誤，而他完全沒有找到！
>
> **B**：我不是這個意思。履歷有其專屬的文法，就像我在「個人簡介」部分給妳看的那樣。妳有沒有注意到 Peter 沒有使用任何句子？
>
> **A**：我怎麼沒發現！

 **Grammar** 片語描述規則

傳達資訊	文法	例句
工作經驗 （單純過去事情）	v-ed 過去簡單式	Opened and closed the store, counted the cash and talked to customers （負責）開店和關店、清點現金以及與顧客交談
工作經驗 （至今仍從事著）	v 現在簡單式	Help manage cases, welcome guests, and do some research 協助管理案件、接待訪客以及做一些研究
技能、能力	n、Able to+v	Superior interpersonal and communication skills （具）卓越的社交與溝通技巧
人格特質	adj、adj+n	Enthusiastic leader and team player （我是一個）充滿熱忱的領導者和團隊合作者

使用動作動詞提升文字說服力 ▼

動作動詞用以描述成就或一個人所做的事情，特色是簡潔有力。

為使句子和陳述更簡潔、更容易理解，求職文件應使用動作動詞。正確的動作動詞也會讓你的陳述看起來更專業。

試比較下列兩種描述：

無動作動詞的句子（11 words）	有動作動詞的句子（7 words）
I was the boss of a team of six service employees 我曾是一個六名客服員工團隊的老闆	Supervised a team of six service employees 曾主管一個六名客服員工的團隊

Ch
3

無動作動詞的句子不太簡潔（11 個字對比 7 個字），也不太生動；有動作動詞的片語以動作開頭，顯得較突出，且看起來更有說服力。

　　為描述你曾做過的事並說服潛在雇主給你面試機會，用字遣詞是至關重要的。記得一定要在頂部列出最重要的成就或工作職責。

Pro Tip

1. 具體且可量化的成就最具說服力，應放在頂部，例如：
   - Accelerated introduction of a new technology, which increased productivity by 15%
     曾加速引進新技術，將生產力提高 15%
   - Organized consumer databases to efficiently track product orders
     曾創建消費者數據庫以有效追蹤產品訂單
   - Supervised a team of six service employees
     曾主管一個六名客服員工的團隊

2. 興趣（Interests）並未提供任何非常有用的訊息，除非你的興趣與所申請的工作類型是有相關的，否則應刪除。另外，若要提供推薦人資料，則應附上聯繫用的電子郵件地址。

履歷範本：最佳（**Best**）

Jellabie (Yi-ran) Dai

0955-5555   jellabie@school.edu

123 Chung Cheung Road, New Taipei City

Objective: Sales specialist

Profile

- Led university debate team for 2 years and won 2 national awards
- Enthusiastic leader and team player with superior interpersonal and communication skills
- Creative, analytical thinker and quick learner with well-rounded knowledge in science, engineering, business, sociology, literature, and art
- Able to work independently and take risks; always ready to accept challenges and respond to changes

Education

BA, Economics, *Banciao University*, New Taipei City   *2019–2022*
- Leader of university Debate Team; organized training about debate procedures and skills, led the team to 2 national championships   *2020–2021*
- Won award for excellent academic performance   2020

Jingmei Girls High School, Taipei   *2016–2019*
- Won award for excellent academic performance   *2018, 2019*

Experience

Intern, Epoch Foundation in Taiwan, Taipei   *Mar 2022–present*
- Assisted communication between governmental, academic, and commercial sectors
- Managed cases, received guests, researched/summarized/translated information

Server, Bartissa Coffee Shop, Banciao, New Taipei City   *2020–2022*
- Opened and closed store, handled all sales, built customer relationships

Skills and Achievements

- Languages: Native speaker of Chinese (Mandarin and Taiwanese); fluent in English (TOEIC 790; 2020)

References

Mr. Chien-Ming Tsao, Bartissa Store Manager, cmtsao@gmail.com

Dr. Mei-hua Wang, Banciao University Professor of Economics, meihua2233@gmail.com

婕拉比（怡然）· 戴

0955-5555　jellabie@school.edu

新北市中章路 123 號

應徵職務：業務專員

個人簡介

- 曾帶領大學辯論隊 2 年並獲 2 個國家級獎項
- 充滿熱忱的領導者和團隊合作者，具卓越的社交與溝通技巧
- 有創造力且學習能力強的分析性思考者，在科學、工程、商業、社會學、文學和藝術等方面具有全面性的知識
- 能夠獨立工作並勇於冒險，隨時準備接受挑戰並應對變化

教育背景

文學學士，經濟學，*板橋大學*，新北市	*2019–2022*
• 曾任大學辯論隊隊長並籌畫辯論程序與技巧培訓，並曾帶領團隊闖進 2 次全國錦標賽	
	2020–2021
• 曾獲書卷獎	*2020*
景美女中，台北	*2016–2019*
• 曾獲書卷獎	*2018、2019*

工作經驗

實習生，台灣大紀元基金會，台北	*2022 年 3 月至今*
• 協助政府、學術和商業部門之間的溝通	
• 管理案件、接待訪客、研究／歸納／翻譯資料	
服務生，Bartissa 咖啡館，板橋，新北市	*2020–2022*
• 開店和關店、經手所有銷售、建立客戶關係	

技能與成就

- 語言：以中文為母語（國語和台語），英語流利（多益 790 分：2020）

推薦人

曹建明先生，Bartissa 店經理，cmtsao@gmail.com

王美華博士，板橋大學經濟系教授，meihua2233@gmail.com

Exercise ⇨ 查看 Jellabie 最佳版履歷（**P.67**）上的應徵職務與個人簡介並回答下列問題（答案見 **P.261**）

1. What job is Jellabie seeking?

_____

2. Does she work well with others? How do you know?

_____

_____

_____

3. Will she be a good worker for a company?

_____

_____

_____

4. Is she a good thinker?

_____

_____

_____

5. Is she probably good at overcoming difficulties? How do you know?

_____

_____

_____

教育背景（Education）　▼

　　你在此部分中輸入的資訊──甚至此部分在履歷中所呈現的位置──很大程度上取決於你畢業的時間點。如果你畢業超過 10 年或 15 年，你的教育背景應該在你的工作經驗之下，因為招募人員會更加關注後者。但是，如果你是最近剛畢業並且沒有什麼工作經驗，那麼你的教育資訊就應該先出現。

　　哪些教育資訊應列於履歷上，請參考下列指南。

資訊	剛剛或即將畢業	畢業＜5 年	畢業 10 ～ 15 年以上
學校名，城市 （若應徵國外工作則加註國家名）	✓	✓	✓
中等教育學位，例如： ▪ 高中畢業 ▪ 職業學校畢業	✓	✓	✓
高等教育學位，例如： ▪ BA（文學學士） ▪ BSc（理學學士）	✓	✓	✓
研究所學位，例如： ▪ MA（文學碩士） ▪ MSc（理學碩士） ▪ MBA（企業管理碩士） ▪ PhD（博士）	✓	✓	✓
主修	✓	✓	✓
副修	✓	✓	✓
畢業年份	✓	✓	可填可不填
榮譽或獎項	✓	✓	
GPA 學業成績平均點數（＞3.5）	✓	✓	
曾參與的課程	✓		
獎學金	✓		

Pro Tip

如果你畢業於一所著名的大學，可將學校名放在前面加粗體以引起注意。不過，2015 年，Google 前人力運營高級副總裁 Laszlo Bock 曾這樣評價名校：「這是評估求職者的缺陷之一。假設你曾就讀於哈佛、史丹福或麻省理工學院，那麼你確實很聰明……但我們發現，你在哪裡求學跟你在 5 年、10 年甚或 15 年的職涯中的表現並沒有關係。所以，我們就不再關注教育背景了。」

　　以下是編寫教育背景的不同方式：簡潔或延伸。如果你不想此部分在履歷上佔用太多空間，就將所有資訊濃縮於 1 行（精簡）。應屆畢業生可使用更延伸的方式，再添加其他訊息，例如所學課程、平均成績（GPA）、獎學金等。

履歷範本 1a：基本而簡潔

Education

High School Diploma, Jingmei Girls High School, Taipei	2019
BA, Marketing, National Chengchi University, Taipei, Taiwan	2020

Or

Harvard University, Cambridge, USA, BSc, Biology	2020

教育背景

中學，臺北市立景美女子高級中學，台北	2019
學士，行銷學，國立政治大學，台北，台灣	2020

或精簡為一行：

哈佛大學，劍橋，美國，理學學士，生物學	2020

履歷範本 1b：基本再延伸

Education

Harvard University – Cambridge, USA *Bachelor of Science, Biology*	2020

教育背景

哈佛大學——劍橋，美國 *理學學士，生物學*	2020

履歷範本 2：兩個以上學位

如果你擁有多個學位，請將最近的學位放在首位。

Education

National Taiwan University, Taipei, Taiwan Master of Business Administration	2022
National United University, Miaoli, Taiwan Mechanical Engineering	2017

教育背景

國立台灣大學，台北，台灣 企業管理碩士	2022
國立聯合大學，苗栗，台灣 機械工程學士	2017

履歷範本 3：主修和副修

如果你擁有主修和輔修的本科學位，請添加片語 "with X Minor" 以示副修科系。

Education

National Taitung University, Taidong, Taiwan BSc, Electrical Engineering with Sociology Minor	2023

教育背景

國立台東大學，台東，台灣 理學學士，主修電氣工程，副修社會學	2023

　　若你即將畢業，可使用 "Expected June 2023"（預計 2023 年 6 月）此片語。假如你沒有相關的工作經驗，你可以添加 "Key courses"（重點課程）或曾參與之專題，以及其他學術資訊，例如獎學金、獎項和 GPA 平均分數（＞3.5），如果看起來還不錯的話則建議填入。

履歷範本 4：相關科目和獎項

添加獲獎紀錄或曾參與的活動時，別忘記使用動作動詞（過去式）。

Education

Ming Chuan University, Taipei, Taiwan 2022

BA, Applied English with Accounting Minor

- **Key Subjects:** *Business Communication, Accounting, English for Economics, Trade, Negotiation*
- Graduated with Honors with GPA 3.8/4.0
- Received ICDF Awards (2020, 2021)

教育背景

銘傳大學，台北，台灣 2022

學士，主修應用英語，副修會計

- 重點科目：*商務溝通、會計、經濟英語、貿易、談判*
- 以優異成績畢業，GPA 3.8/4.0
- 曾獲 ICDF 獎（2020、2021）

Assignment ➡ 寫下你的基本版履歷

記住：

☑ 使用適當的文法以描述技能（Skills），例如 "Able to+v" 或 "adj+n"；描述個性（Personality）用 "adj" 或 "adj+n"；描述工作經驗（Experiences），若是過往從事的職務用動詞過去式，若是現在的職位則用動詞原形。

☑ 在頂部列出較重要的資訊。如果你是應屆畢業生，請將教育背景（Education）置於工作經驗之前；如果你有相當的工作經驗，則將工作經驗置於教育背景之前。

☑ 各應載項目首先列出最近期的資訊。

_____

_____

_____

_____

_____

Figure [11]: Resume apply work form concept photo by rawpixel.com – Freepik.com

Chapter

4

履歷（基本版）Resume (general)

格式與 "KISSES" 守則

Formats and KISSES for your resume

關鍵　Key point

履歷的格式須易於閱讀和掃描，以利招募人員清楚快速地查看：

1. 你是否符合資格

以及

2. 你的實力有多強

學習藍圖　Plan

· 履歷基本格式

· 履歷編寫 "KISSES" 守則

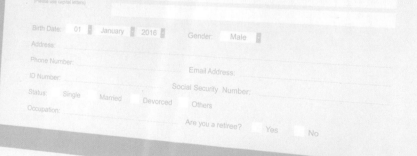

Insight 洞見 ▶

招募人員通常利用大約 7.4 秒鐘的時間掃描一份履歷，他們希望在這短短 7.4 秒鐘內獲得所有相關訊息。（TheLadders，2018 [15]）

💬 Dialog

A: I was searching for resume templates, and I saw a lot of really cool and stylish ones. I think this will help me stand out.

B: Actually, you need to be careful of those beautiful templates that you see on places like MS Word or Canva.com.

A: Is it because they might be difficult to read for the company's ATS?

B: Yes. That is true. And recruiters only want to see clearly and quickly that your resume has most of the key words described in the job ad.

A: They're not impressed by fancy resumes?

B: No, they're not. And sometimes a creative design will take the recruiter more time to scan because it's not a format they usually see.

A: So, I should just focus on making it easy to read.

B: Yes! Don't waste your time on making a beautiful resume. Spend your time making it easy to read and making sure it matches the job ad.

> **A**：我剛在找履歷模板，看到很多很酷、很時尚的樣式。我認為這將幫助我與眾不同。
>
> **B**：實際上，妳要小心那些在 MS Word 或 Canva.com 等網站上看到的那些漂亮模板。
>
> **A**：是不是因為那些模板可能會讓公司的應徵者追蹤系統難以判讀？
>
> **B**：是的，沒錯。招募人員只想清楚、快速地看到妳的履歷中包含徵才廣告中所列出的大部分關鍵字。
>
> **A**：他們不喜歡花俏的履歷嗎？
>
> **B**：不，他們不喜歡。有時候創意設計反而會讓招募人員花費更多時間來掃描，因為不是他們通常看到的格式。
>
> **A**：所以，我應該只專注於讓履歷易於閱讀就好。
>
> **B**：是的！不要把時間浪費在製作精美的履歷上。妳應該花時間讓它好讀並確保它符合徵才條件。

來自 MS Word 和 Canva 等網站的線上履歷模板數以千計，不過，盡量讓履歷能夠被快速掃描是大原則。以下介紹三種主要的履歷格式類型：按時間順序排列（Chronological resume）、依功能性排列（Functional resume）和混合型排列（Combination resume）。（引自 Tomaszewski，zety，2022 [16]）

按時間順序排列	依功能性排列	混合型
• 學生和求職菜鳥 • 求職者尋求的工作與前一份工作相似 • 學術型履歷	• 需要作品集的創意型工作 • 軍職退休人員或過渡時期者 • 不想看起來資歷過高的求職者	• 針對特定職位且經驗豐富的專業人士 • 轉換職涯跑道者 • 有就業空窗期者

Figure [12] from Reference [16]

🗨 Dialog

A: I found out there are different ways to organize information on a resume. But because I don't have much experience, the chronological format seems to be the best one.

B: That's right. But put your education section before your experience section, and list everything in each section from most to least recent.

A: And keep the profile at the top, right?

B: Yes, it is best to follow the KISSES acronym for resume writing—or any writing for that matter.

A: I have heard of KISS before— keep it simple—but what is KISSES?

A：我發現有不同的方式來組織履歷上的資訊。但是因為我沒有太多經驗，所以按時間順序的格式似乎是最好的選擇。

B：沒錯。但是妳要把教育放在經驗之前，並從最近的時間點開始列出各部分中的所有內容。

A：並保持個人簡介置頂，對嗎？

B：是的，編寫履歷最好還是遵循 "KISSES" 守則——任何與求職相關的寫作也一樣。

A：我曾聽說過 "KISS"——保持簡單，但 "KISSES" 是指什麼？

履歷編寫 "KISSES" 守則 ▼

還記得緒論中提到的 "KISSES" 守則嗎？也就是，保持簡單（Simple）、具體（Specific）、引人入勝（Engaging）和可供機器掃描辨識（Scannable）。其中第一項和最後一項對於一份好履歷的格式尤其重要。

有很多格式化履歷的方法，而且很多看起來很酷。只須瀏覽 Microsoft Office 模板或造訪 Canva、Venngage 等設計平台，即可找到大量設計精美的創意履歷。

很酷的履歷格式（資訊圖表風格）	中規中矩的履歷格式

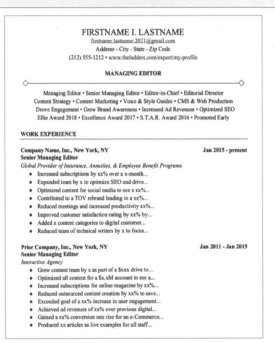

Figure [13]: Infographic resume by Forsey, C – HubSpot.com

Figure [14a] from Reference [7]

請注意，創意履歷格式並不會給招募人員留下深刻印象（除非你應徵的是創意型工作，例如繪圖美編等），且創意格式可能會對 ATS（應徵者追蹤系統）造成混淆，因而導致機器無法擷取相關資訊——這意味著你甚至也許連第一關（非人工）的篩選，都無法通過！

因此，履歷應使用傳統設計並保持簡單，以及確保有足夠的空白使其容易被掃描；此外，也要添加細節使其具有吸引力和具體性。

讓履歷可透過機器辨識且易於被閱讀的方法有：

1. 履歷簡單化

將履歷長度控制在一頁或兩頁之內，而假如你幾乎沒有什麼工作經驗，一頁就好。保留足夠的空白並確保字體不會太小。12 pt 適合主要內容（內文），標題則使用稍微大一點的字體。

2. 提高履歷易讀性

- 將所有關鍵資訊置於靠近頂部的地方並靠左。（更多相關 tips 見下文）
- 用粗體和較大的字體（比如 14 pt）以突顯標題。
- 優先列出與工作最相關的訊息，尤其是在個人簡介或資歷摘要的部分，並將動作動詞置於句首。此外，成就敘述也應該寫在前面，因為英文是從左到右閱讀的。

3. 內容具體且吸睛

- 使用動詞描述具體的工作經驗（參閱第 1 章）——動詞看起來會比名詞來得更有力、更生動。
- 成就部分要添加引人入勝的細節和事實，建議使用量化成果或 "CAR" 敘述法：挑戰→採取的行動→結果。換句話說，基本上就是描述一個有結果的、問題被解決的過程。

可被機器辨識及易讀的重要性

有一種「閱讀引力」吸引讀者的目光。從左到右書寫的英文等語言的讀者是以 Z 或 F 字形瀏覽及掃描文件，如下圖的閱讀熱圖所示：

Figure [14b] from Reference [7] (edited)

上圖意味著履歷上最重要的資訊應該是

- 在頂部

  並且

- 在左側

分析人們如何掃視文件的研究使用熱圖（如上）清楚地顯示文件的頂部三分之一處是關鍵。你的履歷是否通過了「頂部三分之一測試」？是否詳細地回答了下列問題？

- 你是誰？
- 你應徵什麼職位？
- 你的獨特賣點是什麼？

 **Dialog**

A: OK. I've given my resume lots of KISSES.

B: Haha ... great. Let's have a look. The name is bigger, the sections stand out more, and the dates are much easier to read and scan.

A: Yes, I used different font sizes and bold capital letters for the section headings.

B: This is looking quite professional. The recruiter will be able to scan this resume very quickly and comfortably. Good work!

> **A：** OK。我已經給了我的履歷很多 KISSES 了。
>
> **B：** 哈哈……很好。我們來看一下。名字更大了，每一個項目更突出了，也有附上日期讓履歷更易於閱讀和掃描了。
>
> **A：** 是的，我在項目標題使用了不同的字體大小並用大寫字母加粗體。
>
> **B：** 這看起來很專業。招募人員將能夠非常快速和舒適地審視這份履歷。非常好！

履歷範本：加強重點標示

Jellabie (Yi-ran) Dai

0955-555-555   jellabie@school.edu

123 Chung Cheung Road, New Taipei City

OBJECTIVE: SALES SPECIALIST

PROFILE

- Led university debate team for 2 years and won 2 national awards
- Enthusiastic leader and team player with superior interpersonal and communication skills
- Creative, analytical thinker and quick learner with well-rounded knowledge in science, engineering, business, sociology, literature, and art
- Able to work independently and take risks; always ready to accept challenges and respond to changes

EDUCATION

- BA, Economics, *Banciao University*, New Taipei City   *2019–2022*
- Leader of university Debate Team; organized training about debate procedures and skills, led the team to 2 national championships   *2020–2021*
- Won award for excellent academic performance   *2020*

Jingmei Girls High School, Taipei   *2016–2019*
- Won award for excellent academic performance   *2018, 2019*

EXPERIENCE

Intern, Epoch Foundation in Taiwan, Taipei *Mar 2022–present*
- Assisted communication between governmental, academic, and commercial sectors
- Managed cases, received guests, researched/summarized/translated information

Server, Bartissa Coffee Shop, Banciao, New Taipei City *2020–2022*
- Opened and closed store, handled all sales, built customer relationships

SKILLS & ACHIEVEMENTS

- Languages: Native speaker of Chinese (Mandarin and Taiwanese); fluent in English (TOEIC 790; 2020)

REFERENCES

Mr. Chien-Ming Tsao, Bartissa Store Manager, cmtsao@gmail.com

Dr. Mei-hua Wang, Banciao University Professor of Economics, meihua2233@gmail.com

---

婕拉比（怡然）‧戴

0955-5555　jellabie@school.edu

新北市中章路 123 號

應徵職務：銷售專員

個人簡介
- 曾帶領大學辯論隊 2 年並獲 2 個國家級獎項
- 充滿熱忱的領導者和團隊合作者，具卓越的社交與溝通技巧
- 有創造力且學習能力強的分析性思考者，在科學、工程、商業、社會學、文學和藝術等方面具有全面性的知識
- 能夠獨立工作並勇於冒險，隨時準備接受挑戰並應對變化

教育背景

文學學士，經濟學，*板橋大學*，新北市 *2019–2022*
- 曾任大學辯論隊隊長並籌畫辯論程序與技巧培訓，並帶領團隊闖進 2 次全國錦標賽 *2020–2021*
- 曾獲書卷獎 *2020*

景美女中，台北 *2016–2019*
- 曾獲書卷獎 *2018、2019*

工作經驗

實習生，台灣大紀元基金會，台北 *2022 年 3 月至今*
- 協助政府、學術和商業部門之間的溝通
- 管理案件、接待訪客、研究／歸納／翻譯資料

服務生，**Bartissa** 咖啡館，板橋，新北市 *2020–2022*
- 開店和關店、經手所有銷售、建立客戶關係

技能與成就
- 語言：以中文為母語（國語和台語），英語流利（多益 790 分；2020）

推薦人

曹建明先生，Bartissa 店經理，cmtsao@gmail.com

王美華博士，板橋大學經濟系教授，meihua2233@gmail.com

Exercise ➡ 履歷分析（答案見 **P.261**）

你能夠在下方 **K Chen** 的履歷中發現錯誤嗎？針對下列問題回答是（**Y**）／否（**N**）。

_____ **1.** Is there enough whitespace to make scanning easy?

_____ **2.** Is the name clear enough?

_____ **3.** Is the job Objective mentioned?

_____ **4.** Is the contact information concise enough?

_____ **5.** Is there a Profile section?

_____ **6.** Are there clearly visible dates?

_____ **7.** Are there bullets to make it faster to read?

_____ **8.** Are there specific details and numbers?

K Chen

Address: 2F, No.51, Dadong Rd., Shilin Dist., Taipei City 111, Taiwan (R.O.C.)

Tel: 0975299869   Email: kenny83@gmail.com

EDUCATION AND TRAINING

Ming Chuan University, Taipei, Taiwan

BA Finance

Key Subjects: Financial Statement Analysis, Investment, Financial Market, Risk Management, International Financial Management

- I successfully analyzed and presented project of "Impacts of Global Energy Market on International Economy and Taiwan Economy"
- I developed a strong interest in business management and analysis
- I was able to use computer applications to conduct research
- I collaborated with a team and won the volleyball competition in North Finance Cup

WORK EXPERIENCE

Cathay United Bank, Taipei

Intern, Bank Teller

- I performed well as a bank teller intern
- I provided excellent service to build good relations and solve problems
- I was aggressive, enthusiasm, fast-learning, and worked independently to learn standard operating procedures

Ming Chuan University, Taipei

English Tutor

- I tutored and enhanced tutees' English skills
- I designed a survey and successfully interviewed tourists in Shilin Night Market with tutees

LANGUAGE SKILLS

Mandarin, Taiwanese, English

Exercise ➡ 試與下方改良版履歷比較（答案見 **P.262**）

以下關於改良版的敘述是否屬實？正確無誤請打 ✓。

_____ **1.** Is easier to scan

_____ **2.** Is more informative

_____ **3.** Has the most important information in the top 1/3

_____ **4.** Has more numbers and persuasive details

Kenny T.J. Chen

kenny83@gmail.com   0975299869

2F, No.51, Dadong Rd., Shilin Dist., Taipei City 111, Taiwan (R.O.C.)

OBJECTIVE: J.P. Morgan ANALYST

PROFILE

- University graduated with Certificate in International Trade
- Strong interest in business management and analysis
- Able to effectively serve clients and solve their problems
- Aggressive, passionate, fast-learning, team player who works well under pressure
- Fluent business English for communication and presentations

EDUCATION AND TRAINING

TAITRA International Trade Institute, Taipei, Taiwan   **1/2022–6/2022**

Post Bachelors International Trade Program (600+ hours)

Key Subjects: Financial Statement Analysis, Economics, Accounting, Negotiations, Business English, Presentations

- Researched and analyzed the market of the game industry and the relevant companies' financial statements
- Developed strong business presentation and communication skills in English

Ming Chuan University, Taipei, Taiwan   **2018–2021**

BA Finance

Key Subjects: Financial Statement Analysis, Investment, Financial Markets, Risk Management, International Financial Management

- Successfully presented an analysis of the "Impacts of the Global Energy Market on the International Economy and the Taiwan Economy"
- Developed a strong interest in business management and analysis
- Able to utilize SAS, Excel, and other applications to conduct research

Activities

- Collaborated with my department's team and won the volleyball competition in the Finance Cup
- Attended IEFA (International Conference on Economics, Finance and Accounting) & CSBF (The Conference on Cross-Strait Banking and Finance)

EXPERIENCE

Cathay United Bank, Taipei   3/2021–6/2021

Intern, Bank Teller

- Completed a 500-hour internship and worked as a bank teller
- Provided excellent customer service to build good relations and solve problems
- Aggressive, passionate, fast-learning, and worked independently to learn standard operating procedures

Ming Chuan University, Taipei   2018–2020

English Tutor

- Tutored and enhanced tutees' English skills
- Designed tourist survey and interviewed 45 tourists at Shilin Night Market with tutees to practice English

LANGUAGE SKILLS

Mandarin, Taiwanese, English (TOEIC 770)

a. 10 activities	g. invitation cards, posters, clothes, and props
b. 35 countries	h. highly proficient
c. TOEIC 980	i. advanced
d. 80+ high school students	j. 60 attendees
e. 3.96	k. 4 Graphic Artists
f. e.g. Expedium, Airbnb, Booking.com, etc.	

ANTHONY WONG

tw.linkedin.com/in/antwong/ 0975666129 awong@gmail.com

No. 10-5, Aly. 80, Guanter Ln., Pingtung, Taiwan

OBJECTIVE: EXPEDIUM MARKET ASSOCIATE

SUMMARY OF QUALIFICATIONS

- University graduate with Certificate in International Trade
- Fast-learning, detail-oriented, team player who works well under pressure
- Excellent proficiency in business English for presentations, negotiations, and meetings
- **1.** _____ in graphics programs and online travel services
- Strong interest in promoting Expedium products and great passion for travel; visited more than **2.** _____

EDUCATION AND TRAINING

TAITRA International Trade Institute, Taipei, Taiwan   2018

Post Bachelor Certificate in International Trade

- **Key subjects:** Business negotiation, presentation, marketing, social selling, video editing, infographic design, LinkedIn copywriting

National Sun Yat-sen University, Kaohsiung, Taiwan   2013–2017

Bachelor of Department of Foreign Languages and Literature (DFLL)

Cumulative GPA: **3.** _____

- **Honors:** National Sun Yat-sen University Student Award   2014, 2015

VOLUNTEER EXPERIENCE AND ACTIVITIES

Exchange Student   Sep 2016–Aug 2017

Technische Hochschule Nürnberg, Germany

- Successfully organized, launched, and promoted Taiwanese Evening to promote Taiwanese culture, food, and music to over **4. _____**
- Quickly thrived in the new environment and aggressively learned German
- Became familiar with travelling apps and websites, **5. _____**
- Developed a strong interest in traveling and the tourism industry

Director of Graphic Arts   2014–2016

Student Association of DFLL, Kaohsiung, Taiwan

- Supervised the group of **6. _____**
- Collaborated with team members and students from other departments
- Efficiently and successfully organized **7. _____** , including a joint Christmas party for 100+ and an English camp for **8. _____**
- Created a Facebook fan page and designed **9. _____** to promote the activities

SKILLS AND ABILITIES

Canva, Adobe Illustrator, Photoshop – **10. _____** proficiency

Mandarin – Native proficiency, English – Near native (**11. _____** ; CEFR C2),

German – Intermediate (One-year exchange student in Nürnberg, Germany),

Korean – Intermediate

📝 **Assignment** ⇨ 寫下你的基本版履歷

記住：
☑ 使用最適合你現況的履歷格式。
☑ 使用不同的字體大小使標題突出（名字 20–24 pt、標題 14 pt、內文 12 pt）。
☑ 寧可花時間在好的內容上，而不要花俏的資訊圖表樣式。
☑ 盡可能讓履歷看起來專業，完成後利用 "KISSES" 守則檢查一下是否：保持簡單、可被掃描辨識、引人入勝且具體。

5

Figure [15]: Jigsaw puzzles teamwork concept photo by rawpixel.com – Freepik.com

履歷（客製化）Resume (customized)

針對徵才廣告關鍵字編寫

Matching resumes with job ad key words

Key point

求職者的履歷不是由 ATS 追蹤系統，就是由正在積極尋找與徵才條件相匹配的人資專員篩選。如果履歷中的關鍵字少於徵才廣告所提及的 50%，這位求職者甚至不會被列入考慮。

Plan

· 分析徵才廣告並依之建構動作動詞庫
· 客製履歷 4 步驟

── Insight 洞見 ▶

儘管求職者在求職時通常只寫一份履歷，但 63% 的招募人員希望履歷是針對各職缺量身打造的。（引自 Lutov，CareerBuilder，2021 [17]）

A: OK. Now that I finished my resume, what do I do now? Do I just start sending it to companies?

B: The first step is to go to a job bank website and search through its job ads.

A: ... and then send my resume to them, right?

B: Not yet. Most people just do this, but recruiters will first screen out applicants that are not qualified. How do they know which applicants are not qualified? Do you know?

A: If the resume does not match the job ad?

B: Right. You will apply for different jobs and the job ads will have lists of different requirements and qualifications for the job.

A: So, I need to match my resume to the job ad? That sounds like a lot of work.

B: Yes, but this is the reality of job finding. If your resume doesn't have at least 50% of the job ad key words, you will not be called in for an interview.

A: Got it. So how do I do that?

B: Start paying attention to the language in the job ads and build your job finding vocabulary.

 A：OK。現在我完成了我的履歷，接下來要怎麼做？我就直接開始投給各家公司嗎？

 B：第一步是去人力銀行網站搜尋徵才廣告。

 A：……然後投履歷，對吧？

 B：還沒。大多數人都只是這樣做，但招募人員會先刷掉資格不符的求職者。他們怎麼知道哪些人不合格？妳知道嗎？

 A：假如履歷與徵才廣告不匹配的話？

 B：對。妳之後要應徵不同的工作，而徵才廣告會列出各職缺不同的條件與資格。

 A：所以，我需要做的事情是讓履歷與徵才廣告一致？聽起來得下一番工夫。

 B：是的，但這就是找工作的現實面。如果妳的履歷中沒有包含至少 50% 徵才廣告關鍵字，那妳就不會接到面試通知電話。

 A：我懂了。那我該怎麼做？

 B：開始留意徵才廣告的特有語言並建立妳的求職詞彙庫。

如前所述（參閱第 1 章），動作動詞有助於以簡潔有力的方式描述成就或一個人的所作所為。求職履歷應使用動作動詞來描述所有技能、工作，尤其是成就。

履歷關鍵字彙（技能、能力、經驗和成就）的重要資源來自網路徵才版、人力銀行、企業網站、博覽會刊物、報紙或公司內部訊息上的徵才廣告。如果你正在尋找特定的工作，例如 IT 業務、行銷或會計，請找至少 5 個不同公司的徵才廣告並分析其中詞彙以幫助理解：

1. 該公司正在尋找什麼技能、能力和經驗
2. 如何讓你的履歷看起來更專業和更具相關性
3. 你有多適合這份工作

以此方式分析了幾個廣告之後，請列出所有廣告共有的關鍵字；如果你具備這些資格，把它們放在你的履歷上。這些是最有可能被雇主的求職者追蹤軟體（ATS）成功辨識的關鍵字。許多大型國際公司動輒收到數以百計的應徵信，因此他們需要將篩選過程自動化。第一步是減少列入考慮的履歷數量，於是他們經常利用 ATS 篩選履歷，ATS 會刷掉關鍵字與徵才廣告中的職務描述不匹配的履歷。

Pro Tip

注意要確保至少一半的徵才廣告關鍵字出現在履歷上，尤其是職務描述中的關鍵字，因為它們通常是最重要的。

Dialog

B: Here is a four-step process to help you analyze job ads and customize your resume.

A: I guess that for jobs that receive hundreds of job applicants, I need to spend time to really show the recruiter that I'm qualified.

B: Absolutely. Nothing of value in life comes for free. Let's look at an example from a friend of mine who recently applied for a sales job at IBMM.

A: Wow. There must have been many job applicants for that job.

B: Yes. My guess is that there were at least 200. So, the ATS and recruiters have to reduce this number to 6–8 for interviews, and only the best matched resumes will have a chance to earn an interview for those 6–8 interviewees. After going through the following four-step process, I think Peter has a good chance of getting an interview.

> **B：**這裡有一個 4 步驟流程，可幫助妳分析徵才廣告並客製化妳的履歷。
> **A：**要爭取有數百個求職者的工作，我需要花時間好好地向招募人員展示我是合格的。
> **B：**當然。天下沒有白吃的午餐。我們來看一個我朋友最近應徵 IBMM 業務工作的例子。
> **A：**哇。那份工作肯定有很多求職者。
> **B：**沒錯。我猜至少有 200 人。所以，ATS 和招募人員必須將這個數字減少到 6～8 人通知來面試，而只有最符合條件的履歷才能讓這 6～8 人有機會進到面試階段。採用了以下 4 步驟後，我認為 Peter 很有可能獲得面試機會。

Steps 1 & 2：透過查找徵才廣告和利用文字雲工具來鎖定關鍵字

　　從至少 10 個徵才廣告中獲取關鍵字列表的一個快速方法，是將廣告複製貼上到文字雲類的應用程式中，例如 wordart.com、wordclouds.com 或 monkeylearn.com 等，便能呈現出哪些詞彙在徵才廣告中最為常見。文字雲中最大的詞代表在徵才訊息中出現頻率最高，因此你應該在履歷中特別花心思在那些詞彙。

Figure [16]: Word cloud for sales specialist position

Figure [17]: Word cloud for sales specialist position

上面這兩個文字雲是基於 IBMM 的業務專員徵才廣告（見下表左欄）所製成。第一個是從 https://www.jasondavies.com/wordcloud/ 創建的，第二個是從 https://monkeylearn.com 創建的，其中皆包括兩個字或三個字的詞彙，相當實用。由於單字的大小代表該字的使用頻率，故主要關鍵字爲業務（SALES）、建立（BUILDING）、客戶（CLIENT）、顧客（CUSTOMER）、關係（RELATIONSHIP）。對於業務職位來說，這並不足以爲奇，因其基本上就是關於建立關係（relationship building）的工作。另外，從徵才廣告上 "relationship building" 位於上半部「必備條件（Requirements）」底下，也可了解到這項技能的重要性。因此，與建立關係和溝通技巧相關的徵才廣告描述和關鍵字應出現在你的履歷上。

Step 3：更仔細地查看詞組並將其分類

下一步是進行更仔細的分析，不僅要聚焦於單一個字，片語也應多加留意，例如「形容詞＋名詞（adj+n）」或「動詞＋受詞（V+O）」。以下左欄是來自 IBMM 的徵才廣告範例，其中套色字表關鍵字；右欄則爲利用文字雲分析出的關鍵字和更具體的片語列表。

Job ad	Job ad key phrases (job duties, skills, experiences, education, personality traits)
Graduates@IBMM http://www-901.IBMM.com/tw/employment/ graduate/jobopening.html **Available positions in Taiwan** As a future leader in e-Generation, fresh graduates are invited to start your career with IBMM as a trainee. You will receive well- organized and comprehensive training together with invaluable exposure while working with our world-class professionals **Position title:** **Sales Specialist** www-901.IBMM.com/tw/employment/ graduate/1227.html	Sales Specialist

Requirements:

Turn your sales passion into concrete rewards! Learn the ropes in relationship building! The true sales stars at IBMM are the ones who develop that unique rapport. They're the professionals who ask the right questions, listen with both ears and keep the promises they make. Their escalating revenue numbers reflect their commitment to customers. They sell by facilitating their capabilities.

To be a valued business resource to the client, you will need to acquire an in-depth understanding of their business and determine areas where IBMM's business segments can complement theirs. Main industries include banking, finance, security, insurance, transportation, travel, government, manufacturing, distribution, health, education, telecom, utilities and so on. You will establish and maintain an IBMM business relationships with clients. You will recommend solutions to the clients' business problems, enhance their competitiveness and increase their profitability based on your knowledge of their business plans, strategies, goals and the industry marketplace. You will achieve overall customer satisfaction.

Attributes:

1. University graduate interested in selling/promoting information system products
2. Goal oriented and an ability to work under pressure
3. Enjoy client relationship building and coverage
4. Aggressive, self-motivated, fast-learning, work independently
5. Good communication and presentation skills

We are now open to receive applications from fresh graduates or freshman with less than 2 years working experience. We would notify qualified applicants of the interview arrangement after the deadline.

---

sales passion
relationship building

develop unique rapport
ask the right questions
listen with both ears and keep the promises they make
commitment to customers

acquire in-depth understanding of customers' business
determine areas where IBMM can complement business

establish and maintain business relationships with clients
recommend solutions to the clients' business problems

achieve overall customer satisfaction

University graduate interested in selling/promoting information system products
Goal oriented and an ability to work under pressure
Enjoy client relationship building and coverage

Aggressive, self-motivated, fast-learning, work independently
Good communication and presentation skills

徵才廣告

畢業生 @IBMM

http://www-901.IBMM.com/tw/employment/graduate/jobopening.html

台灣職缺

作為 E 世代的未來領導者,誠徵應屆畢業生以實習生身分在 IBMM 開啓職涯。在與我們的世界級專業人士合作的同時,你將獲得組織良好、全面的培訓以及寶貴的接觸機會。

職位名稱:業務專員

www-901.IBMM.com/tw/employment/graduate/1227.htm

必備條件:

將你的銷售熱情轉化為具體的獎勵!學習建立關係的訣竅!IBMM 真正的銷售明星是能夠發展無可取代之關係的人。他們是提出核心問題、全心傾聽並信守諾言的專業人士。他們不斷增加的收入反映出他們對客戶的承諾。他們靠提升自己的能力來銷售。

要成為對客戶而言有價值的業務資源,你需要深入了解他們的業務並判定 IBMM 的業務部門可於客戶的什麼領域裡提供支援。主要產業包括銀行、金融、保全、保險、交通、旅遊、政府、製造、經銷、健康、教育、電信、公共事業等。你將與客戶建立並維持業務關係。你將根據你對客戶商業計畫、策略、目標和對產業市場的了解,為客戶的商業問題推薦解決方案,使他們增強競爭力並提高獲利能力。你要掌握住整體的客戶滿意度。

個性特質:

1. 對銷售 / 行銷資訊系統產品感興趣的大學畢業生
2. 目標明確且能夠在壓力下工作
3. 樂於建立客戶關係及提供專屬服務
4. 積極進取、自我激勵、學習能力強、獨立工作
5. 具良好的溝通和簡報能力

本職缺開放應屆畢業生或工作經驗 2 年以下的社會新鮮人應徵。我們會在截止日期後通知符合條件的求職者前來面試。

Step 4：添加關鍵字，尤其是個人簡介（Profile）部分。

最後一個步驟便是看看這些關鍵字有多少個適合填入履歷。使用這些確切的單字和片語可使你的資格更加亮眼，讓招募人員或 ATS 一秒就看見你。

以下讓我們看看 Peter Chen 如何針對這些關鍵字（套色粗線標示）優化他的履歷，並透過將相關工作經驗和徵才廣告關鍵字放在履歷的上方區塊加以重新排列。

Before and After：客製化（有相當工作經驗者）

Before		After (optimized)

PETER CHEN
123 University Street, Taoyuan, Taiwan
0934 987 654   peterchen@gmail.com

SUMMARY OF QUALIFICATIONS

- University graduate with Certificate in International Trade
- 4 years sales experience
- Aggressive, fast-learning, team player
- Fluent business English

EDUCATION AND TRAINING

TAITRA International Trade Institute, Taipei, Taiwan
Certificate in International Trade,   2020
- **Key Subjects:** Business communication skills, INCO terms, L/Cs
- Familiar with international trade process key terms and documents

Tamkang University, New Taipei City, Taiwan
BA in International Trade (Minor in Finance and Japanese)   2015
- **Key Subjects:** International Marketing, Business Management, Business English, Japanese
- **Honors:** General Service's List, Teaching Staff's List

PETER CHEN
123 University Street, Taoyuan, Taiwan
0934 987 654   peterchen@gmail.com

OBJECTIVE: IBMM SALES SPECIALIST

SUMMARY OF QUALIFICATIONS

- Strong interest in selling IBMM products and achieving sales targets
- 4 years of sales experience building client relationships and achieving sales targets
- Fluent English for sales, negotiations, and business presentations
- Aggressive, fast-learning, team player who works well under pressure
- University graduate with Certificate in International Trade

EXPERIENCE

Shin Kong Mitsukoshi Department Store, Hsin Chu
Sales Specialist   2017–2020
- Provided excellent customer service to maintain and build good relations
- Delivered product presentations to key clients
- Worked under pressure to keep records, inventories, and to increase sales
- Rapidly and aggressively learned product knowledge to promote sales

EXPERIENCE

Shin Kong Mitsukoshi Department Store, Hsin Chu

Sales Representative   2017-2020

- Quickly and aggressively learned product knowledge to promote sales to customers
- Worked under pressure to keep records, inventories, and to increase sales

Hui Meng Hospital, Hsin Chu

Information Counter Representative

2015-2017

- The counter served the hospital's 150 employees in the departments of internal medicine, surgery, obstetrics and gynecology and dentistry.
- Provided friendly service to patients
- Quickly learned standard operating procedures

SKILLS AND ACHIEVEMENTS

Microsoft Office

Mandarin, Taiwanese, English, Japanese

Hui Meng Hospital, Hsin Chu

Information Counter Represntative   2015-2017

- Built and maintained good relations with patients and enjoyed helping clients
- Successfully handled pressure to register patients and arrange anamnesis
- Independently and quickly learned standard operating procedures

EDUCATION AND TRAINING

TAITRA International Trade Institute, Taipei, Taiwan

Certificate in International Trade   2020

- Key Subjects: trade show sales, sales analytics, presentations, negotiations, industry report on pc industry
- Delivered several persuasive IT product presentations in English
- Learned how to find and generate sales leads on LinkedIn and at trade shows
- Developed a strong interest in selling IT products such as those from IBMM

Tamkang University, New Taipei City, Taiwan

BA in International Trade (Minor in Finance and Japanese)

2015

- **Key Subjects:** International Marketing, Business Management, Business English, Japanese

SKILLS and ACHIEVEMENTS

Microsoft Office, CRM software

Mandarin, Taiwanese, English, Japanese

After（經優化）

陳彼得

台灣桃園大學街 123 號

0934 987 654   peterchen@gmail.com

應徵職務：IBMM 業務專員

資歷概要

- 對銷售 IBMM 產品和實現銷售目標有濃厚興趣
- 具 4 年建立客戶關係和實現銷售目標的業務經驗
- 銷售、談判和商務簡報英語流利

- 積極進取、學習能力強、具團隊精神，在壓力下仍然工作良好
- 擁有國際貿易證照的大學畢業生

工作經驗

新光三越百貨，新竹

業務專員   2017–2020
- 提供出色的客戶服務以維持並建立良好的關係
- 向關鍵客戶做產品簡報
- 在壓力下工作，如做紀錄、管理庫存和增加銷售額
- 快速積極地學習產品知識以促進銷售

惠盟醫院，新竹

服務處櫃檯專員   2015–2017
- 與患者建立和保持良好關係，並樂於協助客戶
- 妥善處理為病患掛號和整理病歷的壓力
- 獨立快速學習標準操作程序

教育和培訓

TAITRA 外貿協會培訓中心，台北，台灣

擁有國際貿易證照   2020
- 重點科目：貿易展銷售、銷售分析、簡報、談判、PC 產業報告
- 曾多次以英語完成有說服力的 IT 產品簡報
- 了解如何在 LinkedIn 和貿易展覽會上尋找和開發潛在客戶
- 對銷售來自 IBMM 的 IT 產品有濃厚的興趣

淡江大學，新北市，台灣

國際貿易學士（輔修財務金融和日語）
- 重點科目：國際行銷、企業管理、商務英語、日語

技能與成就

Microsoft Office、CRM 軟體

國語、台語、英語、日語

實例引導：應徵業務專員的客製化履歷（工作經驗甚少者）

💬 Dialog

A: That IBMM sales specialist job sounds interesting, and doesn't require much work experience.

B: If you're interested in sales, you can apply too.

A: Really?

B: Yeah, why not? What do you have to lose?

A: I guess it would be a good learning experience. OK, I'll do it.

B: Why don't you look at the list of key words from the job ad and see if you can add them to the relevant places in your resume?

> **A：**IBMM 業務專員的工作看起來很有趣，而且不要求太多的工作經驗。
>
> **B：**如果妳對銷售感興趣，妳也可以應徵。
>
> **A：**是嗎？
>
> **B：**對啊，為什麼不？妳有什麼好損失的？
>
> **A：**我想這將是一次很好的學習經驗。OK，我來試試。
>
> **B：**妳要不要看一下徵才廣告中的關鍵字列表，看看是否能將它們添加到履歷中的相關位置？

Jellabie 在相關條件旁打勾或用套色粗線標示，發現她符合了許多要求。

`Hint` 請對照第 95 頁徵才廣告的套色部分，並參閱相對應之翻譯以助了解。

Sales Specialist
✓ **Sales passion**
relationship building
~~**develop that unique rapport** / **ask the right questions, listen with both ears and keep the promises they make**~~ / **commitment to customers** / **acquire an in-depth understanding** of their business / **determine areas** where IBMM can complement business / **establish and maintain** an IBMM **business relationships** with clients / **recommend solutions** to the clients' business problems / achieve overall **customer satisfaction**

- ✓ **University graduate**
- ✓ interested in **selling/promoting** information system products
- ✓ **Goal oriented** and an **ability to work under pressure**
- ✓ Enjoy **client relationship building** and coverage
- ✓ **Aggressive, self-motivated, fast-learning, work independently**
- ✓ **Good communication and presentation skills**

Before and After：客製化（社會新鮮人）

注意看 Jellabie 添加了應徵職務、關鍵字（打勾或套色粗線標示項目）並將其個人簡介的優先順序重新排列。

Before		After (optimized)

Before

Jellabie (Yi-ran) Dai

0955-555-555   jellabie@school.edu
123 Chung Cheung Road, New Taipei City

PROFILE

- Led debate team for 2 years and won 2 national awards
- Enthusiastic leader and team player with superior interpersonal and communication skills
- Creative, analytical thinker and quick learner with well-rounded knowledge in science, engineering, business, sociology, literature and art
- Able to work independently and take risks; always ready to accept challenges and respond to changes

EDUCATION

Banciao University, New Taipei City   2019–2022
Bachelor of Arts, Economics
- Leader of university Debate Team; organized training about debate procedures and skills, led the team to 2 national championships
    2020–2021
- Awarded Model Student for excellent academic performance

Jingmei Girls High School, Taipei   2016–2019
- Won awards for excellent academic performance

After (optimized)

Jellabie (Yi-ran) Dai

0955-555-555   jellabie@school.edu
123 Chung Cheung Road, New Taipei City

OBJECTIVE: IBMM SALES SPECIALIST

PROFILE

- **University graduate with passion for sales and persuasion, and strong interest in selling/promoting** information system products
- **Superior interpersonal, communication, and presentation skills**: Led debate team for 2 years and won 2 national awards
- **Goal oriented** and an **ability to work under pressure**
- **Aggressive, self-motivated, fast-learning** team player who is also able to **work independently**
- Creative analytical thinker

EDUCATION

Banciao University, New Taipei City   2019–2022
Bachelor of Arts, Economics
- Leader of university Debate Team; organized training about debate procedures and skills, led the team to 2 national championships
    2020–2021
- **Developed strong leadership and interpersonal communication skills**
- Won award for excellent academic performance

Jingmei Girls High School, Taipei   2016–2019
- Won awards for excellent academic performance

EXPERIENCE

Intern, Epoch Foundation in Taiwan, Taipei
Mar 2022-pres
- Assisted communication between governmental, academic and commercial sectors
- Managed cases, received guests, researched/summarized/translated information

Server, Bartissa Coffee Shop, Banciao, New Taipei City
Summer 2020
- Opened and closed store, handled total sales, developed customer relationships

SKILLS & ACHIEVEMENTS

- Led university debate team to 2 national competitions (2020–2021)
- Languages: Native speaker of Chinese (Mandarin and Taiwanese); fluent in English (TOEIC 790; 2020)

REFERENCES

Professor Jian-Zhe Li, Banciao University, jzli@bcu.tw
Dr. Mei-hua Wang, Banciao University Professor of Economics, meihua2233@gmail.com

EXPERIENCE

Intern, Epoch Foundation in Taiwan, Taipei
Mar 2022-pres
- Assisted communication between governmental, academic and commercial sectors
- Managed cases, received guests, researched/summarized/translated information

Server, Bartissa Coffee Shop, Banciao, New Taipei City
2020–2022
- Opened and closed store, handled total sales, **built customer relationships**

SKILLS & ACHIEVEMENTS

- Languages: Native speaker of Chinese (Mandarin and Taiwanese); fluent in English (TOEIC 790; 2020)
- Led university debate team to 2 national competitions (2020–2021)

REFERENCES

Mr. Chien-Ming Tsao, Bartissa Store Manager, cmtsao@gmail.com
Dr. Mei-hua Wang, Banciao University Professor of Economics, meihua2233@gmail.com

---

After（經優化）

婕拉比（怡然）· 戴

0955-5555　jellabie@school.edu

新北市中章路 123 號

應徵職務：IBMM 業務專員

個人簡介

- 大學畢業生，對業務類和說服他人的工作抱有熱情，且對行銷／推廣資訊系統產品有濃厚的興趣
- 具出色的人際溝通和簡報能力：曾帶領辯論隊 2 年，並獲得 2 個國家級獎項
- 目標明確且能夠在壓力下工作
- 積極進取、自我激勵、學習能力強、具團隊精神並可獨立工作
- 有創造力的分析性思考者

教育背景

板橋大學，新北市　　　　　　　　　　　　　　　　　　　　　　*2019–2022*

文學學士，經濟學

- 曾任大學辯論隊隊長；曾籌畫辯論程序與技巧培訓，並帶領團隊闖進 2 次全國錦標賽

　　　　　　　　　　　　　　　　　　　　　　　　　　　　　　2020–2021

- 培養了強大的領導能力和人際溝通能力
- 曾獲書卷獎

景美女中，台北　　　　　　　　　　　　　　　　　　　　　　*2016–2019*

- 曾獲書卷獎

工作經驗

實習生，台灣大紀元基金會，台北　　　　　　　　　　　　　*2022 年 3 月至今*

- 協助政府、學術和商業部門之間的溝通
- 管理案件、接待訪客、研究／歸納／翻譯資料

服務生，Bartissa 咖啡館，板橋，新北市　　　　　　　　　　　*2020–2022*

- 開店和關店、經手所有銷售、建立客戶關係

技能與成就

- 語言：以中文為母語（國語和台語），英語流利（多益 790 分；2020）
- 曾帶領大學辯論隊參加 2 次全國比賽　　　　　　　　　　　*2017–2019*

推薦人

曹建明先生，Bartissa 店經理，cmtsao@gmail.com

王美華博士，板橋大學經濟系教授，meihua2233@gmail.com

　　Jellabie 能夠從徵才廣告關鍵字列表選出超過 50% 的關鍵字填入履歷，並發現她確實有資格擔任該職位。儘管她沒有從事銷售和建立客戶關係的經驗，但她曾在服務業（Bartissa 咖啡館）工作，因而在履歷增加一筆紀錄。此外，她也利用徵才廣告中的相關軟技能填寫了她的個人簡介。

　　下面我們聚焦於 Jellabie 的個人簡介部分，觀察針對業務專員客製化前後寫法有何不同。請注意，當中的資訊順序不單單只是「量身訂製」，同時也代表根據此職位所需的優先性。

Before and After：比較客製化前後的 PROFILE 差異

Before	After (optimized)
PROFILE • Led debate team for 2 years and won 2 national awards • Enthusiastic leader and team player with superior interpersonal and communication skills • Creative, analytical thinker and quick learner with well-rounded knowledge in science, engineering, business, sociology, literature, and art • Able to work independently and take risks; always ready to accept challenges and respond to changes	**PROFILE** • **University graduate with passion for sales and persuasion, and strong interest in selling/promoting** information system products • **Superior interpersonal, communication, and presentation skills:** Led debate team for 2 years and won 2 national awards • **Goal oriented and an ability to work under pressure** • **Aggressive, self-motivated, fast-learning team player who is also able to work independently** • Creative analytical thinker

 Exercise ⇨ 分析徵才廣告並列出清單（答案見 P.264）

Part 1：分析下列兩則徵求專案經理的廣告並將其中的關鍵字用螢光筆突顯出來。

Part 2：編寫一個更簡潔的列表，最重要的關鍵字置頂，並將突顯的單字分為四類：管理類（Management）、溝通類（Communication）、技術性（Technical）和其他（Other）。

Ad #1: Senior IT Project Manager	Ad #2: Project Manager
The Senior IT Project Manager must be able to oversee large, complex projects, control and understand the business environment and work product, and evaluate technical specifications. Key responsibilities include directing and evaluating project	Our firm has a Project Manager position opening in its Professional Services group. Duties/Responsibilities: • Work with the prospective professional services customer to define the scope of work and provide it to the customer

vision and strategy, accountability for project completion and team management, defining and driving project deliverables, and facilitating development and operations project teams.

The Senior IT Project Manager will be responsible for defining, creating, and maintaining a project plan, managing day-to-day client communication, allocating resources, and maintaining team productivity and morale in high-pressure situations.

Candidates must have IT expertise, a Bachelor's degree in management, engineering, computer science, business or similar field, 4+ years in professional services or consulting, 2–4 years of managerial experience, as well as the ability to manage multidisciplinary projects with 10+ people.

for approval.
- Identify the external resources and if appropriate, internal resources with the necessary skills to develop a detailed Statement of Work.
- Manage the Professional Services team to execute on and complete the deliverables called out in the Statement of Work. Manage the client relationship.

Qualifications:

- Demonstrated management, leadership, communication, motivational and influencing skills.
- Must have a thorough understanding of the software development process, preferably from a system (hardware/software) perspective.
- Must have a proven record of managing software/hardware system integration projects/programs.
- Must feel comfortable in a leadership role in a matrix management environment.
- Must be able to effectively communicate verbally and written with individual contributors, management, executive staff, as well as with the customer.
- Demonstrated commitment to quality.
- Problem solver with the ability to provide primary problem diagnosis and coordination.

Assignment ⇨ 寫下你的客製化履歷

記住：

☑ 將徵才廣告中的工作條件優先列出。

☑ 將最重要的工作條件置頂於個人簡介。

☑ 確保履歷中至少含有 50% 的徵才廣告關鍵字。

PART **2**

LINKEDIN

Chapter

Figure [18]: Woman
holding a LinkedIn icon
photo by rawpixel.com –
Freepik.com

6

LinkedIn 個人檔案 Profile

改良的新世代履歷

The new and improved resume

Key point

尋找工作時,尤其是跨國企業的職缺,你需要註冊並完成一個免費的 LinkedIn 帳戶,主要理由有以下三點:

1. LinkedIn 是大多數中型與大型國際公司招聘員工時所使用的社群平台。

2. LinkedIn 個人檔案可涵蓋比履歷更多的有用資訊。

3. LinkedIn 是 Google 造訪以建立搜尋結果排名的唯一社群媒體平台,完整且經優化的個人檔案和頻繁的發文與留言,可使你在 Google 搜尋引擎上容易被找到。

Plan

· 數位招聘——線上徵才勢在必行

· LinkedIn——資訊時代的新式履歷

· LinkedIn Profile 的標題(Headline):關鍵字與成效

· LinkedIn 個人簡介(About):你的故事

· 編寫技巧:善用平行結構(Parallelism)

· LinkedIn 工作經歷(Experience)

· 編寫 LinkedIn Profile 的加分懶人包

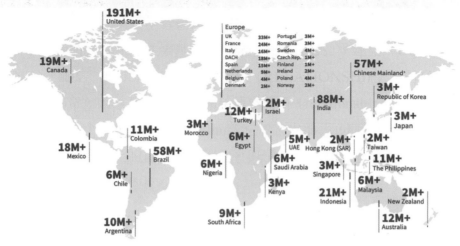

More than 850 million members in 200 countries and regions worldwide*

191M+ United States

19M+ Canada

Europe
UK	33M+	Portugal	3M+
France	24M+	Romania	3M+
Italy	16M+	Sweden	4M+
DACH	18M+	Czech Rep.	1M+
Spain	15M+	Finland	1M+
Netherlands	9M+	Ireland	2M+
Belgium	4M+	Poland	4M+
Denmark	2M+	Norway	2M+

57M+ Chinese Mainland*

88M+ India

3M+ Republic of Korea

3M+ Japan

2M+ Israel

12M+ Turkey

3M+ Morocco

6M+ Egypt

5M+ UAE

2M+ Hong Kong (SAR)

2M+ Taiwan

11M+ The Philippines

11M+ Colombia

18M+ Mexico

58M+ Brazil

6M+ Nigeria

6M+ Saudi Arabia

3M+ Singapore

6M+ Chile

3M+ Kenya

21M+ Indonesia

6M+ Malaysia

2M+ New Zealand

10M+ Argentina

9M+ South Africa

12M+ Australia

*Membership numbers are updated quarterly after Microsoft Earnings. * Numbers reflect InCareer app membership as of December 2021.

Figure [19] from LinkedIn.com

──── Insight 洞見 ▶

- 87% 的招募人員使用 LinkedIn 來檢視求職者，但只有 43% 使用 Facebook、22% 使用 Twitter。（Jobvite Recruiter Nation Report，2016 [3]）
- 70% 的招募人員在社群媒體上搜尋求職者。（CareerBuilder，2018 [8]）
- 66% 的招募人員使用搜尋引擎尋找求職者。（CareerBuilder，2018 [8]）

Figure [20] from Reference [9]

數位招聘——線上徵才勢在必行 ▼

由於線上搜尋十分容易，並且在我們的生活中佔據了如此重要的一部分，因此招募人員也會查看求職者的網路形象。根據 CareerBuilder.com 的調查，41% 的招募人員表示，如果在網路上找不到求職者的任何蹤跡，他們甚至可能不會給予面試機會！單就此原因，認真的求職者應使用 LinkedIn 創建個人線上廣告，這樣當招募人員用 Google 搜尋他們時，他們的名字就會顯示在 Google 搜尋排名中比較前面的位置。

招募人員會在社群媒體上尋找求職者，儘管俗話說「人不可貌相」，但實際上人們仍然免不了這麼做。他們也會從社群媒體來評判求職者，根據 CareerBuilder 和 Jobvite 的調查 [9]，受訪的招募人員表示，如果他們發現挑釁或不當內容的證據，例如酗酒和吸毒（43%）、偏執的評論（33%），過度分享（60%），甚至是批評前公司的貼文（31%）等，便不會將其列入考慮。

此外，Jobvite Recruiter Nation Report [3] 亦指出，72% 的招募人員會因為社群個人資料中的拼寫錯誤而將該求職者判定為不合格。試想若是你的履歷或 LinkedIn 檔案上有此錯誤，你會得到怎樣的回應？

LinkedIn——資訊時代的新式履歷 ▼

自 2003 年以來至今，LinkedIn 是網路上唯一的專業人脈拓展平台。根據 LinkedIn 官方網站的數據 [18]，每週有超過五千萬 LinkedIn 用戶在找工作，而目前 LinkedIn 擁有超過 8.3 億會員。下圖顯示此數據一直在穩定增長，完全沒有放緩的跡象。

為何人們在應徵國際公司職位時應使用 LinkedIn，有以下五個重要原因：

1. 相當於造訪一個巨大求職版，其中包含超過 1,500 萬則職缺訊息，利用關鍵字和地理位置便可搜尋。也就是說，你可以造訪 87% 的招募人員，並且同時也是他們查看的對象之一。

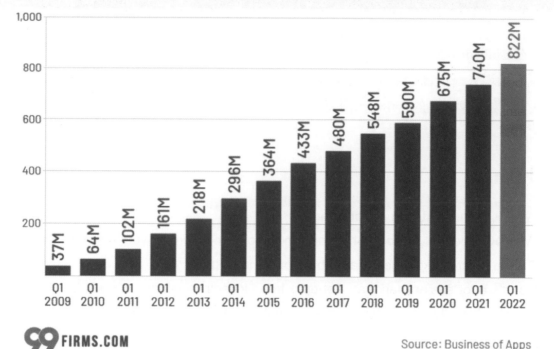

Number of LinkedIn Users Over a 14-Year Period

99FIRMS.COM

Source: Business of Apps

Figure [21] from 99firms.com

2. 透過添加文章、影片或其他數位作品於 LinkedIn 檔案來建立你的個人品牌廣告，以使自己在眾多人之中綻放光芒。這就是為什麼 LinkedIn 檔案是數位時代的新履歷。

3. 一旦你在 LinkedIn 上完成並優化了個人檔案，它將幫助你在 Google 上針對你的名字搜尋的排名大幅往前，甚至比你自己的網站更顯著。這使招募人員能夠輕易地在網路上搜尋到你。

4. 搜尋公司、他們的新聞和他們的員工進行研究，以協助你提交更客製化和個人化的求職申請。

5. 發展出一個亮眼的人脈網和可永存的工作關係。

> **Tip** 當你在 **LinkedIn** 上擁有超過 **250** 個有意義的聯絡人（**connection**）時，人脈效應就會開始產生。（引自 **Career Attraction Team**，**[19]**）

至此，相信你已了解 LinkedIn 對於尋找跨國職務以及開展國際事業的價值，接下來請按照下列步驟來完成你的個人檔案。在此部分，你需要編寫三個主要欄位：標題（Headline）、個人簡介（About）和工作經歷（Experience）。

　　在 LinkedIn 上看到你的照片和姓名後，接著映入瀏覽者眼簾的是標題（Headline），此欄位請填入一段簡短描述來介紹你自己。截至 2021 年，標題字數限制最多 220 個字，其有如一個吸睛的告示牌，簡要地傳達你是誰、你的工作，以及你對它的熱情程度。

🗨 Dialog

A: What is the next step in my job search?

B: Well, even before you look for job openings, you should create your online presence.

A: Do you mean make a personal website or something?

B: No. It's a lot easier than that. Set up a free LinkedIn account—this will be your online resume. Actually, it's much more than an online resume.

A: OK. How do I do it?

B: After you sign up, you'll need to complete the profile section.

A: OK, let's do it!

B: First, sign up for a LinkedIn account and personalize the url to your name, like tw.linkedin.com/in/jellabiedai/, so you will be easy to find on LinkedIn and Google. After that, you'll need a good Headline to catch both the reader's attention, and Google's attention.

> **A：** 我求職的下一步是什麼？
>
> **B：** 嗯，即使在找工作之前，妳也應該把妳的網路形象建立起來。
>
> **A：** 你的意思是做個人網站之類的嗎？
>
> **B：** 不是。比那簡單多了。我是指開設一個免費的 LinkedIn 帳戶——這將是妳的線上履歷。實際上，它不僅僅是一份線上履歷。
>
> **A：** 好。我該怎麼做？
>
> **B：** 註冊後，妳需要填寫個人資料。
>
> **A：** OK，那我們開始吧！
>
> **B：** 首先，註冊一個 LinkedIn 帳戶並將網址個性化為妳的名字，例如 tw.linkedin.com/in/jellabiedai/，這樣妳就很容易在 LinkedIn 和 Google 上被搜尋到。然後，妳需要一個好的標題來吸引瀏覽者和 Google 的注意力。

一個好的標題將說服瀏覽者繼續往下閱讀你的個人簡介（About）。此外，在決定依不同的搜尋或查詢顯示哪些個人資料時，標題強烈影響著平台顯示結果。因此，作為一個求職者，將標題加以優化，能讓 LinkedIn 演算法注意到你，你的名字在 Google 中的排名將會更高，出現在更多搜尋中並獲得更多瀏覽量。這也意味著你會獲得更多的工作機會：

- 出現在招募人員、潛在客戶或任何你的瀏覽者以與你的個人檔案相匹配之關鍵字所執行的 LinkedIn 搜尋結果中。
- 一旦人們造訪你的個人專頁，你就可以推銷你自己、你的價值或你的服務。

你的標題應遵循一個由兩大重點組成的策略：

1. 使用擷取自徵才廣告分析和／或工作經歷的關鍵字
2. 量化你的價值或成果

請看下方範本。

LinkedIn 標題（Headline）範本：關鍵字與量化成果

Zain Kahn
I simplify complex topics — like marketing and psychology — and share my insights here. Scaled products to 8 million+ users | Advisor and Fractional CMO to startups | 100k+ followers on Twitter

贊恩・卡恩
我簡化複雜的主題（例如市場行銷和心理學），並在這裡分享我的見解。量產商品銷售至 800 萬名以上的用戶 | 新創公司的顧問及兼職行銷總監 | Twitter 上擁有 10 萬個以上的關注者

以 Zain 為例，關鍵字包括「量產商品」和「新創公司的顧問及兼職行銷總監」，而量化成果是「量產商品銷售至 800 萬名以上的用戶」和「Twitter 上擁有 10 萬個以上的關注者」。

可惜的是，許多 LinkedIn 用戶並沒有好好利用標題欄位，而僅僅只是寫下他們的職業。最好避免這樣做，而應強調你的優勢和成就。

Before and After：標題（Headline）

Original（28/220 字元）	Revised（96/220 字元）
Sales Executive @ Pandoptics	Passionate Sales Executive @ Pandoptics | Generated $2.1M sales | Increased conversion rate 173%
Pandoptics 業務專員	Pandoptics 熱情的業務專員｜曾創造 210 萬美元的銷售額｜曾提高轉化率 173%

　　在上面的例子中，你會注意到標題並非完整的句子，而是一系列突顯優勢和成就的片語。使用強而有力的詞彙和數字是很棒的選擇（如果它們看起來令人印象深刻）。

 **Grammar** 標題的動詞和片語

我們來看一下 Before and After 兩種版本的標題寫法，並請留意其中的說明。

Original（101 字元）	修改重點 ➡	Revised（102 字元）
I am an Advertising Sales Representative and I help many clients make successful branding strategies. 我是一名廣告業務代表，我幫助許多客戶制定成功的品牌策略。	修改的目的在於避免不必要的文法，並加入更強而有力的用字與數據。 1. 更簡潔——不採用 SVO 句型 2. 添加更有力量的形容詞：winning（制勝的）和 successful（成功的） 3. 添加成功交易的客戶數量（Over 300）	Advertising Sales Rep helping clients create <u>winning</u> branding strategies. <u>Over 300 successful</u> clients. 廣告業務代表，幫助客戶打造制勝的品牌策略，擁有超過 300 個成功的客戶。
〈使用句型〉 SVO		〈使用句型〉 v-ing+n adj+n

　　在修改後的範本中可看到多了一些字和細節。然而，我們仍然希望保持簡潔並快速地傳遞所要表達的意思，因此使用了片語來取代句子。

 **rammar** 標題的動詞和片語

☑ S ＝主詞、V ＝動詞、O ＝受詞、SC ＝主詞補語
　 adj ＝形容詞、n ＝名詞、v-ing ＝動詞現在進行式、v-ed ＝動詞過去式

句子	片語
Who I am 我是誰 I am a Passionate Sales Executive S V O/SC^註	Passionate Sales Executive 　adj　　　　　n
What I (usually) do 我（平常）的職務 I help many clients S V O	helping clients v-ing　O [n]
What I achieved (noun) 我的成就（名詞） I have over 300 successful clients S V O	300+ successful clients 　adj　　　　n
What I did (verb) 我的成功經驗（動詞） I increased the conversion rate by 173% S V O	increased conversion rate 173% v-ed　　　　　O

Ch
6

註：如 "be" 的連綴動詞後面不接受詞（O），而應接主詞補語（SC）。

Pro Tip

提供細節和保持簡短很重要，因此請留意字元數。以下頁 Jellabie 為例（套色字），
她使用了 155 個字元（155/220）。

 **Dialog**

A: For my headline, can I use the key words from my resume Profile?

Jellabie's Profile
- Led university debate team for 2 years and won 2 national awards
- Enthusiastic leader and team player with superior interpersonal and communication skills
- Creative, analytical thinker and quick learner with well-rounded knowledge in science, engineering, business, sociology, literature, and art
- Able to work independently and take risks; always ready to accept challenges and respond to changes

---

B: Yes, that's a good idea. But choose the words carefully because you only have 220 characters.

A: Yes, I know. I'm thinking about looking for a job in sales, so I've written two Headline versions based on the sales specialist job ad. Which one do you think is better?

---

1. Seeking a job in Sales | Excellent team player with superior interpersonal and communication skills | Led university debate team to 2 national championships (155/220)

2. Creative, analytic thinker and quick learner | Excellent leadership and communication skills | Debate team leader | Seeking Sales position (138/220)

B: I think the first one is better. You immediately say what position you are seeking and you have quantified your debate team achievement.

A: Yeah, I thought so, too. Now what?

B: Now you need to write your story in the About section.

> **A**：標題可以用履歷中的關鍵字嗎？
>
> ---
>
> 個人簡介
> - 曾帶領大學辯論隊 2 年並獲 2 個國家級獎項
> - 充滿熱忱的領導者和團隊合作者，具出色的人際溝通技巧
> - 有創意且學習能力強的分析性思考者，在科學、工程、商業、社會學、文學和藝術等方面具有全面性的知識
> - 能夠獨立工作並勇於冒險，隨時準備接受挑戰並應對變化
>
> ---
>
> **B**：可以，好主意。但是要慎選單字，因為妳最多只能寫 220 個字元。

A：嗯，我知道。我正在考慮找一份業務工作，所以我根據業務專員的徵才廣告寫了兩個標題版本。你覺得哪一個比較好？

---

1. 尋找業務工作 | 優秀的團隊合作者，具出色的人際溝通技巧 | 曾帶領大學辯論隊闖進 2 次全國錦標賽（155/220）

2. 有創意、學習能力強的分析性思考者 | 具優秀的領導和溝通能力 | 辯論隊隊長 | 尋找業務職位（138/220）

B：我認為第一個比較好。妳立即說出妳正在尋找的職位，並且也量化了辯論隊的成就。

A：對啊，我也是這麼想。接下來呢？

B：現在妳需要在「個人簡介（About）」欄位寫下妳的故事。

Exercise ➡ 選出最佳標題（答案見 P.266）

下列何者為最理想的版本？

1. Original:

I help companies with innovative ways of doing online marketing by data analytics and visual aids and infographics. I can help companies expand their market. (157/220)

Which is the better revision?

a. Helping companies with online marketing | Able to analyze data and make visual aids and infographics. (104/220)

b. Online marketer with data analytics and data visualization skills. (69/220)

c. Innovative digital marketer | Google and Facebook analytics | Data visualization using R (88/220)

2. Original:

I am a passionate and caring person seeking opportunities to make a difference. I am also highly organized and detail-oriented to make everything become better. (160/220)

Which is the better revision?

a. Passionate about marketing and PR | Presenter in video that won smart pitch competition | Represented university at Model UN | Strong organization skills | Detail-oriented (171/220)

b. Passionate and caring person seeking opportunities in PR to make a difference | Strong organization skills | Detail-oriented personality (139/220)

c. Passionate about marketing and PR | Strong organization skills | Detail-oriented (83/220)

3. Original:

Digital marketer | Business development specialist | Performing artist (70/220)

Which is the better revision?

a. Seeking opportunities in BD | Making changes with arts and technology | Digital marketer | Performing artist (108/220)

b. BD Specialist | Passionate about arts and technology | Digital marketer | Performing artist (94/220)

c. Aspiring business development specialist | Striving to elevate our society with arts and technology | Digital marketer | Dancer | Choreographer (146/220)

Assignment ⇨ 寫下你的 LinkedIn 標題（Headline）

記住：

☑ 關鍵策略就是以下兩點：

　1. 使用擷取自徵才廣告分析或職務概要的關鍵字。

　2. 量化價值或成果。

_____

_____

_____

_____

_____

_____

_____

_____

LinkedIn 個人簡介（About）：你的故事 ▼

善用「個人簡介（About）」此欄位所提供的 2,000 個字元，有助於讓你的形象在瀏覽者的腦海中栩栩如生，不過建議將此部分設定為大約 500 ～ 1,000 個字元為佳，以減輕瀏覽者的負擔——尤其是忙碌的招募人員。

此部分是招募人員和網友在你的個人檔案內閱讀的內容，它將使你有可能在眾多競爭者中超群脫凡。在這裡，你需要描述你過去的經歷、成就，以及你可以做得好的地方。如果你曾解決了什麼問題或克服了什麼困難，則可使用第 2 章中介紹的 "CAR" 敘述法（挑戰－行動－結果）加以闡述。另外，這個部分也是傳達熱情和展現個性的機會。

簡而言之，你需要清楚地表明你能給雇主帶來什麼。

Ch
6

💬 Dialog

B: On to the next section in your LinkedIn profile—the About section. This section is where you can make yourself stand out, so you should spend some time thinking about and writing it.

A: Got it.

B: Because you don't have much work experience, you should concentrate on your accomplishments, personality, and enthusiasm. You need to make yourself sound like someone they want in their company. Someone they want to train. Someone they would like to see every day at work.

A: How do I do that?

B: Let's take a look at Marcus's About section. He's also a recent graduate.

> **B**：我們繼續看 LinkedIn 檔案裡的下一個部分——個人簡介。這個欄位能讓妳脫穎而出，應該花一些時間好好思考再編寫。
>
> **A**：了解。
>
> **B**：因為妳沒有太多的工作經驗，所以應該把重點放在妳的成就、個性和熱忱。妳要讓自己看起來像他們公司想要的人、他們想訓練的人、他們每天上班想見到的人。
>
> **A**：我該怎麼做？
>
> **B**：我們來看一下 Marcus 的個人簡介。他也是剛畢業的學生。

LinkedIn 個人簡介（About）範本：社會新鮮人

簡短很重要，尤其是如果你是剛畢業的學生。看看 Marcus 的完整個人簡介。

With a recent bachelor's in social science, concentrations in economics and politics, and intern experience at Bonami Enterprise Corp, I have sales knowledge and marketing skills.

I am naturally open, hardworking, and a passionate learner and team player who always seeks out challenges and responsibilities to improve myself.

I am now looking for a marketing position at an international company in which I can use my marketing skills to

- Design infographics
- Storyboard and edit videos
- Write and present in English, Vietnamese, and Mandarin.

If any of the above sounds interesting, let's connect. Thank you.

我最近獲得了社會科學學士學位，主要研習經濟和政治，並有在 Bonami 企業有限公司的實習經驗，且具銷售知識和行銷技能。

個性開朗坦率、勤奮，我是一個充滿熱情的學習者和團隊合作者，總是尋求挑戰和責任來提升自己。

現正尋求讓我能夠運用我的行銷技能的國際公司行銷職位：

- 設計資訊圖表
- 寫分鏡腳本和編輯影片
- 越南語和中文寫作與口語表達

如對以上任何一項有興趣，請與我聯繫。謝謝。

由於 Marcus 剛畢業，沒有真正的工作經驗，他便從最能夠行銷的項目下筆：他的教育背景和實習經歷。然後他描述了他的個性，讓他看起來像是公司可能想要的那種新進員工（勤奮、熱情的學習者、團隊合作者）。最後，他描述了他正在尋找的工作（行銷），以及他可以帶來哪些技能（設計和影片製作）。

💬 Dialog

A: According to LinkedIn, I have 2,000 characters to use. That's good—I can say more than Marcus, right?

B: You can, but it's actually better to be as brief as you can. The shorter it is, the more likely someone will finish reading it. Try to keep it to about Marcus's length of about 600 characters.

A: Oh, OK. Do I just use the information on my resume?

B: Yes. Use the vocabulary and ideas that represent your strengths and uniqueness, and how they make you suitable for the job you're looking for.

A: Like we did when we customized my resume for the sales specialist position?

B: Exactly.

A: But how do I organize the information?

B: Typically, most people do what Marcus did—simply describe their main strengths first, then their accomplishments, and finally what they can contribute to the company. This style we can call expository. But you could also tell a personal story.

A: That sounds interesting.

B: It is, and stories will create a deeper impression on readers. They will also remember a story more easily.

A: Before I write my About section, do you have an example of these types?

B: I do. Sauron wrote an expository style and Symphia wrote in a more story-like style.

A：根據 LinkedIn，我有 2,000 個字元可以使用。很好——我可以寫比 Marcus 更多，對吧？

B：是可以，但實際上最好盡可能簡短。愈簡短，就愈有可能有人讀完它。盡量保持像 Marcus 大約 600 個字元的長度。

A：噢，OK。我就只用履歷上的資訊嗎？

B：是的。使用能表現妳的優勢和獨特性、並且適合妳正在尋找的工作的詞彙和內容。

A：就像我們根據業務專員職位客製化履歷時所做的那樣嗎？

B：沒錯。

A：但是我該如何組織這些資訊？

B：通常，大多數人都會像 Marcus 那樣——先簡單地描述他們的主要強項，然後成就，最後是他們能為公司做出什麼貢獻，這種可稱之為說明文風格。但妳也可以講述個人故事。

A：聽起來很有趣。

B：是的，故事會讓瀏覽者留下更深刻的印象，也會更容易被記住。

A：在我寫我的個人簡介之前，你有這些類型的例子嗎？

B：有。Sauron 寫的是說明文風格，而 Symphia 寫的是更像故事的文體。

務必將此部分保持簡短，以獲得最大的迴響——除非你有很多相關的經驗、技能或創造力，而你認為分享這些很重要。在上面 Marcus 的範本中只用了四個句子。

接下來的兩個範本來自有工作經驗的人。第一個範本是以偏說明文或履歷風格編寫，而第二個範本則更像一段故事。

LinkedIn 個人簡介（**About**）範本：說明文風格

以 Sauron 為例 (1,518/2,000)

[1] I thrive on challenges. I love to find my limits and push them along the way.

[2] I also love working with people. My experience working with cross-functional, international teams has taught me the importance of building trusted relationships and creating a shared project vision.

[3] As a project manager in charge of 2 automotive parts projects, I analyzed risk projections and performed strategic analyses for the projects. In 2020, I was responsible for increasing the number of bidding cases from 68% to 80%.

[4] I developed metrics to define the scope and goals of new projects and kept employees on track with assigned responsibilities. I coordinated with clients to factor in their expectations and needs, kept them informed, and solicited their feedback, while at the same time improving cross-functional communications. I also created monthly progress reports and estimated costs of launching new products.

[5] While facilitating the execution of projects and directing my team, I earned specific recognition from my colleagues for my ability to effectively delegate and keep myself and my teammates calm under pressure.

[6] With an eye for detail and passion for organization, I can help you
   • develop and execute successful project plans,
   • communicate expectations clearly,
   • build team enthusiasm even in the late stages of the project cycle.

[7] If any of the above sounds interesting, and you think I could contribute to your organization, please send me an invitation to connect. I'd love to hear from you.

[1] 我在挑戰中茁壯成長。我熱愛探尋自己的極限並挑戰極限。

[2] 我也喜歡與人合作。我與跨部門的國際團隊合作的經驗，教會了我建立信任關係和創建共享專案願景的重要性。

[3] 作為負責兩個汽車零件專案的專案經理，我對專案做了風險預測和策略分析。2020 年，我負責將標案的數量從 68% 增加到 80%。

[4] 我制定了指標來定義新專案的範圍和目標，並讓員工按照指定的職責與進度進行。我與客戶端協調以將他們的期望和需求列入考慮，讓他們了解情況並徵求他們的反饋，同時改善跨職能溝通。我還建立了每月進度報告，以及估計發售新產品的成本。

[5] 在推動專案的執行和帶領團隊的同時，我獲得了同事們明確的認可，因為我知人善任，以及讓我自己和團隊成員在壓力下保持冷靜。

[6] 注重細節和對組織的熱情，我可以協助以下項目：
- 制定並執行成功的專案計畫
- 清楚地傳達預期目標
- 即使在專案的後期階段也能建立團隊熱情

[7] 如對以上任何一項有興趣，並認為我能夠為貴公司貢獻一己之力，請與我聯繫。靜候佳音。

Sauron 正在尋找與他之前的專案經理職位類似的工作。他的個人簡介有七個段落：

- 前兩段總結他的主要專業特色
- 接下來的三段分享他的專業成就
- 第六段解釋他能夠如何以專案經理一職幫助公司
- 最後一段表達他積極想為公司做出貢獻，並希望能獲得公司聯繫

Sauron 的個人簡介是成功的，因為：

- 強而有力的開場白傳遞專業熱情並以此吸引招募人員的注意力
- 令人印象深刻的量化成就
- 真誠地表明他想為招募人員所屬公司做出貢獻

LinkedIn 個人簡介（**About**）範本：故事風格

以 Symphia 爲例 (1,079/2,000)

My life changed in 2017.

That was the year my father passed away. Since death is a taboo subject for most people, no one ever taught me how to face the death of a loved one. For the first time, I experienced helplessness. I experienced devastation.

Because of this experience, I decided to help people to learn more about death, so they didn't have to go through what I went through. I joined the One-Way Travel Agency, a YouTube channel that promotes death education. This was the start of my life as a content creator.

In my working period at the One-Way Travel Agency, I once created a video script for a video that got 700,000 views and I produced articles to help attract 3,000 visitors a day from Google search to our company's website.

Content creating became part of my life. I enjoy writing and turning complex concepts into words that are easy to understand. I love it when people find my articles and videos online and think they are useful.

If you like content writing and creating, or if you are looking for a content creator, I would love to hear from you!

Let's connect!

我的人生在 2017 年發生了變化。

那年我父親去世。由於死亡對大多數人而言是禁忌話題，沒有人教我如何面對親人的離去。那是第一次，我感受到了無助，我經歷了毀滅。

因為這次經歷，我決定幫助人們對死亡有更多的了解，這樣他們就不必經歷我所經歷過的。我加入了「單程旅行（One-Way Travel Agency）」，一個推廣死亡教育的 YouTube 頻道。這是我作為內容創作者生活的開始。

在「單程旅行」工作期間，我曾經為一個獲得 700,000 次瀏覽量的影片創作了影片腳本，並撰寫文章成功吸引了一天 3,000 名訪客從 Google 搜尋造訪我們公司的網站。

內容創作成為我生活的一部分。我喜歡寫作並將複雜的概念轉變為易於理解的文詞，尤其是當人們在網上找到我的文章和影片並認為它們有用時。

如果您喜歡寫作和創作，或者您正在尋找內容創作者，衷心期待收到您的來信！

歡迎聯繫！

Symphia 正在尋找與她之前的行銷推廣作家職位類似的工作。她的個人簡介和 Sauron 的一樣有七個段落：

- 前兩段分享一個關於死亡並奠定其工作經歷的個人故事
- 下一段描述她如何開始爲一個關於死亡教育的 YouTube 頻道撰寫內容
- 第四段量化她作爲作家的工作成就
- 第五段顯露她對寫作和創作的熱情
- 最後兩段表達她希望與公司或志同道合者聯繫的熱情

Symphia 的個人簡介之所以成功，是因爲它的開場白「我的人生在 2017 年發生了變化（當年她的父親去世）」相當戲劇性。接著，這段個人故事串聯起她的內容寫作工作（與死亡教育有關）。對於從事創意產業的人——尤其是涉及寫作者——個人簡介不僅能夠展示成就，還可以展示寫作技巧。對於像 Symphia 這樣的人來說，故事風格非常有影響力。

LinkedIn 個人簡介（About）範本：工作經驗尚不足者

以 Jellabie 爲例 (1,013/2,000)

💬 Dialog

A: OK, I finished my About section. The story style was a bit too difficult, so I just described my strengths.

B: That's fine. Can I see it?

A: Sure. Here it is.

ABOUT

I joined the debate team in university because I enjoyed analyzing ideas. Two national championships later, I became fascinated with interpersonal communication and the ability to persuade people.

With my experiences as the debate team leader and as a customer service representative at Bartissa coffee, I learned how important it is to listen to others and make useful suggestions and contributions. I love working on a team and doing my part to be useful and help the team be successful.

I am now looking for a job in sales to put my strengths and passions to work. In a sales or sales assistant position, I can offer

- Diligence and ~~aggressive learning~~ to understand and promote products
- Passion for working with people on a team and also for ~~building customer relationships~~
- Strong listening and ~~presentation skills~~ in English and Chinese to build relationships with customers.

If this sounds interesting, please connect with me. I'd love to have the opportunity to learn how I can contribute to your company.

B: Perhaps a bit long at 1,013 characters, but it's easy to read with the white space created by the short paragraphs and bullets. It also contains the main key words from your customized resume.

A: It's hard to write something short when you have a lot to say.

B: That's true. You know, I think you can mention your TOEIC score in the About section, too.

A: That's a good idea.

A：OK，我的個人簡介完成了。故事風格有點太難了，所以我只是描述了我的強項。

B：沒關係。我可以看嗎？

A：當然可以。在這裡。

個人簡介

因為喜歡分析觀點，我在大學時加入了辯論隊。經歷過兩次全國冠軍賽後，我開始著迷於人際溝通和說服人的能力。

身為辯論隊隊長和 Bartissa 咖啡館服務生的經驗讓我了解到傾聽他人的意見並提出有用的建議和貢獻是多麼重要。我喜歡在團隊中工作，以及盡本分幫助團隊成功。

現正尋找一份讓我發揮優勢和熱情的業務工作。在業務或業務助理職位上，我能夠提供：

- 勤奮和積極的學習以了解和推廣產品
- 團隊合作與建立客戶關係的熱情
- 強大的中英文聽力和表達能力以建立客戶關係

如對上述內容有興趣，請與我聯繫，期盼有機會學習如何為貴公司貢獻一己之力。

B：1,013 個字元可能有點多，但是用短段落和條列式的寫法，中間留有空白，很容易閱讀。這段簡介還包含妳客製化履歷中的主要關鍵字。

A：當你有很多話要說時，很難寫出簡短的東西。

B：沒錯。不過，我想妳也可以在個人簡介提及妳的多益成績。

A：好主意。

個人簡介範本：Resume (PROFILE) vs. LinkedIn (ABOUT)

Jellabie's resume	LinkedIn ABOUT section (1,159/2,000 characters)

PROFILE

- University graduate with passion for sales and persuasion, and strong interest in selling/promoting information system products
- Superior interpersonal, communication, and presentation skills: Led debate team for 2 years and won 2 national awards
- Goal oriented and an ability to work under pressure
- Aggressive, self-motivated, fast-learning team player who is also able to work independently
- Creative, analytical thinker and quick learner

EDUCATION

Banciao University, New Taipei City   2019–2022
Bachelor of Arts, Economics
- Awarded Model Student for excellent academic performance

Jingmei Girls High School, Taipei,   2016–2019
- Leader of Jingmei HS Debate Team; organized the training program, conducted lectures on debate procedures and skills
- Developed strong leadership and interpersonal communication skills
- Won award for excellent academic performance

EXPERIENCE

Intern, Epoch Foundation in Taiwan, Taipei   Mar 2022-pres
- Assisted communication between governmental, academic and commercial sectors
- Managed cases, received guests, researched/summarized/translated information

Server, Bartissa Coffee Shop, Banciao, New Taipei City
          Summer 2020
- Opened and closed store, handled total sales, built customer relationships

SKILLS AND ACHIEVEMENTS

- Languages: Native speaker of Chinese (Mandarin and Taiwanese); fluent in English (TOEIC 790; 2020)
- Led university debate team to 2 national competitions (2020–2021)

ABOUT

I joined the debate team in university because I enjoyed analyzing ideas. Two national championships later, I became fascinated with interpersonal communication and the ability to persuade people. This interest continued when I worked at Bartissa in customer service to develop customer relationships that helped with customer loyalty.

With my experiences as the debate team leader and as a customer service representative at Bartissa coffee, I learned how important it is to listen to others and make useful suggestions and contributions. I love working on a team and doing my part to be useful and help the team be successful.

I am now looking for a job in sales to put my strengths and passions to work. In a sales or sales assistant position, I can offer

- Diligence and aggressive learning to understand and promote products
- Passion for working with people on a team and also for building customer relationships
- Strong listening and presentation skills in English (TOEIC 790) and Chinese to build relationships with customers.

If this sounds interesting, please connect with me. I'd love to have the opportunity to learn how I can contribute to your company.

個人簡介

因為喜歡分析觀點，我在大學時加入了辯論隊。經歷過兩次全國冠軍賽後，我開始著迷於人際溝通和說服人的能力。此興趣延續至我在 Bartissa 咖啡館從事客服工作，以發展有助於提高客戶忠誠度的客戶關係時。

身為辯論隊隊長和 Bartissa 咖啡館服務生的經驗讓我了解到傾聽他人的意見並提出有用的建議和貢獻是多麼重要。我喜歡在團隊中工作，以及盡本分幫助團隊成功。

現正尋找一份讓我發揮優勢和熱情的業務工作。在業務或業務助理職位上，我能夠提供：

- 勤奮和積極的學習以了解和推廣產品
- 團隊合作與建立客戶關係的熱情
- 強大的中、英文（多益 790 分）聽力和表達能力以建立客戶關係

如對上述內容有興趣，請與我聯繫，衷心期盼有機會學習如何為貴公司貢獻一己之力。

編寫技巧：善用平行結構（Parallelism） ▼

Sauron 和 Symphia 都使用空白來讓簡介更易於閱讀。請注意短段落和條列式的寫法，其中 Sauron 在重複的 V-O 現在式動詞－受詞片語中使用了平行結構。請看下面的例子：

範本：使用片語的平行結構語法

With an eye for detail and passion for organization, I can help you

- develop and execute successful project plans,
- communicate expectations clearly,
- build team enthusiasm even in the late stages of the project cycle.

注重細節和對組織的熱情，我可以協助以下項目：

- 制定並執行成功的專案計畫
- 清楚地傳達預期目標
- 即使在專案的後期階段也能建立團隊熱情

上例便是平行結構，因為所列出的項目皆使用相同的文法或字詞類型："develop ..."、"communicate ..." 和 "build ..."。這種寫法易於閱讀，並滿足了我們對整齊形式的喜愛。注意，條列式也有文法不同的寫法，如下所示：

> With an eye for detail and passion for organization, I can help you
> - to develop and execute successful project plans,
> - communicate expectations clearly,
> - with team enthusiasm even in the late stages of the project cycle.

這樣的寫法在文法上並沒有錯，但要多花一點時間閱讀，而且看起來比較亂。第一項的文法（to+V-O）與後兩項（V-O、with+n）不同，整個段落也不流暢。

Symphia 則是使用另外兩種類型的平行結構：子句和句子。請看下面的例子：

範本：使用子句的平行結構語法

> If you like content writing and creating, or if you are looking for a content creator, I would love to hear from you!

如果您喜歡寫作和創作，或者您正在尋找內容創作者，衷心期待收到您的來信！

範本：使用完整句子的平行結構語法

> For the first time, I experienced helplessness. I experienced devastation.

那是第一次，我感受到了無助，我經歷了毀滅。

人們天生會被樣本和次序所吸引，我們喜歡井然有序的廚架、衣櫥和書架。瀏覽者也偏好模板和列表，在寫作中這稱為平行結構，也就是列表各部分都用相同的寫法。

Pro Tip

使用條列式和平行結構寫法，讓段落更清楚、更專業且更易於閱讀，如上段所示。

 **Grammar** 平行結構的並列句式與文法類型

平行結構可分為下列幾種類型：名詞、名詞片語、名詞子句或 V-O（動詞－受詞）。

☑ V＝動詞、O＝受詞、n＝名詞、nc＝名詞子句、np＝名詞片語

文法分類	非並列句 → 並列句
名詞 n, n, and n	a. LinkedIn users are mostly American, Europeans, and many are from the Asian Continent. → LinkedIn users are mostly <u>American</u>, <u>European</u>, and <u>Asian</u>. LinkedIn 用戶主要是美國人、歐洲人和亞洲人。
動詞 v, v, and v V-O, V-O, and V-O	b. Successful companies identify their clients, they know they have to learn about their needs, and also try to solve the customers' problems. → Successful companies <u>identify their clients</u>, <u>learn about their needs</u>, and <u>solve their problems</u>. 成功的公司辨識他們的客戶，了解他們的需求，並解決他們的問題。
名詞子句 nc and nc	c. The recruiter wanted to know which companies we worked for and our previous job duties. → The recruiter wanted to know <u>which companies we worked for</u> and <u>what our job duties were</u>. 招募人員想知道我們在哪些公司上班以及我們的職責是什麼。
名詞片語 np ... np	d. The artistic skills of students in the fine arts are not the same as graphic design. → The <u>artistic skills of fine arts students</u> are not the same as <u>those of graphic design students</u>. 美術科系學生的術科技能與平面設計科系學生的不一樣。

Exercise ➡ 平行結構並列句判斷與寫作練習（答案見 **P.266**）

1. Which of the following are parallel sentences?
   a. To excel at website design, one should be good at JavaScript and to know how to use SEO.
   b. To excel at website design, one should be good at JavaScript and SEO.

2. Which of the following are parallel sentences?
   a. All products must be tested, approved, and packaged carefully.
   b. All products must be tested, approved, and we should also package them carefully.

3. Which of the following are parallel sentences?
   a. Not only is this app expensive but also not reliable.
   b. Not only is this app expensive but it is also unreliable.

4. Which of the following are parallel sentences?
   a. Either you chair the meeting or take the minutes.
   b. Either you chair the meeting or taking the minutes is something you can do.

5. Which sentence **lacks** parallelism in the paragraph below? Which sentence has good parallelism?

   > [a] Amelia Earhart once said, "A single act of kindness throws out roots in all directions, and the roots spring up and make new trees." [b] As the owner of a small dry cleaning and tailoring business, I live by this motto. [c] I make it my mission to get to know my clients, their needs, and provide top-notch service. [d] Whether it's cleaning a favorite outfit, tailoring a wedding gown, or sewing a custom patch onto a backpack, I take pride in providing the best service in record time while always leading with kindness. [e] When I'm not running my small business, you can find me out exploring the world with my husband and two amazing kids.

6. Rewrite this sentence using parallelism. (**Hint** use 3 parallel to+V-O phrases)
   • I make it my mission to get to know my clients, their needs, and provide top-notch service.

Assignment ⇨ 寫下你的 LinkedIn 個人簡介（**About**）

記住：

☑ 使用說明文或故事風格。

☑ 盡量突顯你的成就並使用 "CAR" 敘述法（挑戰－行動－結果）。

☑ 添加求職關鍵字以優化 LinkedIn 個人檔案。

☑ 當提到兩個或多個經驗、技能或人格特質時，使用平行結構的寫作風格較加分。

LinkedIn 的「工作經歷（Experience）」並非履歷的副本，因為它們有不同的用途。履歷應根據所應徵的工作來客製化，但 LinkedIn 的工作經歷不僅應突顯你的專業成就和資格，同時也應傳達你是如何的一個人。

💬 Dialog

A: OK, I've added my Headline and About sections to my LinkedIn profile, but it tells me it is not complete yet. What else do I need to do?

B: There are still a few more sections left, but an important one is the Experience section.

A: But I don't have much experience.

B: That's OK. You can talk about your volunteer work or internships here. Try to add as many relevant key words as you can because recruiters will notice these more quickly.

A: Can I mention my debate team experiences?

B: Absolutely. You can even add some media to showcase any skills that you have relating to your experiences and accomplishments, like PDFs of articles or reports, images and infographics, or videos.

A: Actually, I have videos of my debate performances at the national competitions. One of them isn't bad.

B: Then edit it and definitely attach it. This is one powerful way that your LinkedIn Profile is a much more improved version of your resume. It can be both a list of your professional experiences but also a portfolio of your successes and works.

A: So, do I just copy and paste my resume information?

B: No. Just select the best of the best of your accomplishments or experiences. Let me show you some examples.

> **A：** OK，我已經把標題和個人簡介添加到我的 LinkedIn 檔案中，但它顯示尚未完成。我還需要做什麼？
>
> **B：** 還有幾個欄位要填，其中一個重頭戲是工作經歷。
>
> **A：** 但我沒有太多經驗。
>
> **B：** 沒關係。妳可以在這個欄位聊聊妳的志工活動或實習經驗。盡可能試著添加多一點相關的關鍵字，這樣招募人員會更快地注意到。
>
> **A：** 我能夠談談我的辯論隊經歷嗎？

B：當然可以。妳甚至可以添加一些媒體來展示與妳的經驗和成就相關的任何技能，例如文章或報告的 PDF、圖像和資訊圖表或影片。

A：其實，我有我在全國辯論比賽中登場的影片。其中一個內容還不錯。

B：那就編輯一下，一定要附上。這是讓 LinkedIn 檔案變成履歷的大幅改良版本的一種有效方式，它既可以是專業經驗清單，也可以是展現成功的作品集。

A：那麼，我把履歷上的資訊複製貼上就可以了嗎？

B：不是的。只要從妳最棒的成就或經驗中選擇最亮眼的填入就好。我給妳看一些例子。

「工作經歷」為過往至今的工作經驗總結，應突顯其中主要的成就；重要的是，曾有過什麼經驗或成就，就寫出具體的細節和數據來加以佐證支持。此時，"CAR" 敘述法非常實用。以下我們回顧一下第 2 章當中採取了 "CAR" 的例子。

工作經歷（Experience）範本：用 "CAR" 敘述法談論時間管理

To organize and manage my school, work, and volleyball schedules, I used a planner for school assignments, set aside time for homework, and kept up with my volleyball schedule. I also communicated regularly with my supervisor to avoid conflicts between work and my volleyball practice and game schedule. As a result, I was able to maintain a 3.5 GPA in school, work 10 hours a week, and be a contributing member of my department volleyball team.

為妥善管理學校、工作和排球事務的行程，我使用了一個計畫工具來安排學校作業、家庭功課以及排球練習、比賽的時間。同時我也經常與主管溝通，以避免工作與排球日程發生衝突。因此，我能夠在學校維持學期平均成績 3.5，每週工作 10 小時，並成為系排球隊的一名積極貢獻的球員。

如何將履歷的工作經驗改寫為 LinkedIn 版本？

下列三個基本步驟能引導你將履歷的工作經驗修改為更適合 LinkedIn 的寫法。

Step 1：複製資訊

將履歷中按公司或職位條列式寫出的工作經驗複製到 LinkedIn 檔案。

Step 2：重新整理格式

首先刪除項目符號。然後從中選擇主要成就（盡可能量化）並刪除其餘內容。將最重要的資訊放在前四行，以符合瀏覽 LinkedIn 時螢幕上的一頁長度。

Step 3：編輯

讓內容引人入勝，並使用如對話一般的語言風格。建議採用 "I did XYZ."（我曾做過何事）的寫法。敘述轉換成第一人稱可能需要一點時間重寫，但這麼做會使其更易讀，且更加口語化。

工作經歷（**Experience**）範本①：**Resume vs. LinkedIn**

以下對照列出如何從履歷擷取資訊改為 LinkedIn 檔案中的「工作經歷」。

Resume	LinkedIn Experience
Sales Executive • Work directly with the VP of Sales to supervise key accounts • Organize meetings to deliver proposals and demonstrate brand value propositions • Successfully closed large deals totaling more than $20M+ in sales	In my current role, I manage a significant account base in collaboration with the VP of Sales. By organizing meetings, I am able to deliver proposals and demonstrate our brand's value propositions. As a result, I have successfully closed large deals that brought multimillion-dollar sales to the company.
業務主管 • 直接和業務副總工作，監督重要客戶 • 安排提案會議，展示品牌價值主張 • 成功促成總銷售額超過 2 千萬元的大案子成交	我在目前的職位與業務副總共同管理一個重要的客戶群。透過安排會議，我能夠做提案以展示我們品牌的價值主張。就成果而言，我曾經成功促成為公司帶來數百萬元銷售額的大案子成交。

由上表可見履歷條列式的寫法變成一個包含完整句子的段落。此外，你可能還注意到 LinkedIn 版本遵循了 "CAR" 敘述法：

- 挑戰（Challenge）：做提案以展示品牌的價值主張
- 行動（Action）：安排會議
- 結果（Result）：促成大案子成交

「工作經歷」應聚焦於成功事蹟、成果和影響。此部分如同你的專業能力告示牌，展示人們之所以會想給你工作機會或與你一起共事的理由。

💬 Dialog

A: I don't have many achievements, but I added my experience as debate team leader from university.

B: That's perfectly OK since you don't have much work experience. You can still focus on school experiences and achievements.

A: Here it is.

EXPERIENCE

As debate team leader for 2 years, I developed strong interpersonal communication, presentation, and leadership skills. As leader, my goal was to enter the national debate championships, so I organized frequent training and practice sessions with my teammates and teachers. As a result, we competed in the national championships two years in a row and came in second place both times.

B: That is pretty good. I see you used the CAR structure like I showed you before.

A: Yes, I first said what skills I developed as team leader. I also described my challenge, which was to enter the national championships, and then the action I took to achieve it. Finally, the results of getting to the championships and coming in second place.

B: Well done! That looks good.

> **A：**我沒有什麼成就，但我添加了我大學辯論隊隊長的經驗。
>
> **B：**很 OK 啊，畢竟妳沒有太多工作經驗。不過，妳還是可以把重點放在學校的經歷和成就。
>
> **A：**像這樣。
>
> ---
>
> 工作經歷
> 作為辯論隊隊長兩年，我培養了強大的人際溝通、演講和領導能力。身為隊長，我的目標是進入全國辯論錦標賽，所以我經常和隊友、老師安排訓練和練習。結果，我們連續兩年闖進了全國錦標賽，兩次都獲得第二名。
>
> ---

B：相當不錯。我看到妳使用了我之前給妳看過的 "CAR" 敘述法。

A：是的，首先我說我作為隊長培養了哪些技能。我也描述了我的挑戰，也就是進入全國錦標賽，然後是我為了實現它而採取的行動。最後則提及了闖進錦標賽並獲得亞軍的成果。

B：非常好！看起來很不錯。

工作經歷（Experience）範本②：Resume vs. LinkedIn

Resume

EDUCATION

- BA, Economics, Banciao University, New Taipei City   *2019–2022*
- Leader of university Debate Team; organized training about debate procedures and skills, led the team to 2 national championships   *2020–2021*

EXPERIENCE

Server, Bartissa Coffee Shop, Banciao, New Taipei City   *2020–2022*
- Opened and closed store, handled all sales, built customer relationships

LinkedIn Experience
Note 實際編寫時*毋*須標註粗體。

As **debate team leader** for 2 years, I developed strong **interpersonal communication, presentation, and leadership skills**. As leader, my goal was to enter the national debate championships, so I **organized frequent training and practice sessions** with my teammates and teachers. As a result, we competed in the **national championships** two years in a row and **came in second place** both times.

As a barista and server, I improved my **customer service** skills and learned how to **build rapport** with our clientele to encourage them to become **loyal customers**. I also managed transactions with customers at the cash register and tracked transactions and balance sheets.

作為辯論隊隊長兩年，我培養了強大的人際溝通、演講和領導能力。身為隊長，我的目標是進入全國辯論錦標賽，所以我經常和隊友、老師安排訓練和練習。結果，我們連續兩年闖進了全國錦標賽，兩次都獲得第二名。

作為咖啡師和服務生，我增進了客服技巧，並學會如何與客戶建立融洽的關係以鼓勵他們成為忠實顧客。同時我也在收銀台管理客戶交易，並追蹤交易和收支報表。

現在，讓我們來比較兩位主廚 Penny 和 Tai 的工作經歷當中最近期的部分，看看不同寫法重點有什麼優劣之處。

工作經歷（**Experience**）範本③：**Bad vs. Good**

Penny (no successes)	Tai (successes)
Executive chef, Pasta Bistro • Manage a restaurant specializing in Italian cuisine, • control inventory weekly, • oversee food production and, • manage overall budget.	Executive chef and owner, Tai Styling Restaurant • I create memorable dining experiences that connect people to traditional Taiwanese culture through food, music, and 1960s pop culture. • I own and operate The Tai Styling Restaurant, where our goal is to immerse you into the lighter and more joyful sides of Taiwan history and cuisine one bite at a time. • We won two Taiwan Restaurant Awards for Outstanding Chef and Best New Restaurant, and we're just getting started. • I've built this business from the ground up in less than three years and have increased profits more than 60%.
行政主廚，義大利麵餐館 • 經營一家專門供應義大利美食的餐廳 • 每週控管庫存 • 監督餐點製作 • 管理整體預算	行政主廚兼老闆，台時尚餐廳 • 我創造令人難忘的用餐體驗，透過食物、音樂和 1960 年代流行文化將人們與台灣傳統文化串聯起來。 • 我擁有並經營台時尚餐廳，我們的目標是讓顧客慢慢沉浸於台灣歷史和美食更輕鬆、更愉快的一面。 • 我們曾獲得兩項台灣餐廳獎，傑出主廚獎和最佳新餐廳獎——我們才正起步而已。 • 我在不到三年的時間裡白手起家創業，並已增加超過 60% 的收益。

簡短的片語 vs. 完整的句子

Penny 在她的工作經歷中使用簡短的片語，而 Tai 使用完整的句子。對經驗不足或不習慣描述自己的人來說，片語是一個不錯的選擇。如果你沒有好的故事或令人印象深刻的成就可分享，瀏覽者會更喜歡閱讀較簡短的工作經歷。

與 Penny 不同，Tai 成功地將重點放在他正在產生的影響，他強調了他對創造難忘用餐體驗的奉獻精神和熱情。他講述了一個精彩的成功故事，其中包括獲獎、餐廳成長以及他如何白手起家。

你的履歷就是你的人生故事，所以它與時間有關；而由於英語是一種時間語言，故正確使用動詞時態非常重要。

在前面 Tai 的例子中，他使用了多少個動詞時態？ 2、3、4、5 還是 6 ？

接下來請進一步分析 Tai 的工作經歷當中的四個句子，並選擇正確答案。

Exercise ⇨ 選出正確的動詞時態（答案見 P.267）

a. Present   b. Present continuous   c. Past   d. Present perfect   e. Future

_____ **1.** I <u>create</u> memorable dining experiences that <u>connect</u> people to traditional Taiwanese culture through food, music, and 1960s pop culture.

_____ **2.** I <u>own</u> and <u>operate</u> The Tai Styling Restaurant, where our goal <u>is</u> to immerse you into the lighter and more joyful sides of Taiwan history and cuisine one bite at a time.

_____ **3.** We <u>won</u> two Taiwan Restaurant Awards for Outstanding Chef and Best New Restaurant, ...

_____ **4.** ... and we'<u>re</u> just <u>getting</u> started.

_____ **5.** I'<u>ve built</u> this business from the ground up in less than three years and <u>have increased</u> profits more than 60%.

以下是動詞時態表，須特別注意填色網底的部分，因為它們是最常見的。

動詞時態 / 功能	例子
現在簡單式 (Present) 動作 / 狀態反覆發生（習慣、事實等）	I create memorable dining experiences. 我創造難忘的用餐體驗。
現在進行式 (Present continuous) 動作正在發生	We're just getting started. 我們才正開始。
過去簡單式 (Past) 動作 / 狀態已經完成	We won two Taiwan Restaurant Awards. 我們獲得了兩項台灣餐廳獎。
現在完成式 1 (Present perfect 1) 動作 / 狀態從過去開始並持續到現在	I've built this business from the ground up in less than three years. 在至今不到三年的時間裡，我從無到有地創立了此事業。
現在完成式 2 (Present perfect 2) 一般指過去曾發生的經驗	I've been to Thailand. 我曾去過泰國。
現在完成進行式 (Present perfect continuous) 動作 / 狀態從過去開始並一直持續到現在	We've been researching this product for two months, but we still need more time. 我們已經研究這個產品兩個月了，但我們還需要更多的時間。
過去完成式 1 (Past perfect 1) 動作 / 狀態在過去某時間點之前就已發生	I had a business trip to Singapore last year. Previously, I had been to Singapore two times on vacation. 去年我去新加坡出差了一趟。此前，我曾去過新加坡渡假兩次。
過去完成式 2 (Past perfect 2) 動作 / 狀態從過去開始並持續到過去某時間點為止	Before my current job, I had worked at Acer for ten years. 在現在的工作之前，我曾在 Acer 工作了十年。

過去完成進行式 (Past perfect continuous) 動作／狀態從過去開始並持續不止至過去某時間點	They had been working continuously on their PowerPoint presentations till 4:30 this morning. 他們一直在忙他們的 Power Point 簡報直到今天早上 4:30。
未來簡單式 (Future) 動作／狀態將來會發生	We'll probably play basketball on Sunday, if the weather is nice. 天氣好的話，我們可能將會在星期天打籃球。
未來完成式 (Future perfect) 動作／狀態從過去開始並將在未來某時間點結束	I'll have lived in Hanoi for ten years by next June. 明年六月起，我將會住在河內十年。

Note 有些動詞時態在生活中甚少使用，但上面以填色網底突顯的五個時態（現在簡單式、現在進行式、過去簡單式、現在完成式和未來簡單式）建議在 LinkedIn 個人檔案中多加活用。

📝 **Exercise** ➡ 選出正確的動詞時態（答案見 P.267）

1. He _____ an employee of this company ever since he first started working.
   a. has been   b. had been

2. The marketing ideas that he introduced at the meeting _____ very interesting.
   a. will not be   b. were not

3. Our business _____ and we are hiring many new people.
   a. rapidly expands   b. is rapidly expanding

4. Mr Richardson _____ for that company for three years, from 2009 to 2012.
   a. has worked   b. had worked

5. The visitor, who we are expecting to arrive in a few days, _____ help finding a good hotel.
   a. needs   b. had needed

6. I have read your request and _____ it to the manager to get her approval.

    a. send   b. sent

7. We have so many meetings that we _____ not have enough time to focus on our main work tasks.

    a. do   b. will

8. This qualification exam last week was easy. The two previous ones _____ a failure rate of 30%.

    a. had had   b. have

9. I need to take my daughter to a doctor tomorrow afternoon so I _____ be able to attend the meeting.

    a. was not able   b. am not able

10. John _____ the employee-of-the-year award four times.

    a. receives   b. has received

11. While I _____ at college, I started my own company.

    a. was studying   b. am studying

12. At my previous job, I _____ a team of six sales staff.

    a. led   b. lead

📝 Assignment ⇨ 寫下你的 LinkedIn 工作經歷（Experience）

記住：

☑ 不要只是複製貼上履歷的工作經驗——將重點放在你的成就並盡可能使用 "CAR" 敘述法。

☑ 使用完整句子並以段落的形式編寫；注意動詞時態。

☑ 利用職缺關鍵字來優化你的 LinkedIn 檔案。

☑ 當要提及兩個或多個經驗、技能或人格特質時，善用平行結構語法是比較好的寫作風格。

_____

_____

_____

_____

這裡還有一些額外的技巧可進一步強化你的 LinkedIn 帳戶。

- 客製化 URL，使其更容易被記住。
- 主動發送好友邀請以建立人脈。
- 為你的聯絡人的技能背書；他們可能也會回來認證你的職能。

  Tip 在 LinkedIn 頁面有一個欄位可讓用戶寫出自己所擁有的技能。你可以「認證」其他人的技能，這意味著你認同他們擁有這項技能。為提升你的個人檔案的可信度，獲得他人的背書對求職有所幫助。

- 選擇一些徵才廣告中的職能關鍵字，若符合你實際所具備的技能，邀請你的聯絡人為你認證。
- 在「個人簡介（About）」欄位添加附件，例如獎項、線上課程證照、案例研究、曾做過的相關報告或推薦信等，PDF 檔案、照片或影片都可以。

Ch
6

現在你已經掌握了編寫出色的 LinkedIn 個人檔案的訣竅，那就動手做吧！加入 LinkedIn 這個專業社群網站，它能幫助你與超過八億用戶聯繫，包括招募人員、獵人頭公司，甚至潛在客戶和商業夥伴。

7

LinkedIn 人脈經營 Networking

建立人脈網並開始關注公司、招募人員和意見領袖。

Build your personal network and start following companies, recruiters, and thought leaders.

Figure [22]: LinkedIn icon line connection photo by natanaelginting – Freepik.com

Key point

關鍵

在 LinkedIn 上透過結交許多相關聯絡人所建立的良好人脈網有朝一日將為自己敞開許多工作機會的大門。在 LinkedIn 上建立人脈的最佳策略就是編寫有意義的交友邀請,並評論他人的貼文;此外,關注、聯繫和評論欲應徵公司之招募人員或員工的貼文也是重要的一環。

Plan

學習藍圖

· 在 LinkedIn 上拓展人脈
· LinkedIn 人脈經營 1:發送交友邀請
· 挑選主動出擊的對象
· 用「5P 原則」寫訊息邀請加好友
· 5 大基本情境的交友邀請寫法與模板
· LinkedIn 人脈經營 2:評論動態
· 你在評論動態上付出的努力會帶來回報
· 如何寫出有價值的評論?
· 動態評論的 6 種加分寫法

Insight 洞見 ▶

- 你需要 250 個聯絡人,才能從中獲得 LinkedIn 上的「人脈效應」。[19] 意思是,重要的不是你的 1 度聯絡人,而是你聯絡人的聯絡人;不是你認識的人,而是他們所認識的人。
- 820 個 1 度聯絡人可能相當於超過 1,100 萬個 2 度和 3 度聯絡人![19]

在 LinkedIn 上拓展人脈

　　許多招募人員使用 LinkedIn 搜尋求職者，當你擁有的人脈愈多，你看起來就愈專業。換句話說，龐大的 LinkedIn 人脈網可能為你帶來許多工作機會，而且由於大多數從事國際業務的中大型公司都有開設 LinkedIn 帳戶，因此公司的頁面往往是非常有用的資訊來源，求職者能夠從中了解公司及其員工，例如招募人員或人資部職員。

　　在送出應徵文件或參加面試之前，對該公司甚至他們的員工做一下研究，將大大提高你成功的機會。

💬 Dialog

A: Now that I've finished my LinkedIn Profile, what's next?

B: You need to build up your network, or number of connections on LinkedIn. Try to get to at least 250 as soon as you can.

A: How do I do that? I don't know anybody there!

B: The fastest way is to import your contacts list from your email with LinkedIn's "add connections." This will show you which of your email contacts have LinkedIn accounts. You can also use LinkedIn's alumni tool to find your classmates. Connect with them.

A: OK, but this seems a bit limited.

B: Right. So, you can also discover thought leaders or KOLs [Key Opinion Leaders] in the industry you are interested in and "follow" them. You can also research companies in the industry you would like to work in and follow them and any of their employees if they post on LinkedIn.

A: What is the difference between "connecting" and "following"?

B: When you want to connect with someone, you send them a connection request or invitation to connect. However, if you find someone who posts a lot on LinkedIn or is a celebrity or thought leader, you may simply only want to "follow" them so that their posts show up on your LinkedIn news feed.

A: I see. OK, my goal is to get at least 80 connections this week.

B: That sounds reasonable. But, if possible, send a message with your connection request to make it sound more sincere.

A: Got it. See you later.

A：現在我已經完成了我的 LinkedIn 個人檔案，下一步是什麼？

B：妳需要在 LinkedIn 上把人脈網建立起來，也就是增加聯絡人的數量。試著盡快達到至少 250 個。

A：我該怎麼做？我在 LinkedIn 上根本不認識任何人！

B：最快的方法是利用 LinkedIn 的「添加聯絡人」按鈕匯入電子郵件聯絡人清單，這麼做將顯示妳的哪些電子郵件聯絡人擁有 LinkedIn 帳戶。妳也可以使用 LinkedIn 的校友工具來尋找同學。去跟他們聯繫。

A：好的，但這似乎有點侷限。

B：沒錯。所以妳可以在妳感興趣的產業中挖掘意見領袖、KOL 並「關注」他們，還可以研究一下妳想投身的行業的公司，並關注他們和他們的任何員工，只要他們有在 LinkedIn 上發文。

A：「建立關係」和「關注」有什麼區別？

B：當妳想與某人聯繫時，就向他們發送交友邀請。然而，如果妳發現有人在 LinkedIn 上發布很多貼文，或者他們是名人或意見領袖，妳可能只想「關注」他們，以便他們的貼文會出現在妳的 LinkedIn 動態上。

A：我懂了。OK，我的目標是這個禮拜至少獲得 80 個聯絡人。

B：聽起來很合理。但是，可以的話，發送交友邀請時要附上一段訊息，才會讓人感覺更真誠。

A：了解。晚點見。

LinkedIn 人脈經營 1：發送交友邀請 ▼

快問快答：Hao-yun 會更願意接收哪一則交友邀請？

I'd like to add you to my professional network on LinkedIn

Hi Hao-yun! I just finished reading your excellent article on digital marketing and SaaS.

I made several notes and learned some useful ideas that I hope to put into practice at my company. I'd love to connect on LinkedIn and keep learning from you. Have a great Friday and weekend! – Nigella

我想加你到我的 LinkedIn 人脈網	嗨，Hao-yun！我剛讀完你關於數位行銷和 SaaS（軟體即服務）的精彩文章。
	我做了一些筆記，並學到了一些有用的想法，希望在我的公司付諸實踐。我很想在 LinkedIn 上與你取得聯繫並繼續向你學習。祝週末愉快！– Nigella

顯然，Hao-yun 會比較喜歡訊息 b，因爲它展現了對收件者的尊重和興趣。既然如此，爲什麼有這麼多人發送沒有溫度、系統自動產生的訊息 a？

許多專業人士使用 LinkedIn 的主要目的是經營人脈，或者套句 LinkedIn 上的術語是「建立關係（to connect / make connections）」：招募人員希望找到求職者，買家希望與賣家聯繫，賣家希望找到潛在顧客，敬業的專業人士則關注著其所在領域之領導者和公司。

挑選主動出擊的對象 ▼

邀請他人成爲聯絡人以及接受他人交友邀請的原因眾多。假設你還不太確定，下表列出幾個你會想要聯繫並接受交友邀請的人員類型。

應主動發出交友邀請的對象	建議接受交友邀請的對象
▪ 和你一起工作的人	▪ 和你一起工作的人
▪ 你在活動中認識的人	▪ 對方提及你熟識的人
▪ 你所加入之 LinkedIn 社團中的人	▪ 你曾在一次活動中見過對方
▪ 你的客戶或潛在客戶	▪ 你所加入之 LinkedIn 社團中的人
▪ 值得學習的領導者	▪ 對方在你的所屬產業中
	▪ 能幫助你成長的人
	▪ 能讓你學習的人
	▪ 值得學習的領導者

發送交友邀請時要小心！若使用智慧型手機，則無法進行個人化的交友邀請。系統預設的邀請訊息是 "I'd like to add you to my professional network on LinkedIn"（我想加你到我的 LinkedIn 人脈網），而許多人並不喜歡收到這樣的訊息。

Watch out!

關於編寫交友邀請訊息，LinkedIn 講師 Michaela Alexis（2021 [20]）列出了 6 個你不應該做的事情：

1. 不要發送沒有添加訊息的交友邀請。
2. 不要寫太多關於你自己的事或東聊西聊。
3. 不要在交友邀請中宣傳產品或服務。
4. 不要尋求幫助，因為你還沒有這個權力。
5. 不要炫耀自己有多少聯絡人。
6. 不要利用 AI/Chatbot 等來自動化這個過程。

在交友邀請訊息中添加幾句你給對方的話，是被認為更有禮貌和尊重的作法。就像你永遠不會在不解釋你是如何知道對方的情況下傳送 email 給陌生人一樣，你應該提供一個你想要與對方聯繫的理由，如此才能讓收到訊息的人對你的邀請敞開心胸。

要在交友邀請訊息中添加個人化的留言，請使用電腦連至欲聯繫者的個人檔案頁面。如果對方的檔案照片下沒有 "Connect"（建立關係）按鈕，則它可能位於 "more"（更多內容）按鈕下的選單中。

💬 Dialog

A: I'm thinking about connecting with someone I met last month at a conference in Taipei. Her name is Teresa and from her business card I found her on LinkedIn. She is a successful sales executive, and I would like to ask her for some advice about sales. But I'm a bit nervous about sending a connection request to her. Can you take a look at it for me?

B: Of course.

A: Here it is.

> Teresa,
>
> Do you remember we met at the IELTA conference in Taipei last month? I want to connect with you.
>
> – Jellabie

B: Hmm.

A: Too direct?

B: Yes. Short is good, but it sounds a bit rude. Is that what you would say to her face if you bumped into her on the street?

A: No, I guess not.

B: Right. When you write your connection requests, remember the 5 P's.

A: What are those?

A：我正在考慮與上個月我在台北的一次會議上認識的人聯繫。她的名字叫 Teresa，我從她的名片上找到了她的 LinkedIn 頁面。她是一個成功的業務主管，我想向她請教一些銷售方面的建議。但我對向她發送交友邀請有點緊張。你能幫我看看嗎？

B：沒問題。

A：在這裡。

> Teresa，
>
> 妳還記得我們上個月在台北的 IELTA 會議上見過面嗎？我想和妳聯繫。
>
> – Jellabie

B：嗯……

A：太直接？

B：對。雖然簡短是好的，但看起來有點沒禮貌。如果妳在街上碰到她，妳會這樣當面對她說嗎？

A：不，我想不會。

B：這就對啦。當妳編寫交友邀請時，請記住「5P 原則」。

A：那是什麼？

用「5P 原則」寫訊息邀請加好友 ▼

清楚了什麼不該做之後，一則簡潔而真誠的訊息應包含網路行銷公司創始人 Larry Kim（2021 [21]）所說的 5P：

1. **Polite** 有禮貌的
2. **Professional** 專業的
3. **Pertinent** 相關的
4. **Personalized** 個人化的
5. **Praiseful** 讚美的

首先，你要有禮貌，就像在專業活動中與陌生人面對面時一樣。你所編寫的訊息應該要有專業性，並且與你希望建立關係的人相關。LinkedIn 用戶不喜歡在不了解原因，且不知道此人與他們的職業生活如何相關的情況下接受交友邀請。再者，訊息也應該是個人化的，也就是說你應該說明為什麼要與他們聯繫。最後，也是非常重要的一點，對接收者表達讚賞之意相當有幫助。

更具體地說，我們可以將這 5 個 P 視為成功交友邀請的五個必備元素：

- **Personalized greeting** 個人化的問候
- **Professional recognition** 專業認可（你是如何知道對方的）
- **Pertinent reason** 相關原因（為什麼想和對方聯絡）
- **Praise their professionalism** 讚賞對方的專業
- **Polite sign-off at end** 禮貌性結語

LinkedIn 交友邀請範本：5P 原則分析

接下來讓我們再看一次 Nigella 的交友邀請，這次是更仔細的分析。在此例中，我們可以看到上述 5 個 P 是如何組合在一起形成一個有效的訊息。

Personalized connection request	5-P Functions
Hi Hao-yun! I just finished reading your excellent article on digital marketing and SaaS.	1. **Personalized** greeting 2. **Professional**—How you know the person + Praise
I made several notes and learned some useful ideas that I hope to put into practice at my company.	3. **Praise** + **Pertinent**—Why you want to connect
I'd love to connect on LinkedIn and keep learning from you.	4. **Pertinent**—Why you want to connect
Have a great Friday and weekend! – Nigella	5. **Polite** signoff

個人化的交友邀請	5P 功能
嗨，Hao-yun！ 我剛讀完你關於數位行銷和 SaaS（軟體即服務）的精彩文章。	1. 個人化的問候 2. 專業性表述──你如何知道此人＋讚賞
我做了一些筆記，並學到了一些有用的想法，希望在我的公司付諸實踐。	3. 讚賞＋相關性──為何你想與其建立關係
我很想在 LinkedIn 上與你取得聯繫並繼續向你學習。	4. 相關性──為何你想與其建立關係
祝週末愉快！ – Nigella	5. 禮貌性結語

Exercise ➡ 分析下列兩個交友邀請（答案見 **P.268**）

在每個句子之後的括弧內寫出該句的功能編號（1、2、3、4、5），答案可能不只一個。

1. Personalized greeting
2. Professional - How you know the person
3. Praise
4. Pertinent - Why you want to connect
5. Polite signoff

[A] Hi Gyllis, You have lots of great advice in your article on tips for the ELT sales process.（**a.**　）Many thanks for the educational read—I learned a lot.（**b.**　）I'm also in this industry and I hope we can connect.（**c.**　）Have a wonderful week, Antony（**d.**　）

[B] Hi Jaime, I just finished your terrific course on LinkedIn!（**a.**　）You are a terrific presenter and I learned a fair bit from just watching how you organized and presented your ideas.（**b.**　）You gave great advice and I have a lot of notes and even more inspiration. :)（**c.**　）I hope we can connect so that I can learn more from you in the future.（**d.**　）Have an awesome day! - Pete（**e.**　）

5 大基本情境的交友邀請寫法與模板　▼

一般而言，你可能會想要向下列這五種人發送交友邀請：

1. 你認識或曾經一起求學的人
2. 你在會議或活動中遇到的人
3. 招募人員
4. 你在 LinkedIn 上找到其內容者
5. 你所屬產業的業界名人、網紅或意見領袖

以下是基於 Michaela Alexis 的 "6 Message Templates for LinkedIn Connection Request Success"（2021 [22]）改寫的模板，請根據自身具體情況、個性和語氣加以個人化再套用。如果你想要一個正面的答覆，展現友好和熱情的態度是很重要的。

模板：適用於大多數情況的交友邀請訊息

情況 1：同校校友（自己目前正就讀該校）

Hi _____!

I see that you graduated from my current university, _____ (name of school). It's fantastic to see alumni having such a positive influence on LinkedIn! I'm a _____ major and would love to learn more about your work with _____ (person's current employer).

Thanks so much, _____

嗨，___對方名字___！

我看到你畢業於我現在就讀的大學，___學校名稱___。看到校友對 LinkedIn 產生如此正面的影響真是太棒了！我目前主修 ___科系名稱___，很想了解更多關於您在 ___對方目前的雇主___ 旗下的工作。

非常感謝，___署名___

情況 2：你在會議或活動中遇到的人

Hi _____, it was great meeting you at the _____ (event name). Our conversation about _____ (specific topic) really got me thinking more about _____ (general topic)! I'd love to stay in touch and stay in the loop of what you're up to.

嗨，___對方名字___，很高興在 ___活動名稱___ 見到你。我們關於 ___特定主題___ 的談話真的讓我對 ___一般主題___ 有更多的想法！我很想與你保持聯繫以隨時了解你的最新動態。

情況 3：招募人員

Hi _____,

I see that you work for _____ (name of recruiting agency). I wanted to reach out because I'm currently exploring new opportunities. I've been working professionally in _____ (name of industry) for _____ (number of years), and I think I'm ready for my next big challenge! If you have time, I'd love to talk about whether my background would make me a fit for any openings you have. Thanks!

Hope to talk soon,

_____

_____ 對方名字 _____ 您好，

我看到您在 _____ 徵才機構名稱 _____ 工作。我目前正在探索新的機會，因此想與您聯繫。我已經在 _____ 產業名稱 _____ 從事專業工作 _____ 年數 _____，我想我已經準備好迎接下一個重大挑戰了！如果您有時間，我很想和您談一談我的背景，看看是否貴公司有適合我的任何職缺。謝謝！

希望盡早與您聊聊，

_____ 署名 _____

情況 4：你在 LinkedIn 上看到了此人的貼文

Hi _____,

I recently came across your LinkedIn article/post/video about _____ (topic), and I was amazed. I couldn't agree more about your take on _____ (topic), and knew I needed to try and reach out. I'd love to connect and keep up-to-date with your inspiring content.

Sincerely, _____

____對方名字____ 您好，

我最近無意間看到您關於 ____主題____ 的 LinkedIn 文章／貼文／影片，讓我十分驚豔。對於您在 ____主題____ 方面的見解，我完全同意，並且知道我需要嘗試聯繫您。我很想要與您建立關係，並接收您啟發靈感的最新內容。

____署名____ 敬上

情況 5：你所屬產業的業界名人、網紅或意見領袖

Hi _____,

I've been following your content and I'm really impressed with your work and accomplishments. I recently read your article / listened to your interview / watched your video about _____ (topic), and I'd love to discover more about your work and support you!

_____

嗨，____對方名字____，

我一直都有在關注你的內容，你的工作和成就令我留下了深刻的印象。我最近讀了你關於 ____主題____ 的文章／聽了你關於 ____主題____ 的採訪／觀看了你關於 ____主題____ 的影片，我想了解更多關於你的工作並支持你！

____署名____

讓招募人員更容易注意到的一種有效方法是在 LinkedIn 上向他們主動發送訊息，只要他們有 LinkedIn 帳戶。如果他們會定期發文，那麼你就可以套用前面情況 3 或 4 的模板。

🗨 Dialog

B: Did you revise your connection request to Teresa?

A: Yes. I made some revisions to the connection request based on the templates from Michaela Alexis that you showed me. Here it is ...

Hi ____Teresa____, it was great meeting you at the ____IELTA event____ last month. Our conversation about __your work in sales__ really got me thinking more about __a career in sales__! I'd love to stay in touch and maybe ask you some for some advice in this area.

B: That sounds perfect. Asking for Teresa's advice is a kind of praise. Most people respond well to that kind of request.

A: Great. I'll send it out.

> **B**：妳有修改妳要發給 Teresa 的交友邀請了嗎？
>
> **A**：有。我根據你給我看的 Michaela Alexis 的模板把交友邀請修改了一下。在這邊……
>
> ---
>
> 嗨，____Teresa____，很高興上個月在 ___IELTA 活動___ 中見到妳。我們那段關於 ___妳的業務工作___ 的談話真的讓我對 ___業務這一行___ 思考許多！我想與妳保持聯繫，也許會在這方面向妳請教一些建議。
>
> ---
>
> **B**：看起來很完美。徵求 Teresa 的意見是一種讚美。大多數人對這種要求反應都很好。
>
> **A**：太好了。我就這樣發送出去。

[A] Conference/event

Scrambled request	Correct order
a. Best, Alphie	1. ___b___
b. Hi Fabrize!	2. _____
c. It was great meeting you at the NLP Conference in Madrid last week.	3. _____
d. I hope we can connect.	4. _____
e. I look forward to following your work and learning more!	5. _____
f. I really enjoyed hearing about how you're using machine learning to improve your gamified marketing.	6. _____

[B] Recruiter

Scrambled request	Correct order
a. I wanted to reach out to discuss potentially working together.	1. _____
b. I'd love to find out if I may be a fit for any of your current openings.	2. _____
c. Hi Haruki,	3. _____
d. I'm a freelance copy writer with 15 years of experience and currently seeking new opportunities.	4. _____
e. I noticed that you are a recruiter in the Osaka area.	5. _____
f. Hope to chat soon, Ruru	6. _____

Ch
7

Assignment ⇨ 參考前面的模板寫下五則不同情境的交友邀請訊息

請掌握以下 5P 原則：

☑ Personalized greeting 個人化的問候
☑ Professional recognition 專業認可（你是如何知道對方的）
☑ Pertinent reason 相關原因（為什麼想和對方聯絡）
☑ Praise their professionalism 讚賞對方的專業
☑ Polite sign-off at end 禮貌性結語

_____

_____

_____

_____

_____

_____

_____

_____

_____

_____

_____

_____

_____

_____

_____

_____

_____

_____

快問快答：

在 LinkedIn 上建立人脈甚至產生影響的最佳方式是什麼？

a. 撰寫很多動態和文章

b. 分享很多文章

c. 發布影片

d. 多評論

你對自己的答案有多大信心？

許多人可能會認為答案是 a。然而，如果你這麼做（或像 b 和 c 那樣），並無法確保穩定且不斷增加的受眾。在 LinkedIn 上被注意與否更多地取決於發表評論的頻率，而不是發文的數量。正確答案是 d。

發表評論就像坐下來進行討論一般，是最直接的獲得關注的方式。

💬 Dialog

A: Good news. Teresa replied to my invitation and accepted my connection request.

B: How many connections do you have now?

A: Only 34, and these are mostly my classmates, friends, and family members.

B: Well, that's a good place to start. But if you really want to expand your network, you need to get active on LinkedIn and start commenting on people's posts.

A: But my news feed has nothing interesting.

B: That is because LinkedIn doesn't know what you like yet. So, start to follow companies and thought leaders and join groups about topics you are interested in, like sales. Then you'll start to get more interesting posts on your news feed.

A: But what posts should I comment on? I don't have much experience or knowledge to say anything interesting.

B: That's OK. Don't be intimidated by the impressive comments you read. There are still many comments that are simpler and easier to write. Now go and start following people.

A: Will do!

> **A：**好消息。Teresa 回覆我了，並接受了我的交友邀請。
>
> **B：**妳現在有多少聯絡人？
>
> **A：**只有 34 個，這些大多是我的同學、朋友和家人。
>
> **B：**嗯，這是一個很好的開始。但如果妳真的想拓展妳的人脈，妳需要在 LinkedIn 上活躍起來，開始評論別人的貼文。
>
> **A：**但是我的動態消息沒有什麼有趣的。
>
> **B：**那是因為 LinkedIn 還不知道妳喜歡什麼。所以，開始關注公司和意見領袖，加入關於妳感興趣的話題的社團，比方說業務。然後，妳就會開始在妳的動態消息上看到更多有趣的發文。
>
> **A：**我應該評論哪些貼文？我沒有太多的經驗或知識可以寫任何有趣的評論。
>
> **B：**沒關係。不要被妳所閱讀的一些厲害的評論嚇倒。還是有很多比較簡單好寫的評論。現在就開始去關注別人吧。
>
> **A：**好的！

你在評論動態上付出的努力會帶來回報　▼

對他人貼文的富有見解的評論會引起注意並獲得回覆，彷彿就像在網路上進行真正的專業對話一樣。藉由持續的努力，評論和回覆一來一往，不僅能夠與發文者建立線上關係，還可以與在同一領域發表評論的其他人建立線上關係。

正如 Bliss（2019 [23]）所指出，LinkedIn（及其演算法）將評論視為建立對話的方式，該機制並透過擷取評論將之置入你的人脈網動態消息中作為獎勵，因此事實上其他人也可以看到你的評論，進而提升你在 LinkedIn 上的能見度。

如果你正在行銷自己或你的業務，並且如果你正在嘗試拓展人脈，你應該每週多次評論你所屬產業中的人的相關貼文。

為什麼？

求職者應瀏覽 LinkedIn 並定期發表評論有兩個主要原因：

1. 建立更多關係

如果你經常評論同一個人的發文、更新或文章，他們很快就會知道你是誰。這是與意見領袖，甚至其他相關行業的人脈或潛在客戶建立關係的特別有用的策略，並可以為工作面試和專業合作創造機會。

2. 開發新機會

評論欄位並不是讓你直接宣傳自己或所屬組織的地方——這是 LinkedIn 用戶所無法容忍的。然而，足夠多的有意義評論會帶來新的機會，比如產生商機和客戶，以及創造更多的品牌能見度。

因為很多人都能看到你的評論，所以確保它們是有意義的很重要。記得只有在你對該貼文／文章有所貢獻或想對自己從中學習良多表達真誠感謝時才發表評論，這意味著你的評論應盡量具體說明你之所以對該文按讚的理由。

Pro Tip

即使 "Great post. Thanks for sharing.（很棒的貼文，感謝分享）" 是你的肺腑之言，像這樣的評論也不會引起發文者注意。

那麼，怎樣才能寫出展現深度、引起注意並開啟對話的評論？

撰寫有建設性的評論有三個基本要素：

1. 保持專業、大方、禮貌和尊重。LinkedIn 是一個專業的平台，
   不會容忍誹謗、侮辱、酸民發言或包藏仇恨的粗魯言論。
2. 從你的知識或經驗中添加一些有價值的分享來讓每個人多學習一點。
   內容務必與你的專業領域相關。
3. 要散播積極的感受和正能量。

然而，除了上述三點之外，Morgan（2019 [24]）還列出了一些可加入有效評論的重要元素：

- 提交評論前務必檢查文法、標點符號和拼寫
- 加入你對主題／議題的想法以增加貼文的價值
- 不要自我推銷
- 避免文長
- 不要全部使用大寫

別忘了，你的 LinkedIn 檔案（姓名、照片和標題）也會隨著你發表的每則評論一起顯示。

🗨 Dialog

A: Guess what?

B: What?

A: Remember the IBMM job ad that Peter and I applied for? Well, I found the recruiter for IBMM Taiwan on LinkedIn. Her name is Isabelle Lee.

B: That's terrific.

A: Should I send her a connection request? That seems a bit direct, right?

B: Yes, it is a bit. Does she post on LinkedIn?

A: Sometimes. Actually, I noticed an interesting article she recently shared about job interviews.

B: Great. You can use this as a better and more indirect way to get her attention before you send a connection request.

A: How?

B: Write a comment. Now, before you ask, there are six types of comments you can write, and some of them are very easy.

A: Good, what are they?

> **A**：你知道嗎？
>
> **B**：怎麼了？
>
> **A**：你還記得我和 Peter 應徵了 IBMM 的職缺嗎？我在 LinkedIn 上找到了 IBMM Taiwan 的招募人員。她的名字是 Isabelle Lee。
>
> **B**：太棒了。
>
> **A**：我應該向她傳送交友邀請嗎？會不會有點太直接？
>
> **B**：嗯，有點。她有在 LinkedIn 上發文嗎？
>
> **A**：偶爾。事實上，我注意到她最近分享了一篇關於求職面試的有趣文章。
>
> **B**：很好。在發送交友邀請之前，妳可以把這件事當作一種比較間接、比較好的方式來引起她的注意。
>
> **A**：怎麼做？
>
> **B**：寫評論。現在，在妳詢問之前，妳有六種評論可以寫，而且其中一些很簡單。
>
> **A**：好，是什麼？

動態評論的 6 種加分寫法 ▼

為協助撰寫恰到好處的評論，mann-co.com（2018 [25]）和 carreerattraction.com [26] 這兩個網站建議採用以下六種最常見的評論類型；其中幾種相當簡單，下表左欄內的便是屬於比較容易的類型，因為並不需要提供專業知識或技能。

簡易型的評論	有難度和產業特定性
a. Offer a compliment 　給予讚賞	d. Offer constructive feedback 　提供具建設性的反饋
b. Make a promise to share 　承諾分享	e. Answer reader questions 　回答讀者問題
c. Ask follow-up questions 　提出後續問題	f. Add value to the post 　為貼文增加價值

Exercise ➡ 連連看。將下列評論與上述六大類型配對。（答案見 **P.268**）

1. Is it okay if I leave a link to a resource? I think it's relevant to the topic at hand and could add value for your readers.

ⓐ

2. @Arvind, I noticed that En-Tai said something relating to your question ... @En-Tai, are you able to answer @Arvind's question about ...?

ⓑ

3. Hi Jon. If you don't mind, perhaps I could help answer your question. ...

ⓒ

4. This was a great read, Arvind. I was just wondering if you thought about covering _____ because it seems relevant to the topic at hand.

ⓓ

5. You mentioned _____. This is a good point, and I know it is very true because I remember encountering an instance where _____.

ⓔ

6. I thought your post was interesting and insightful. I'm going to share it on my news feed.

ⓕ

如果你想寫出引人入勝的評論來發展人脈和影響力，你需要練習下列幾項重要準則：

- 標記作者並解釋你認同其言論之原因
- 添加其他觀點
- 延伸文章中的某個主題
- 標記你認識的、其他可能有幫助的人（使用 "@" 此符號，例如 @JellabieDai）
- 添加相關資源的數據或連結（除非有先問過發文者，否則不要寫上你自己的）
- 提出問題請求進一步說明以幫助理解
- 敘述你如何成功應用文章中的建議
- 包含替代解決方案（附上數據或實例）

接下來讓我們看一些修訂示例（根據 Bliss 改寫，2019）和語言策略，以使你的評論更有力並令人印象深刻。

LinkedIn 貼文評論範本：添加相關「細節」為原文加值

藉由評論對貼文做出貢獻的一種方法是向作者提出問題請求釐清文中某個觀點，同時要確保提問應使作者能夠進一步擴充闡明其原文。

Original 幾乎沒有反饋什麼細節或價值	Revised 回應較多相關細節，對原文有加值
Do you think your method for increasing the number of leads in sales really works?	Miguel, many thanks for the interesting post. Do you think your method for increasing sales leads would work in other industries, like the field I work in—publishing? And in your experience, did you find any common obstacles in the process?
你認為你增加潛在客戶數的方法真的有效嗎？	Miguel，非常感謝你的這則有趣貼文。你認為你增加潛在客戶的方法是否適用於其他產業？比如我工作的領域——出版？根據你的經驗，你在過程中是否曾發現任何共同的瓶頸？

左邊原本的評論態度冷淡又直接，甚至還很無禮；它提出的問題如此籠統，以至於顯得毫無意義——它沒有為讀者增加任何價值。作者可能也不想參與其中。

另一方面，修訂後的評論提出了更具體的問題，並促使 Miguel 能夠繼續對話。它還可能會吸引更多的評論，進而 LinkedIn 將透過讓更多人看到該貼文來獎勵這些評論。若 Miguel 了解 LinkedIn 此機制，他一定會感到很高興。

LinkedIn 貼文評論範本：添加相關「實例」為原文加值

Rachel 寫了一篇關於其人力資源解決方案如何幫助 IT 企業留住工程人才的文章。但你身處於出版業的人資部門，這似乎是一個完全不同的產業／市場。你是否依然能夠發表相關評論？

Original 幾乎沒有反饋什麼細節或價值	Revised 回應較多相關細節，對原文有加值
Rachel, that was a wonderful post. In publishing we have a different problem, but I still liked your article. Thanks.	Rachel, that was a wonderful post. I can see how this HR solution would be beneficial for the IT industry. For me, working in publishing, we have encountered a different HR challenge. *[Explain the different challenge.]* The approach to a solution has also been different. Still, the results seem to be the same. Great insights and thanks for sharing a solution that can help all of us think more clearly about the different challenges we face.
Rachel，這則貼文真棒。在出版界，我們的問題不太一樣，但我還是很喜歡妳的文章。謝謝。	Rachel，這則貼文真棒，讓我看到這種人力資源解決方案將如何對 IT 產業有益。對我來說，在出版業工作我們遇到了不同的人力資源挑戰。〔*解釋你所遇到的挑戰是如何不同法*〕尋找解決方案的方法也有所不同。然而，結果似乎是一樣的。妳的見解十分精闢，感謝分享可幫助大家更清楚地思考我們所面臨的不同挑戰的解決方案。

左邊原本的寫法提及個人並給予了讚美，但看起來很空洞，並且未提供作者或任何其他評論者可回應的任何資訊。

相較之下，右邊的修改版指出了即使身處不同產業，你仍然能夠補充一些自己所屬領域的細節，並藉由與作者的以及你自己的讀者相關之內容，促成進一步的對話。

Dialog

B: Have you thought about what kind of comment you want to make on Isabelle's post?

A: I think I will thank Isabelle for posting the article.

B: OK. What are you going to write?

A: How about ...

Isabelle, thank you for sharing the post. I thought the advice in the article was very useful.

B: Well, it's a little bland and she might not notice it. How about adding a question? If it's a good one, she'll probably answer you.

A: Like what?

B: You're interested in sales, right?

A: Yeah.

B: Maybe ask her if the interview questions and advice in the article can also be applied to a field like sales. And if you ask for her advice as someone who needs it and wants it, she will surely pay more attention to it. How about ...

Isabelle, thank you for sharing the post. As a recent graduate, the advice about interview questions was eye opening for me. I'm interested in entering the IT area and sales in particular, so I was wondering: does the advice in the article apply to these fields too? As an experienced recruiter yourself, I hope you can give me some guidance. Thank you so much. I'm looking forward to hearing your ideas.

A: I see. That should catch her attention.

B: And who knows? If she answers with some generous advice, you may even ask her some follow-up questions to learn more. And then even mention you will be applying for a job in her company.

A: Won't she think that is weird?

B: Not if you do it sincerely. She will probably be impressed with your initiative. This could help you stand out from the other candidates.

A: All right. Let me send out the comment to her post.

B: Good luck.

B：妳有沒有想過妳要對 Isabelle 的貼文做什麼樣的評論？

A：我想我會感謝 Isabelle 發表這篇文章。

B：OK。妳要寫什麼？

A：這樣如何……

Isabelle，謝謝您分享這篇文章。我認為文章中的建議非常有用。

B：嗯，有點乏味，她可能不會注意到。加一個問題怎麼樣？如果問得好，她可能會回答妳。

A：比如什麼？

B：妳對銷售感興趣，對吧？

A：對啊。

B：也許問她文章中的面試問題和建議是否也適用於銷售領域。如果妳請教她就像妳很需要她的意見的話，她肯定會更加注意。像這樣……

Isabelle，謝謝您分享這篇文章。我是一個剛畢業的學生，關於面試問題的建議真是讓我大開眼界。我對進入 IT 界和銷售特別感興趣，所以我想知道：文章中的建議是否也適用於這些領域？作為一名經驗豐富的招募人員，希望您能給我一些指導。非常感謝。期待了解您的想法。

A：我懂了……這應該會引起她注意。

B：天曉得？如果她大方地回覆妳一些建議，妳甚至可以問她後續問題學更多。然後甚至提及妳將會應徵她公司的工作。

A：她不會覺得很奇怪嗎？

B：如果妳問得很真誠，就不會。她可能會對妳的主動性印象深刻。這可以幫助妳從其他候選人當中突圍而出。

A：好的。我要把評論發送到她的貼文了。

B：祝妳好運。

個人化和禮貌性的讚賞

- Many thanks for the post, Peter. 非常感謝你的貼文，Peter。
- Peter, great post. Peter，這則貼文太棒了。
- Great insights—thanks for sharing, Peter. 精闢的見解—感謝分享，Peter。
- Peter, very useful and informative. Thank you for sharing.
  Peter，文章非常有用且內容豐富。感謝你的分享。

與特定文章內容有關

- Peter, I especially liked what you said about X. I totally agree.
  Peter，我特別喜歡你對 X 的說法。我完全認同。
- Peter, I think you made a great point about X. I'd never thought of that before.
  Peter，我認為你對 X 提出了一個很好的觀點。我以前從未想過這一點。
- Peter, I rarely <u>think about / do</u> X. I will need to <u>consider / do</u> it more in the future.
  Peter，我很少考慮 / 做 X。將來我要考慮 / 做更多。

提出後續問題

- Peter, I don't think I fully <u>get / understand</u> your comments on X. Could you please give some more details or perhaps an example? Many thanks.
  Peter，我想我沒有完全理解你對 X 的評論。你能不能提供更多的細節或實例？非常感謝。
- Peter, I think your point about X sounds quite interesting/important, but I'm not sure I understand it completely. Could you <u>explain a bit more / give an example / provide some more details</u> to help me better understand? I really appreciate it.
  Peter，我認為你對 X 的觀點很有趣 / 很重要，但我不確定我是否完全理解它。你能不能再解釋一下 / 舉個例子 / 提供更多細節以幫助我更清楚地理解？非常感激你。

為貼文增加價值

- Peter, you mentioned that X (S+V). I know this is true because I remember encountering an instance where Y (S+V).
  Peter，你提到了 X（主詞＋動詞）。我知道這是真的，因為我記得我也遇過 Y（主詞＋動詞）的例子。

- Peter, is it OK if I leave a link to a resource? I think it's relevant to the topic at hand and could add value to your readers.

  Peter，我可以留下資源連結嗎？我認為它與目前的主題相關，能夠為你的讀者增加價值。

- This was a great read, Peter. I was just wondering if you thought about <u>covering / discussing / including</u> X because it seems relevant to the topic.

  這篇文章很棒，Peter。我只是想知道你是否考慮過報導／討論／涵括 X，因為它似乎與主題相關。

📝 Assignment ⇒ 試寫幾則 LinkedIn 評論

請掌握以下四大原則：

☑ 個人化和禮貌性的讚賞
☑ 與特定文章內容有關
☑ 提出後續問題
☑ 為貼文增加價值

Figure [23]: Asian influencer filming photo by DCStudio – Freepik.com

Chapter

8

自我介紹影片 Self-introduction on video

展現你的表達技巧、個性甚至創造力！

Show your presentation skills, personality, and even creativity!

Key point

如果你正在應徵一份有很多競爭者的工作，你得多做一些什麼才能讓你在人群中大放異彩。錄製一支精心設計的自我介紹影片便可達成此目標，因為很少有人這麼做。一段簡短、有溫度、自然的 60 ～ 90 秒自介影片重點在於介紹你的技能、成就和熱情，讓招募人員更全面地了解你這個人。

Plan

· 自我介紹影片是指？求職者為何應準備？
· 錄製自介影片的「3P 確認清單」
· 規畫發表內容以及如何呈現
· 腳本要簡潔、口語化、分段

─── Insight 洞見 ▶

相較於標準履歷，影片讓招募人員或人資主管能夠更徹底地進行篩選，因為影片展示了求職者的表達技巧、個性和創造力。（indeed.com，2021 [27]）

💬 Dialog

A: I read an article offering job application tips and it suggested making a self-introduction video. Is that really important?

B: Not really. Most companies don't ask for one and don't expect it. And that's why most people don't make them. But a good self-introduction video can really set you apart from other applicants.

A: That's what the article said, but it sounds complicated.

B: Yes, there are many steps involved to make a self-introduction video. But by this time, you know the type of job you want to apply for and you know your strengths and relevant experiences, so most of the hard work is done.

A: OK. So, what do I need to do?

B: Write your script, practice, use your phone to film it, and edit it on your phone.

A: That sounds simple enough.

B: Yes, but it will take a long time to make a video you are satisfied with. You don't want to show any recruiter a bad video self-introduction, because it might even lower your chances of getting an interview.

A: Yikes. Well, I want to try to make one. And then I'll decide if I use it or not.

B: All right. Let's get started. By the way, even if you don't use the video, the brief self-introduction will still be useful during interviews when you are usually asked this question anyway.

A：我看了一篇提供求職技巧的文章，它建議製作一個自我介紹影片。這真的很重要嗎？

B：倒不盡然。大多數公司不要求、也不期望。這就是為什麼大多數人沒有錄製影片的原因。但是一個好的自我介紹影片真的可以讓妳和其他求職者區隔開來。

A：那篇文章也是這麼說的，但聽起來很複雜。

B：是的，製作一個自我介紹影片有很多步驟。不過，現在妳已經清楚了妳想應徵的工作類型、自己的強項和相關經驗是什麼，所以大部分的艱難工作都已經完成了。

A：OK。那我要怎麼做？

B：寫腳本、練習，用手機拍攝，然後在手機上剪輯。

A：聽起來蠻簡單的。

B：是的，但是錄製一個令人滿意的影片會花很多時間。妳不會想要向任何招募人員展示糟糕的自我介紹影片，因為它甚至可能會降低妳獲得面試的機率。

A：唉呀！好吧，我想試著錄一個，然後再決定要不要使用。

B：嗯，我們開始吧。順帶一提，即使妳不使用影片，準備一段簡短的自我介紹在面試中仍然很有用，因為不管怎樣通常妳都會被問到這個問題。

自我介紹影片是指？求職者為何應準備？

現在你已經思考過將會使用客製化履歷應徵的工作類型，並且你的 LinkedIn 檔案也已經準備就緒。因此，是時候考慮製作一段 60 ～ 90 秒簡短的自我介紹影片，並將其附加於履歷或上傳至 LinkedIn 個人頁面。

自我介紹影片應簡短、有溫度，並包含關於你的個性、技能和成就的資訊。與標準履歷、LinkedIn 檔案或求職信不同，自我介紹影片能夠讓招募人員看到並聽到你究竟是「何方神聖」。

求職者應認真考慮錄製自我介紹影片（以下簡稱自介影片）有四個原因：

1. 許多公司動輒收到數百份應徵文件，因此要求提供自介影片以篩減大量求職者之趨勢變得愈來愈普遍。
2. 有一個好的自介影片能夠讓你與其他未準備的求職者區隔開來。
3. 影片可以讓你有效地展現自我，讓招募人員清楚地看到你的表達技巧、個性甚至創造力。
4. 為自介影片所做的寫作和口語練習有助於擬出一份簡潔的自我介紹講稿，而這是求職面試中的基本任務。

Ch
8

錄製自介影片的「3P 確認清單」

要製作一支精彩的自我介紹影片，你需要仔細策畫（Plan）、呈現（Present），然後進行後製（Post-produce）。在執行此三個步驟時，精心編寫的腳本、錄製和編輯影片的基本技術以及拍攝影片的合適地點缺一不可。事實上，你並不需要多厲害的相機、影片編輯技能或任何其他藉口。使用手機拍攝和編輯影片便已足夠；有許多優秀的影片剪輯應用程式（例如 CapCut 等）讓影片編輯變得簡單。

接下來就讓我們來逐一確認上述三個步驟的要點。

Step 1：策畫 Planning ——呈現你的真實面貌就好

你將需要：

- 先有一個好的腳本，之後再調整成練習的筆記或提詞；最好設定 60 秒或大約 140 個字，但如果你真的需要傳達更多訊息，盡量保持在 90 秒或 230 個字以內。（詳見範例）
- 智慧型手機（使用內建相機即可），如果可能的話，最好有麥克風。
- 一個安靜、光線充足的地方（例如自然光下的窗戶前），以及適合拍攝影片的素面背景；如果沒有自然光，那就放兩盞燈分別在你的左右臉斜前 45 度角，確保光源不在你的身後（不要背光），因為這會讓你的臉顯得太暗。

Step 2：呈現 Presenting ——自然且討喜

你將需要：

- 從腰部以上取景，以便展示你的手勢。
- 自然的語速和清晰的對話風格，就像你在與觀眾交談一樣。
- 自然、放鬆的臉部表情和微笑；你必須多練習幾次才能做到這點，否則你的眼睛會不由自主地左右飄移，透露出你正在努力背腳本。
- 與相機鏡頭眼神交流；如果覺得尷尬，就在鏡頭前放一張讓你感覺舒服的人的照片。（先在照片上剪個洞！）
- 穿著適合你應徵的工作類型的衣服。
- 再多試幾次；寫好腳本，練習再練習，然後在錄製前做簡單明瞭的筆記。你可能需要錄好幾次，才能獲得你滿意的成果。

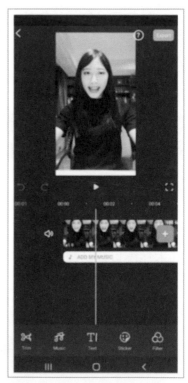

Figure [24] from CapCut

Step 3：後製 Post-producing ——順暢流利

你將需要：

- 檢視影片以確保影像和聲音穩定清晰，沒有任何干擾。
- 影片剪輯 1：去除「嗯」和停頓，甚至也可以將不同次拍攝的片段組合起來，以獲得最順、最流暢、最賞心悅目的自我呈現。
- 影片編輯 2：如果你對剪輯軟體比較熟悉，也可以添加濾鏡以調整色調，或利用聲音的「壓縮（compression）」功能來改善音質。

規畫發表內容以及如何呈現 ▼

這是最重要的階段，也是最耗時的。但是，花時間在面試中以及讓看到自介影片的招募人員留下好印象是非常值得的。

首先，你不應該只是根據履歷照本宣科。這裡的內容應該更像是一個好的 LinkedIn 檔案的「個人簡介（About）」部分：重點在於過去的成就、才能、個性和熱情（參閱第 6 章）。建議先做筆記（清單或簡圖），然後從中採用能夠將你最棒的一面呈現出來並且最適合你正在尋找的工作類型的點子。記得要在影片中放一些可展示你個人有趣或獨特之處的片段，也就是所謂的「鉤引點（hook）」。

Ch
8

自介影片腳本範例：鉤引點（hook）

Elizabeth's notes

Hook: music, viola = bridge
Education: music → Viola
Personality: team player, loves challenges and stepping out of comfort zone, adaptable, patient, detail-oriented
Experience: flight attendant - interact with lots (#) of people
Accomplishment: letter of commendation
Goal: sales and marketing
Back to school: # hrs of ITI English and Chinese business classes

Elizabeth 的筆記

鉤引點：音樂、中提琴＝橋樑
教育：音樂 → 中提琴
個性：有團隊精神、樂於挑戰並跳脫舒適圈、適應力強、有耐心、注重細節
經驗：空服員──與很多（#）人互動
成就：感謝信
目標：銷售和行銷
進修：# 小時 ITI 中英商務課程

如果你有「鉤引點（hook）」，那就好好利用。

以上資訊來自 Elizabeth。她打算將她的中提琴天賦之於她在團隊中的人際交流能力做隱喻。（參閱下頁）那是一個很棒的 hook！這點是獨一無二的，相較於其他單純敘述他們是具強大協作能力之優秀團隊合作者的求職者，Elizabeth 將會更容易被記住。

在 Elizabeth 的例子當中，起初她擬定的想法是將個性、經驗、教育、工作和未來目標結合在一起平鋪直述。經過深思熟慮、寫了又改寫之後，她想出了她的中提琴 hook 和一個獨特的故事，其中包含強調她的協作個性和強大的溝通技巧的具體細節（中提琴、服務過的乘客數量、培訓時數）。她發現這些對於她計畫將來投身的銷售行銷職涯有其重要性與相關性。

自介影片腳本範例：腳本（**script**）

Hi, my name is Elizabeth Chao.

A few years ago, I graduated from NTNU with a bachelor's degree in Music and a major in viola. Although no longer part of my career plan, the viola has deeply impacted who I am. Between the violin and cello, the role of the viola in an orchestra is a bridge.

This is like me: I am an excellent team player and I am a good mediator between different people in a group.

I like to step out of my comfort zone, so after graduating, I became a flight attendant. I once served about 600 passengers in one day and often collaborated with more than 70 cabin crew in a month.

This work experience gave me the opportunity to interact with hundreds of different people every day and trained me to quickly observe and react to ever-changing work environments. In my first five months, I even received a letter of commendation from a VIP passenger who praised my attention to detail and warm and patient service.

With a goal to improve my knowledge and skills in sales and marketing, I joined TAITRA's International Trade Institute for over 250 hours of business content courses in Chinese and more than 400 hours of Business English communication skills. I am now ready to enter sales and marketing, and perhaps make a contribution to your organization.

Thank you.

(230 words, <90 secs)

嗨，我的名字是伊麗莎白·趙。

幾年前，我畢業於國立臺灣師範大學，取得音樂學士學位，主修中提琴。雖然不再是我職涯藍圖的一部分，但中提琴深深地影響了我。在小提琴和大提琴之間，中提琴在管弦樂隊中的作用有如一座橋樑。

這就像我：我是一個優秀的團隊合作者，我在團隊中不同人之間擔任稱職的調解人角色。

我喜歡跳脫舒適圈，所以畢業後，我成為了一名空服員。我曾經在一天內服務了大約 600 位乘客，並且經常一個月內與 70 多名機組人員共事。

此工作經歷讓我有機會每天與數百名不同的人互動，並訓練我快速觀察和應對不斷變化的工作環境。在就職前五個月內，我甚至收到了一位 VIP 乘客的感謝信，稱讚我注重細節和熱情耐心的服務。

為精進我在銷售和行銷方面的知識和技能，我加入了 TAITRA 外貿協會培訓中心，進修了超過 250 小時的中文商務課程和超過 400 小時的商務英語溝通技巧。現在我已經準備好進入銷售與行銷領域，或許我能夠為貴公司做出一番貢獻。

謝謝。

💬 Dialog

A: I wrote a script for my introduction video. Could you take a look?

B: Sure ... Hmm ... hmm ....

A: Is something wrong?

B: Well, it is a pretty good first draft but we can make it better.

A: OK. How?

B: First, imagine you are actually talking to someone like a recruiter, so at least start off with a greeting. And you can end with what we call a "call to action," which means you ask them to do something, like contact you.

A: Got it. Anything else?

B: I think you can focus on your skills and experiences that are relevant to the type of sales position you want to apply for.

A: So, I don't need to mention my cashier experience?

B: Right. Some of your sentences seem like a shopping list. They don't seem to be very connected with each other. And you don't have to mention your TOEIC score—the viewer will see and hear your good English.

A: Got it. Anything else?

B: The sentences and grammar are sometimes like written grammar. Spoken grammar and vocabulary is simpler.

A: What do you mean?

B: Here, let me revise it for you and show you.

A：我為我的自介影片寫了一個腳本。你能幫我看看嗎？

B：當然……嗯……嗯……

A：有什麼不對勁嗎？

B：嗯，這是一個相當不錯的初稿，但我們可以讓它變得更好。

A：好。要怎麼做？

B：首先，想像一下妳實際上是在和像招募人員這樣的人交談，所以至少一開始要先打個招呼。結尾則可以套句所謂的「行動呼籲」，這意味著妳要求聽者做某事，例如聯繫妳。

A：懂。還有其他要注意的嗎？

B：我認為妳可以把重點放在妳想應徵的業務類職位相關的技能和經驗。

A：所以，我不需要提我的收銀經驗嗎？

B：對。妳的一些句子看起來像是一個購物清單，彼此之間的串聯似乎不是很緊密。而且妳不必提及妳的多益分數——觀看影片的人自然會看到並聽到妳說得一口好英語。

A：了解。還有嗎？

B：妳用的句子和文法有時像書面寫法。口語上的文法和字彙比較簡單。

A：什麼意思？

B：來，我來幫妳修改看看。

Exercise ➡ 下列何者為經修訂過的自我介紹？（答案見 **P.269**）

Version A	Version B
My name is Jellabie Dai.	Hi, my name is Jellabie Dai.
I have a degree in Economics, which made me interested in business.	I have a degree in Economics and strong interest in business.
I love to do research, present it, and collaborate with people.	I also have a passion for researching, presenting, and collaborating.
In university, I joined the debate team, and we went to two national championships.	I think this started in university when I joined the debate team. Two national championships later, I became fascinated with ~~interpersonal communication~~ and the ability to persuade people.
I became interested in ~~interpersonal communication~~ and the ability to persuade people.	
I had a job at Bartissa as a server and barista in which I served customers. I was also a cashier with the responsibility of tracking and balancing the cash.	This interest continued when I worked at Bartissa in customer service. I loved to develop customer relationships and customer loyalty.
~~I love working on a team~~ and doing my part to be useful and help the team be successful.	~~I love working on a team~~ and doing my part to be useful and help the team be successful.
I am now looking for a job in sales where I can use my strengths to ~~aggressively research~~ and promote products and use my strong listening and ~~presentation skills in English (TOEIC 790)~~ and Chinese to build customer rapport.	I am now looking for a job in sales where I can use my strengths to ~~aggressively research~~ and promote products and to use my communication and ~~presentation skills in English~~ and Chinese to build customer rapport.
Thank you.	If this sounds interesting, please connect with me. I'd love to have the opportunity to learn how I can contribute to your company.
(143 words)	(154 words)

Assignment ➡ 為你的自我介紹寫下一些筆記

如果你能像 Elizabeth 一樣想出一個夠吸引人的鉤引點（hook），那就加一個上去吧。

Hook?

_____

_____

_____

Education:

_____

_____

Personality:

_____

_____

Experience:

_____

_____

Goal:

_____

_____

Other:

_____

_____

自介影片腳本 Tip 1：口語化

　　一旦你有了想法並完成了初稿，接著便需要簡化句子，讓它們聽起來就像是在與人對話一般。讓我們看一下剛畢業的大學畢業生 Misty 寫的初稿。雖然它沒有吸引人的 hook，但它很清楚且所提供的資訊沒有離題。

Watch out!

你會注意到劃底線的部分十分正式，它們比較適合書面英文，不適合我們在自我介紹中想要的對話式風格。可惜的是，許多英語學習者，尤其是進階的學習者，在學校經常被教導用過於正式的風格書寫，往往都不口語化。

自介影片腳本範例：過於正式的風格（**Misty** 的草稿）

My name is Misty Tseng. I graduated from McGill University in Canada with a bachelor's degree in arts. I majored in Psychology and minored in Commerce.

Having a background in Psychology has helped me to be more open-minded and sensitive to differences among individuals, which has strengthened my interpersonal and communication skills.

Moreover, during my university studies, I worked as a teaching assistant in the summers. This experience gave me the opportunity to interact closely with people and taught me the importance of collaborating on teams in a professional setting.

Although I earned a minor in Commerce, I still desired to advance and broaden my knowledge in international business.

Therefore, I decided to participate in the six-month intensive business training course at TAITRA's International Trade Institute to further enhance my skills in several areas, for example, international trade, marketing, sales, negotiation, and business English.

<u>In such a way</u>, I have become more confident and am eager to apply my skill sets to the international trade industry. <u>It is my hope</u> to have <u>the opportunity</u> to meet with you and show you how I can contribute to your company. <u>Thank you for your time</u>.

(193 words, 75 secs)

我叫米斯蒂・曾。我畢業於加拿大麥吉爾大學，具文學士學位，主修心理學，輔修商學。

擁有心理學背景幫助我更加心胸開闊，對個體差異能夠以較高的敏感度覺察，這加強了我的人際交往與溝通的技巧。

除此之外，在大學求學期間，我曾於暑假擔任助教。這段經歷讓我有機會與人密切互動，並令我深刻體會到在專業環境中團隊合作的重要性。

雖然我輔修了商學，但我仍然渴望增廣國際商務的知識。

為此，我做了一個決定去參加 TAITRA 外貿協會培訓中心為期六個月的商務密集培訓課程，以進一步強化我在多個領域的技能，例如國際貿易、行銷、銷售、談判和商務英語。

透過這樣的方式，我變得更加有自信，並殷切期盼將自己的技能應用到國際貿易產業。我希望有機會與您見面並向您展示我可以如何為貴公司做出貢獻。感謝您撥冗觀看。

當撰寫正式的書面英文時，我們有比較多的時間思考用字遣詞和語氣，所以文字通常會比較長，並且使用比較不常用的詞彙和文法。但是當我們說話時，我們並沒有太多時間去思考語言層面的問題，所以我們使用較短的單字和較簡單的文法，而這也有助於讓聽眾較容易理解。

在上面 Misty 的例子當中，劃底線的詞語不是過長，就是包含贅字（"During my university studies"、"It is my hope"、"Thank you for your time"），或者對日常的口語溝通而言過於正式（"opportunity"、"Therefore"）。

下面的修訂版本比較口語化，修改部分以全大寫的粗體字表示，方便讀者清楚對照箇中差異。

自介影片腳本範例：口語化的風格

修改後讓語言更簡潔、更自然且更易於理解。（根據 Misty 的草稿修訂）

HI! My name is Misty Tseng.

I graduated from McGill University in Canada with a bachelor's degree in arts, **WITH** a major in Psychology and minor in Commerce.

MY background in Psychology has helped me to be more open-minded and sensitive to differences among individuals, **AND THIS** has strengthened my interpersonal and communication skills.

IN university, I **ALSO** worked as a teaching assistant in the summers. This experience gave me the **CHANCE** to interact closely with people and taught me the importance of **TEAMWORK** in a professional setting.

I had a minor in commerce, **BUT** I still **WANTED** to **LEARN MORE ABOUT** international business. **THIS IS** why I decided to **JOIN** the six-month intensive business training course at TAITRA's International Trade Institute to **IMPROVE** my skills in areas **LIKE** international trade, marketing, sales, negotiation, and business English.

NOW I AM more confident and eager to apply my **SKILLS IN** international trade.

IF YOU THINK I CAN MAKE A CONTRIBUTION TO YOUR COMPANY, I WOULD LOVE TO HEAR FROM YOU. Thank you.

(171 words, 70 secs)

嗨！我叫米斯蒂・曾。

我畢業於加拿大麥吉爾大學，獲得文學學士學位，主修心理學，輔修商學。

我的心理學背景使我更加客觀，對個體之間的差異敏感，這增強了我的人際交往和溝通技巧。

在大學裡，我也在暑假期間擔任助教。這段經歷，讓我有機會與人密切互動，並教會了我團隊合作在專業環境中的重要性。

輔修了商學，但我仍然想了解更多關於國際商業的資訊。這就是為什麼我決定參加 TAITRA 外貿協會培訓中心為期六個月的強化商務培訓課程，以提升我在國際貿易、行銷、銷售、談判和商務英語等領域的技能。

現在我更加自信並希望將我的技能應用到國際貿易中。

如果您認為我可以為您的公司盡一份心力，我很樂意聽取您的意見。謝謝你。

下表擷取自 Misty 腳本的原版（P.184）和修訂版（P.186），試比較並於底線填入相對應的詞語。

Language type	Formal written English [usually longer, less common]	Informal Spoken English [usually shorter, common]
Sentence grammar	1. _____	and this
	Although/though	2. _____
	Moreover / In addition / Furthermore	3. _____
	4. _____	This is why / so
Vocabulary	5. _____	In university
	Opportunity	6. _____
	collaborating on teams	7. _____
	8. _____	Want
	Advance and broaden my knowledge of	9. _____
	10. _____	join
	11. _____	improve
	For example	12. _____

💬 Dialog

A: The second version is much better. Thanks. So, do I just memorize the script?

B: Yes, but in stages.

A: What do you mean?

B: If you just try to memorize the script, you will probably sound like a robot and speak in a monotone voice. This is not the Jellabie you want to show to the recruiter, right?

A: Right! That will give a bad impression. So, how can I memorize the script to make me sound more natural and relaxed?

B: You need to make it sound conversational, which I have already helped you with. But for memorization, you should first chunk your sentences and practice several times. And then you should pick out key words and practice several more times.

> **A**：第二個版本好多了。謝謝。所以，我只要把腳本背起來就好嗎？
>
> **B**：是的，但妳要循序漸進。
>
> **A**：什麼意思？
>
> **B**：如果妳只是想記住腳本，妳可能會聽起來像個機器人，說話很單調。這不是妳想展示給招募人員的印象吧？
>
> **A**：沒錯！這會給人留下不好的印象。那麼，我要怎麼背腳本才能讓我聽起來更自然、更放鬆呢？
>
> **B**：妳需要讓講稿口語化一點，我已經在協助妳這個部分了。但是為了方便記憶，妳應該先把句子分段並多練習幾次。接著從中選出關鍵字，然後再多練習幾次。

自介影片腳本 Tip 2：分段

回到 Misty 的例子。你會注意到第二個初稿的流暢度更好——比較容易被聽進去，同時也比較好說。它也以「嗨！」作為開場白，就像 Misty 是在和觀眾說話一樣。

在正式錄製自介影片之前，Misty 應該將段落分解成句子、將句子分解成區塊，以幫助她知道如何以更自然的方式將講稿大聲唸出來。所以撰寫腳本時的第二個技巧就是 Chunking（分段），亦即斷句。

自介影片腳本範例：將 **Misty** 口語化的講稿分段處理

Hi! My name is Misty Tseng.

I graduated from McGill University in Canada

with a bachelor's degree in arts,

with a major in Psychology and minor in Commerce.

Mu background in Psychology

has helped me to be more open-minded and sensitive

to differences among individuals,

and this has strengthened

my interpersonal and communication skills.

In university,

I also worked as a teaching assistant in the summers.

This experience gave me the chance

to interact closely with people

and taught me the importance of teamwork

in a professional setting.

Although I have a minor in commerce,

I still wanted to improve my knowledge

in international business.

This is why I decided to join

the six-month intensive business training course at

TAITRA's International Trade Institute

to improve my skills in areas such as

international trade, marketing, sales,

negotiation, and business English.

Now I am more confident and eager

to apply my skills in international trade.

If you think I can make a contribution

to your company,

I would love to hear from you.

Thank you.

(171 words, 70 secs)

完成了腳本分段之後，練習大約 10 到 20 次以掌握節奏和語調。在影片中，你需要聽起來比平時更有活力、更活潑，因爲影片不比實際對話，往往會弱化溝通能量——相反的是，影片會讓你的臉和身體看起來比較胖。要做好這點，你應該將腳本簡化爲一個以關鍵字或片語組成的短清單（見下方範例），多練習一些，然後再錄影。

以上這些技巧能夠有效預防你只是平淡地朗讀腳本，讓你有餘裕看著鏡頭與觀眾進行眼神交流，並且幫助你盡量放鬆到自然微笑。試著讓自己聽起來很友善，像是其他人想要網羅到他們團隊的那種人。

自介影片腳本範例：提詞關鍵字

Hi
Graduated McGill – psych and commerce
Open-minded and sensitive
Interpersonal and communication skills
Improve knowledge – ITI
Int'l trade, marketing …
Confident and eager to apply
Make a contribution to your company
Love to hear from you
Thank you

時間是值得投資的

總之，記住「3P 確認清單」：策畫（Plan）、呈現（Present）、後製（Post-produce）。按照上述步驟，花時間寫一個相關的、詳細的、獨特的（如果可能的話）且其中包含鉤引點（hook）的故事。接著將腳本口語化並將句子分段，避免只是用單調的語調大聲唸腳本。然後練習腳本，練習再練習。

接下來，將腳本簡化爲筆記並再次練習。待準備就緒，確保你的拍攝空間安靜且光線充足後再按下錄影鍵。看著鏡頭、微笑，展現眞實的你。

即使做足了準備，你也需要錄很多次才有辦法對鏡頭感到自在並看起來像是在進行一段自然的對話。當你能夠做到這一點時，再將影片放在你的 LinkedIn 檔案上，並附上履歷或其他求職文件的連結，至此你已經遙遙領先於競爭對手。

錄製自我介紹影片是一個被絕大多數求職者忽視的策略。不過，許多有製作自介影片的人往往沒有做好充分的準備，結果呈現出來的影片品質很差，這實際上反而可能會減損他們獲得工作面試的機會。然而，為何不利用這些人的疏忽，好好花心力依「3P 確認清單」拍攝一個好的自介影片？這將是你投資時間可獲得的最佳回報之一，並有助於提升接獲面試通知的機會。

📝 Assignment ⇨ 寫下你的自介影片腳本

記住：

☑ 保持在 150 ～ 180 字左右。

☑ 描述關於你的個性、經歷或教育背景的細節，這些資訊對你而言是獨一無二的；務必與你應徵的工作類型相關。

Notes

PART **3**

LETTERS and EMAILS

Figure [25]: Checking emails photo by pressfoto – Freepik.com

9

信件與電子郵件 Letters & Emails

求職活動期間的有效溝通

Job application conversations

關鍵

Key point

身為求職者第一次直接與招募人員溝通是透過電子郵件和信件，你肯定想留下專業的第一印象。為此，你需要知道如何架構一封信或電子郵件，以及如何利用這些聯繫在面試前後提升好感度。

學習藍圖

Plan

面試前：

· 信件——職缺詢問信（Inquiry Letter）

· 信件——求職信（Cover Letter）

· 電子郵件—— Follow-up Email（提交履歷後無回應時）

面試後：

· 電子郵件——面試後的感謝信

· 電子郵件——回覆雖然遺憾未獲錄取但感謝對方撥冗面談

· 電子郵件——回覆工作機會：拒絕

· 電子郵件——回覆工作機會：接受

──── Insight 洞見 ▶

CareerBuilder.com 調查了招募人員刷掉求職者的原因。以下是與求職過程中的電子郵件和信件相關的主因（[2]）：

▪ 84% - 應徵資料中未提及聯繫窗口之姓名

▪ 45% - 未附求職信

▪ 57% - 面試後未捎去感謝信

▪ 37% - 面試後未跟進與雇主聯繫

Dialog

A: Now that I know how to customize my resume and have a LinkedIn profile, I need to start applying for jobs. Do I just visit job banks and send my resumes to companies?

B: That's part of it, but you also need to write letters and get ready to write emails.

A: Like a Cover Letter, right?

B: Right. Resumes and even job interviews are only parts of the job application process. The other parts happen in letters, emails, and telephone calls. These different types of communication can give you a chance to speak in your own personal, but professional, voice.

A: Hmm. That sounds complicated.

B: It is a bit, but you'll get used to it. Sometimes you will submit a resume with your Cover Letter, and you won't hear any news, so you will need to write a follow-up email. And if the company thinks they might want to interview you, they might phone you first for a chat, and if that goes OK, they will then call you in for an interview.

A: And then they tell you if you got the job?

B: Not usually. After the interview, you should send the interviewer a thank you note. And then they might call you back for a few more rounds of interviews. And then you might get a job offer ... or not. Either way, you need to write emails and continue the conversation to the end.

A: OK. That is really complicated.

B: Don't worry. We will go through these letter and email conversations step by step.

A：現在我知道怎麼客製化履歷了，也有了 LinkedIn 個人檔案，我要開始應徵工作了。再來我只要去看人力銀行網站然後丟履歷給公司就好了對吧？

B：對一部分，妳還需要寫信並準備寫 email。

A：就像求職信 一樣，對嗎？

B：沒錯。履歷甚至面試都只是求職過程的一部分，其他部分還包括信件、email 和電話。這些不同類型的溝通管道可以讓妳有機會呈現真實而專業的自我。

A：嗯，聽起來有點複雜。

B：是有一點，但妳會習慣的。有時妳會隨求職信一起提交履歷，但是妳不會收到任何回應，所以妳需要寫一封 follow-up email 跟進了解狀況。如果那家公司想與妳面談，他們可能會先打電話給妳聊聊，如果聊得不錯，他們會再打電話跟妳安排面試。

A：然後他們會通知我有沒有被錄取嗎？

B：通常不會。面試結束後，妳應該給面試官發一封感謝信。然後他們可能會再跟妳進行好幾輪的電話面試。然後，或許妳會得到一份工作……也可能不會。無論哪種方式，妳都要透過 email 繼續和面試單位保持互動到最後。

A：OK。這真的很複雜。

B：別擔心。我們一步一步來，看看這些信件和 email 該怎麼寫。

Letters vs. emails　▼

在求職期間，你可能需要寫兩種類型的信件：職缺詢問信（inquiry letter）和求職信（cover letter）。這兩種溝通管道在內容和目的上往往更像是正式的獨白，因此我們稱之為信件。此外，你還需要寫一些電子郵件（email），因為面試前後通常都會有透過電子郵件互動的過程，所以電子郵件更像是招募人員和求職者之間的對話。

寫信技巧

- 為了看起來更專業，請將履歷和信件中的格式（如字形、字體大小）統一，以創造一個具一致性的個人品牌。
- 記得寫下聯繫資訊，尤其是你的電話號碼、電子郵件和 LinkedIn 網址。

寫信和電子郵件的技巧

- 藉由從徵才廣告分析得來之技能、經驗方面的關鍵字突顯你是合格的人選。
- 依循 "KISSES" 守則使其簡潔、具體、引人入勝以及可供 ATS 機器掃描。

就整體而言，在包括信件、電子郵件、電話和面試在內的求職溝通中，你需要始終如一地表達兩件事：

1. 你的熱情／興趣
2. 你對該公司的潛在貢獻

🗨 Dialog

A: I was scrolling on LinkedIn and came across this company called GreenTexx. They make pretty cool green technology products and wrote some interesting articles. They really seem to care about reducing waste and increasing recycling in their products. I think it would be cool to work there.

B: So, why don't you send them an email to ask if they are hiring?

A: I already checked their website, and they are not currently seeking employees.

B: That's OK. You can still send what we call an Inquiry Letter to express your interest in working with the company. Who knows, they might soon be recruiting.

A: OK. How what do I need to write?

B: In this case, you need to write an Inquiry Letter.

> **A：**我在滑 LinkedIn 時發現了這家名為 GreenTexx 的公司。他們製作很厲害的綠色科技產品,並分享了一些有趣的文章。他們似乎真的很關心減少浪費和增加產品的回收利用。我覺得在那裡工作應該很酷。
>
> **B：**那妳為什麼不給他們發一封 email 詢問他們有沒有在徵人?
>
> **A：**我已經看過他們的網站,他們目前並沒有在招募員工。
>
> **B：**沒關係。妳還是可以發送我們所說的詢問信來表達妳想服務於那家公司的興趣。說不定他們可能很快就會徵人。
>
> **A：**OK。我要怎麼寫?
>
> **B：**在這種情況下,妳要寫的是職缺詢問信。

職缺詢問信（Inquiry Letter） ▼

　　職缺詢問信（Inquiry Letter）,又稱為 Letter of Interest（以下簡稱詢問信）,是一種針對目前可能正在徵才,但沒有你所屬領域的有效職位,但你仍然可主動聯繫公司的一種方式。在詢問信中,你可以直接聯繫潛在雇主解釋你的技能如何能夠使該公司受益,並詢問他們是否有職缺。活用詢問信亦有助於拓展人脈,更重要的是,當該公司未來有職缺時,你可能就會被優先納入考慮。

　　根據 Indeed.com（2021 [28]）,詢問信的結構應包含以下四個部分:

Part 1. 使用聯繫窗口的姓名（Dear ...）

正如「Insight 洞見」所述，84% 的招募人員希望求職者的應徵資料是指名寄給他們的，而非籠統的通稱 "To whomever it may concern"（敬啟者）或 "Dear Hiring Manager"（敬愛的招募經理）。

> *Pro Tip*
>
> 如何得知收件者的姓名？詢問親朋好友是否有人認識你想應徵的公司裡的員工，或者，如果是一家小公司，甚至不妨直接致電詢問負責窗口是哪位。至於較大的公司，則建議造訪他們的網站並試著用 LinkedIn 來搜尋他們的招募人員。若能在詢問信中顯示你知道這些資訊，相當於展現你的研究技能、奉獻精神和對該公司的興趣。

Part 2. 創建令人難忘的開場白

在開場白部分，試著與該公司和聯繫窗口「拉關係」。如果你是經由一個共同熟人得知對方的聯繫資料，提及此事有助於立即拉近彼此的關係。如果你不認識聯繫窗口，就說明你是如何得知他們，以及你寫這封信的原因。如果你關注此聯繫窗口或公司已有一段時間了，例如在 LinkedIn 上，務必讓這點和你對該公司的熱情一覽無遺。

Part 3. 突顯技能

在這第二段中，你需要描述足以使你成為該職缺之有力候選人的本事。大方地自我行銷並展示你的技能、資格和經驗如何為公司做出一番貢獻。

> *Pro Tip*
>
> 這段要簡短和夠有趣，促使他們向你詢問更多資訊。

為了給人留下深刻印象，仔細研究欲應徵之公司，不僅要了解其優勢，還要找出其弱點和需求。如果你做得到這點，極其有禮地提出他們可改進之處，以及你或許能夠助一臂之力的方式。同樣地，這裡不需要寫得太具體，只要道出足夠的細節以勾起他們對你的好奇心。而如果你有完整的策略，則可於被錄取後再提供詳細的建議方案給對方。

Part 4. 簡短的結論

在拉近雙方關係並描述你的相關價值後，信末應傳達：

- 你有興趣與他們會面
- 感謝他們撥冗閱讀

以下是職缺詢問信的標準刊頭。確保你的聯繫資訊置頂於信件上方；信件的格式須與履歷一致，以營造專業的風格。

YOUR NAME

0 Fl, No123, Lane 45, Street Name, Area Name, City, Taiwan

LinkedIn address　　+886-02-12345678　　name@emailaddress.com

寫完強而有力的最後一段後，務必使用專業且有禮貌的結語，例如：

- Respectfully（尊敬地）
- Sincerely（誠摯地）
- Thank you（感謝）
- Best Regards（最好的問候）

讓我們看幾個範本。

職缺詢問信範本 1：應屆畢業生

1. 使用聯繫窗口的姓名

2. 創建令人難忘的開場白

3. 突顯技能

4. 簡短的結論

Seo-jun Kim

Apt. 102-304 Sajik-ro-3-gil 23 Jongno-gu, Seoul 30174

sjkim@gmail.com   82 123 4568   www.linkedin.com/in/seojunkim/

Dear Ms. Park,

As a recent honors graduate in finance, I am eager to find a position where I can learn and grow with the best in the finance industry. I have been following your company in the news and on LinkedIn for some time and am impressed with your team's ability to maintain steady financial portfolio growth and provide excellent trading advice to your clients. I am highly motivated and would love to be part of your team as a financial analyst if a position opens.

At college, I completed two internships–one at a financial institution and the other at a bank–where I developed my skills in financial accounting, auditing, investment banking, and trading. My final year honor's thesis focused on the stock market and the best times to trade, buy, or sell (this thesis can be accessed from my LinkedIn account above). I am meticulous in my attention to detail and take great pride in logging accurate accounting books. I'm dedicated to delivering high-quality work ahead of deadlines.

I hope we can set up a time to meet to discuss how my qualifications can be a benefit to your company. If you have any questions regarding my skills, please call or email me at the contacts listed at the top of the letter. Thanks again for reviewing my resume. I look forward to hearing from you.

Respectfully,
Seo-Jun Kim

金書俊

30174 首爾鐘路區社稷路三街 23 號 102 公寓 304 室

sjkim@gmail.com   82 123 4568   www.linkedin.com/in/seojunkim/

朴女士您好：

我是一名最近畢業於金融專業的榮譽畢業生，十分渴望能夠找到一個可以與金融產業之佼佼者一起學習和成長的職位。我在新聞和 LinkedIn 上已經關注貴公司一段時間了，並且對貴團隊保持穩定的金融投資組合成長，以及為客戶提供絕佳交易建議的能力印象極為深刻。若貴公司有開放職缺，個性積極進取的我很希望以金融分析師之身分成為您團隊的一員。

在大學裡，我完成了兩次實習，一次在金融機構，另一次在銀行，期間我培養了財務會計、審計、投資銀行和貿易方面的技能。我最後一學年的榮譽論文側重於股票市場和交易、買入或賣出的最佳時機（此論文可於我上面的 LinkedIn 帳戶查看）。我對細節一絲不苟，並深以記錄準確的會計帳簿為榮；我致力於在截止日期之前交付出高品質的工作成果。

希望我們可以安排時間會面討論我的能力如何為貴公司增色。若您對我的技能有任何疑問，請透過信件頂部的聯繫資訊來電或發電子郵件。再次感謝您審閱我的履歷。靜候佳音。

金書俊 敬上

職缺詢問信範本 2：經驗豐富的專業人士

Miki Yamaguchi

2-7-2 Marunouchi, Chiyoda-ku, Tokyo 100-8994

Myamaguchi001@gmail.com   080-1234-5678   www.linkedin.com/in/myamaguchi/

1. 使用聯繫窗口的姓名

Dear Mr. Lee,

I have been following the recent growth of XYZ Corp. after the launch of your new ABC product line. These products really look like they will be able to improve your customer's lives and continue to grow your consumer base. I am writing to ask

2. 創建令人難忘的開場白

if you have considered adding a strategist role to your marketing team. I have a demonstrated record of implementing marketing strategies to reach new consumers who would love the product. I believe my innovative marketing skills would be a good fit for your innovative product team.

3. 突顯技能

I have seven years' experience as a senior marketing strategist with a local brand, where I led a team of four junior marketing analysts and the company's highest gross profit segment. During my first year in this role, I increased website page views by 130% and continued to grow views by 5% each year since. With SEO and content marketing strategies, I have helped the website rank in the top 5 for key words related to our main product lines. I also led our company's social media marketing campaign (Facebook, IG, and Tik Tok), where we saw an average of 12,000 traffic redirects to our website from the social media postings. Additionally, the sales revenue of my segment increased by 50% over my seven years on the team as a marketing strategist.

I would be grateful if you could add my name to your list of potential candidates for future marketing roles, especially relating to marketing strategy. My resume and work samples are attached, and please let me know if I can provide any additional references. I would welcome the opportunity to speak with you regarding a marketing career with XYZ brand. Thank you for your time and consideration.

Sincerely,
Miki Yamaguchi

山口美紀

100-8994 東京都千代田區丸之內 2-7-2

Myamaguchi001@gmail.com　080-1234-5678　www.linkedin.com/in/myamaguchi/

李先生您好：

自從您們推出新的 ABC 產品線後，我一直在關注貴公司的近期成長。此產品看起來真的能夠改善您們客戶的生活，並繼續擴大您的消費群。我寫這封信是想探詢您是否考慮過在您的行銷團隊中增加一個策略師的角色。我在實施行銷策略以吸引喜愛公司產品的新消費者方面有相當不錯的實績。相信我創新的行銷技能與您的創新產品團隊是絕佳組合。

作為本土品牌的資深行銷策略師，我有七年的實戰經驗，我曾領導由四名新進行銷分析師組成的團隊，我們是公司毛利潤最高的部門。在我執行此職務的第一年，我使公司網站的瀏覽量增加了 130%，並且從那之後，每年以 5% 的量繼續上漲。透過 SEO 和內容行銷策略，我幫助了該網站在與我們主要產品線相關的關鍵字中排名前 5。我還領導了我們公司的社群媒體行銷活動（Facebook、IG 和 Tik Tok），平均有 12,000 次流量從社群媒體上的貼文重新導向到我們的網站。此外，在我擔任行銷策略師的七年時間裡，我們部門的銷售收入整整增長了 50%。

若能將我加入您未來行銷團隊的潛在候選人名單中，尤其是與行銷策略相關的職位，本人不勝感激。隨信附上我的履歷和工作樣本，如果我可以提供任何其他參考資料，麻煩請告知。十分樂意有機會與您討論 XYZ 品牌的行銷職務。感謝您的時間及考慮。

此致
山口美紀

Dialog

A: After looking at the examples you showed me, I'm not sure what qualifications I should emphasize for an Inquiry Letter to GreenTexx.

B: Well, what have you learned about the company?

A: I found them on LinkedIn. They are a new Taiwanese company who makes IT products and computer peripherals, like keyboards and mouses. They use a lot of recycled plastics and metals to make their products.

B: OK, so that's why they are called GreenTexx—green technology.

A: Right. And they try to reduce waste and carbon emissions and design their products to be easily repairable.

B: Sounds like an innovative and caring company. So, what kind of position would you like? Sales, like with the IBMM job you're applying for?

A: Sure, or customer service or marketing.

B: For sales and customer service, you can emphasize your knowledge of economics and your experience serving customers at Bartissa. You also have good research and presentation skills from your experience with the debate club. Mention those.

A: OK. How about my English ability?

> **A：**看了你給我的範例後，我不確定在給 GreenTexx 的詢問信中我應該強調什麼資格。
>
> **B：**嗯，妳對這公司有什麼了解？
>
> **A：**我在 LinkedIn 上有找到他們。他們是一家新的台灣公司，生產 IT 產品和電腦周邊設備，例如鍵盤和滑鼠。他們使用大量再生塑膠料和金屬來製造產品。
>
> **B：**OK，所以這就是為什麼他們取名為 GreenTexx —— 綠色技術。
>
> **A：**對。他們致力於減廢和減碳，並將他們的產品設計成易於維修的。
>
> **B：**聽起來像是一家創新且充滿愛心的公司。那麼，妳想做什麼樣的職位？業務？就像妳應徵的 IBMM 工作一樣？
>
> **A：**沒錯，要不然就是客服或行銷工作。
>
> **B：**針對業務和客服工作，妳可以強調自己的經濟學知識和在 Bartissa 咖啡館為顧客服務的經驗。從辯論社的經驗中，妳還擁有很棒的研究和表達技巧。這些都要提到。
>
> **A：**好的。那我的英語能力呢？
>
> **B：**絕對要提及！如果他們是一家開發實用和創新產品的新興本土公司，他們會希望在國際市場上發展業務。他們肯定會想要找到英語能力良好的員工。
>
> **A：**聽起來不錯。我現在知道該在詢問信中寫什麼了。

Ch
9

職缺詢問信範本 3：Jellabie 詢問一家綠色科技公司的職缺

Jellabie (Yi-ran) Dai

jellabie@school.edu   0955-555-555   tw.linkedin.com/in/jellabiedai/

As a recent graduate in economics and an ecofriendly tech enthusiast, I am eager to find a position in an innovative and green company. I recently discovered your company on LinkedIn and have read about your products and really admire your creativity and corporate values of reducing waste, reusing materials, and making your products repairable. I am highly motivated and hardworking, and I would love to be part of your sales or customer service team if a position opens.

From my experiences in customer service at a coffee shop, I learned the importance of interpersonal communication skills and I enjoyed making an effort to remember people's names and orders to increase customer loyalty. I developed my research and persuasive presentation skills in university when I was leader of the debate club. We went to the national championships twice and we came in second both times. My degree in economics gives me a solid understanding of business and with my high English proficiency (TOEIC 790), I am ready to start a career in international sales or customer service. I look forward to using my strengths and experiences to contribute to an excellent company like GreenTexx.

I hope we can set up a time to meet to discuss how my qualifications can be a benefit to your company. If you have any questions regarding my skills, please call or email me at the contacts listed at the top of the letter. Thank you so much for reviewing my resume. I look forward to hearing from you.

婕拉比（怡然）戴

jellabie@school.edu   0955-555-555   tw.linkedin.com/in/jellabiedai/

作為一名剛畢業於經濟學的環保技術愛好者，我熱切希望能夠於一家創新的綠色公司覓得一職。我最近在 LinkedIn 上找到了貴公司，並參閱了貴公司的產品，真的非常欣賞您們在減廢、重複使用材料、設計易維修產品等方面的創造力和企業價值。我個性主動積極且工作勤奮，如果貴公司有開放職缺，我很希望成為貴公司的銷售或客服團隊的一員。

從我在咖啡館的客服經驗中，我了解到人際溝通技巧的重要性；我盡力記住客人的名字和他們的訂單品項以提高顧戶忠誠度。當我在大學期間擔任辯論社社長時，我發展了研究和具說服力的表達技巧。我們曾兩度闖進全國錦標賽，並且都獲得亞軍。我主修經濟學，使我對商業有紮實的理解，加上我優異的英語能力（多益 790 分），我已經準備好在國際業務或客服領域開啓職涯。我期待能夠利用我的優勢和經驗為像 GreenTexx 這樣的傑出公司做出一番貢獻。

希望我們可以安排時間會面討論我的能力如何為貴公司增色。若您對我的技能有任何疑問，請透過信件頂部的聯繫資訊來電或發電子郵件。非常感謝您審閱我的履歷。靜候佳音。

From paragraph 1

1. What are the two connections Jellabie makes with the company?

   a) _____

   b) _____

2. What are her qualifications? Check (✓) the relevant ones.
   _____ Economics graduate
   _____ Ecofriendly tech enthusiast
   _____ Highly motivated
   _____ Hardworking
   _____ Wants to work in customer service or sales

3. What position is she interested in?

From paragraph 2

4. What is the order of the five skills she listed? Put a number next to them.
   __3__ presentation skills
   _____ Interpersonal communication skills to boost customer service and loyalty
   _____ English proficiency
   _____ research skills
   _____ knowledge of economics and business

5. Why did Jellabie rank the skills in that order?
   a. no reason
   b. most important skills first for job
   c. most important skills last

ANTHONY WONG

No. 10-5, Aly. 80, Guanter Ln., Pingtung, Taiwan

tw.linkedin.com/in/antwong/   0975666129   awong@gmail.com

Feb. 22, 2021
Mike Chow, Hiring Manager
Agoda
4F, 7 Wan-Hwa Rd.,
Taipei City, Taiwan

Dear Mr. Chow,

Paragraph 1

___3___ I would love to be part of your team in sales, marketing, or customer service.

_____ I have used your service several times on my travels in Europe and admire your first-class technology and marketing.

_____ With a degree in Foreign Languages and Literature and certificate in International Trade and passion for travel, I am eager to find a position in the travel industry.

Paragraph 2

_____ These travel experiences convinced me to choose a career in the tourism industry.

_____ I have a TOEIC score of 980 out of 990, which is considered native-like, or C2 according to the CEFR. While I was earning my Bachelor's Degree in Foreign Languages and Literature, I was an exchange student in Germany where I improved my German (Intermediate, CEFR A2-B1) and traveled to 15 countries in Europe.

_____ In this program, I was able to use my strong interpersonal skills and a detail-oriented personality as well as skills in image and video editing that I developed in college.

_____ To improve my business knowledge and communication skills, I enrolled in a six-month intensive post-bachelor's program in International Trade where I completed several marketing projects, made frequent sales presentations, and participated in numerous negotiations.

Paragraph 3

_____ If you have any questions regarding my skills, please call or email me at the contact information at the top of the letter.

_____ I hope we can set up a time to meet to discuss how my skills and experience can contribute to your company.

_____ Thank you for taking the time to review my resume. I look forward to hearing from you.

Sincerely,
Anthony Wong

📝 Assignment ⇨ 寫下你的職缺詢問信

記住：

☑ 使用聯繫窗口的姓名（Dear Mr./Ms. ...）。

☑ 第一段，創建令人難忘的開場白，拉近你與公司之間的距離。

☑ 第二段，突顯你的相關能力，但不需要太詳細。點到為止讓招募人員對你產生好奇心。

☑ 第三段，表達你有興趣與他們會面，並感謝對方的時間。

Ch
9

求職信（Cover Letter）▼

求職信（Cover Letter）是你在應徵工作時隨履歷附上的信函。

　　將求職信想像成一篇短文，訴說你之所以就是所應徵職位之最佳人選的三大強項。在第一段開場白點出此三大強項為何，再於接續的段落詳細說明加以佐證。一封理想的求職信內容約分為五段，簡潔即可，其中包含一些未列於履歷上的具體細節。和詢問信一樣，盡量找出將負責審閱求職信之招募人員的姓名。

💬 Dialog

A: I have customized my resume for the IBMM job ad, so now I have to write a Cover Letter, right?

B: Yes. This is where you can focus on your main strengths for the job, and even some less important strengths.

A: So, I need to copy-and-paste my profile information from my customized resume.

B: Yes, but you need to put these phrases into sentences that logically connect to each other.

A: How many paragraphs do I need? Is it three, like for the letter of inquiry?

B: Actually, you can write more because you know what job you are applying for and you can list all of your relevant qualifications, like experiences, skills, and personality traits. I suggest five paragraphs.

> **A：**我已經為 IBMM 徵才廣告客製化我的履歷，所以現在我必須寫一封求職信，對吧？
>
> **B：**是的。妳可以強調妳對這份工作的主要優勢，甚至一些比較不重要的強項也都可以寫進去。
>
> **A：**所以，我需要從我的客製化履歷把個人資訊複製貼上。
>
> **B：**對，但是妳要把那些片語放在符合邏輯的前後文中。
>
> **A：**要寫幾段？三段嗎？跟詢問信一樣？
>
> **B：**其實，妳可以寫更多，因為妳知道自己應徵的是什麼工作，妳可以列出所有的相關資格，例如經驗、技能和人格特質。我建議五段。

第一段：開場白（說明你是一個優質求職者的三個原因）

　　這個段落就像一篇短文的引言，點出此文的三大要點——即針對該職位你最亮眼的三個能力／資格。條列式寫法有助於突顯所寫內容並使之更易於閱讀。

- 表明欲應徵之工作為何以及從何得知招聘資訊
- 使用徵才廣告中的關鍵字提及針對該工作個人最適任的能力／資格

第二～三段：正文（支持前述三大要點並補充其他原因）

　　在第二段中，利用兩到三句話，詳細說明你的資格（qualifications）、技能（skills）、能力（abilities）、工作經驗（experience）和人格特質（personality traits）是如何與所應徵之工作相匹配。

　　雖然筆者強調應利用徵才廣告中的關鍵字，但仍應避免多次重複同一個詞。因此，建議使用不同的字詞形態（下例 A）或同／近義字（下例 B）來換句話說第一段中的資訊，例如：

例A｜ assist、assisted、assisting、assistance、assistant（協助／助理）

例B｜ helped（幫助）、coordinated（統籌）、facilitated（促進）、organized（規畫）、arranged（安排）＊記得使用過去式

　　你可以繼續寫第三段來添加三～五個其他強項，建議使用句子加條列式名詞片語清單，例如：

Other key strengths that I possess for success in this position include the following:
- qualifications, skills, experience, personal qualities – use NOUN phrases
- qualifications, skills, experience, personal qualities – use NOUN phrases
- qualifications, skills, experience, personal qualities – use NOUN phrases
- qualifications, skills, experience, personal qualities – use NOUN phrases

讓我能夠勝任此職位的其他強項包括：
- 資格、技能、工作經驗、人格特質——使用名詞片語（下略）

第四段：更多資訊請參閱附件

本段大意為告知審閱者可參考隨附的履歷以獲取更多資訊，例如：

Please see my attached resume for additional information on my qualifications and experience.

關於我的資格與工作經驗，欲知更多資訊，請參閱隨附履歷。

第五段：結論

在最後一段中，簡單地感謝審閱者，表現出欲會面之意，並提及自己的聯繫方式，例如：

Thank you for your time and consideration. I look forward to speaking with you about this employment opportunity. I can be reached anytime via the contact information above.

感謝您的時間和考慮。期待與您討論此工作機會。歡迎透過上面的聯繫資訊隨時聯絡我。

📱 Dialog

A: I think I have it. For the IBMM sales specialist job, I want to use key words from the job ad and highlight my

- Strong interpersonal and persuasive communication skills
- Goal-oriented personality and ability to work under pressure both independently and on a team
- Passion for sales and IT products

B: That sounds good, but I think you might want to put your "passion for sales and IT products" first because it shows your enthusiasm, which is a recent graduate's main USP or selling point.

A: Got it.

B: What about the second paragraph? What details or examples can you give to support the three main qualifications in the first paragraph?

A: Well, for my "passion for sales" I can describe my efforts to remember my customers' names and order to create customer loyalty. That was a fun game for me. I will then mention my debate club experiences that helped me develop my interpersonal communication and presentation skills.

B: Sounds good. Any other qualifications you can mention in the third paragraph?

A: My English ability and Bachelor's degree ....

B: ... and your research skills and personality traits, like being a quick learner, having a responsible attitude, and don't forget your detail-oriented personality.

A: Great. I'll get to work and write it out.

> **A**：我想我有的。針對 IBMM 業務專員的工作，我想用徵才廣告中的關鍵字來突顯我
>
> -----
>
> - 強大的人際互動能力和具說服力的溝通技巧
> - 目標導向的個性和在壓力下獨立工作與團隊合作的能力
> - 對銷售和 IT 產品的熱情
>
> -----
>
> **B**：看起來相當不錯，但我建議把「對銷售和 IT 產品的熱情」放在首位，有助於顯示妳的熱忱，這是應屆畢業生的主要賣點。
>
> **A**：了解。
>
> **B**：那第二段呢？妳能給出什麼細節或例子來支持第一段中的三大強項？
>
> **A**：嗯，針對「對銷售的熱情」，我可以描述我為記住顧客的姓名和訂單品項以建立顧客忠誠度所做的努力。那對我來說是一場有趣的比賽。然後，我會提到我的辯論社經歷，那些經歷幫助我培養出人際溝通和表達技巧。
>
> **B**：不錯喔。妳還有其他資格可以在第三段中提及嗎？
>
> **A**：我的英語能力和學士學位……
>
> **B**：……還有妳的研究能力和人格特質，比如學習速度快、有責任感等，別忘了還有妳注重細節的個性。
>
> **A**：太好了。我現在就去把這些加上去。

求職信範本

Jellabie (Yi-ran) Dai

jellabie@school.edu   0955-555-555   tw.linkedin.com/in/jellabiedai/

May 22, 2022
Michael Tan
IBMM
4F, 7 Song-Jen Rd.,
Taipei City, Taiwan, 11044

Dear Mr. Tan,

This letter is to express my interest in the sales Specialist position at IBMM posted on your website. I believe that I am a very competitive candidate for this position thanks to my
- Passion for sales and IT products
- Strong interpersonal and persuasive communication skills, and
- Goal-oriented personality and ability to work under pressure both independently and on a team.

My experience in customer service at a coffee shop taught me how to build customer relationships and create more loyal customers. I made an effort to remember customer names and preferred orders, which allowed me to anticipate their order and ask them about it even before they spoke. I think customers appreciate this personalized service. I also developed strong analytic and communication skills when I was the leader of the debate club in university. I organized several trainings and worked closely with my teammates to prepare for debates and competitions. Through our teamwork and effort, we went to the national championships twice and came in second place both times.

Other key strengths that I possess for success in this position include the following:
- A bachelor's degree in Economics
- An aggressive and learning attitude
- Very good English proficiency (TOEIC 790)
- Strong research skills
- A responsible and detail-oriented personality.

Please see my attached resume for additional information on my qualifications and experience.

Thank you for your time and consideration. I look forward to speaking with you about this employment opportunity. I can be reached anytime at the contact information above.

Sincerely
Jellabie (Yi-ran) Dai

jellabie@school.edu
0955-555-555
123 Chung Cheung Road, New Taipei City

婕拉比（怡然）· 戴

jellabie@school.edu　0955-555-555　tw.linkedin.com/in/jellabiedai/

2022 年 5 月 22 日

麥克 · 譚

IBMM

11044 台灣台北市

松仁路 7 號 4F

譚先生您好：

這封信是為了表達我對您網站上發布的 IBMM 業務專員一職的興趣。我相信針對此職位我是一個極具競爭力的候選人，這要歸功於我：

- 對銷售和 IT 產品的熱情
- 強大的人際互動能力和具說服力的溝通技巧
- 目標導向的個性和在壓力下獨立工作與團隊合作的能力

過去我在咖啡館的客服經驗讓我學習到如何建立顧客關係，以及創造更多的忠誠顧客。我努力記住顧客姓名與其訂單偏好，甚至在他們說話之前，我就能夠預測他們要點什麼，我認為顧客們很欣賞這種個人化的服務。當我擔任大學辯論社的隊長時，我也培養了強大的分析和溝通能力。我規畫了幾次培訓，並與我的隊友密切合作為辯論和比賽做準備。透過我們的團隊合作和努力，我們兩度闖進了全國錦標賽，並且獲得了第二名。

讓我能夠勝任此職位的其他強項包括：

- 經濟學學士學位
- 主動積極的學習態度
- 優異的英語能力（多益 790 分）
- 出色的研究能力
- 有責任心和注重細節的個性

關於我的資格與工作經驗，欲知更多資訊，請參閱隨附履歷。

感謝您的時間和考慮。期待與您討論此工作機會。歡迎透過上面的聯繫資訊隨時聯絡我。

婕拉比（怡然）戴
敬上

jellabie@school.edu
0955-555-555
新北市中章路 123 號

ANTHONY WONG

No. 10-5, Aly. 80, Guanter Ln., Pingtung, Taiwan
tw.linkedin.com/in/antwong/   0975666129   awong@gmail.com

Feb. 2018
Catherine Chan, Hiring Manager
Expedium
47F, 7 Hsin Yi Rd., Sec 5,
Taipei City, Taiwan, 11077

Dear Ms. Chan,

_____ **[a]** After years of studying English by myself and in school and completing my bachelor's degree in foreign languages and literature, I received a TOEIC score of 980 out of 990, which is considered native-like ability, or C2 according to the CEFR. I was an exchange student in Germany for one year, and I traveled to 15 countries in Europe during my free time and developed a strong interest in travelling and the tourism indus try. After I returned to Taiwan, I decided to improve my business knowledge and business communication skills, so I enrolled in the six-month intensive Post-bachelor's Program in International Trade from the Taiwan External Trade Development Council's Institute of International Trade. This increased my knowledge of international trade processes and key terms and concepts, and also gave me the chance to undertake marketing projects, sales presentations, and negotiations.

_____ **[b]** Thank you for your time and consideration. I look forward to speaking with you about this employment opportunity. I can be reached anytime via the contact information above.

_____ **[c]** This letter is to express my strong interest in the Market Associate position at Expedium posted on the website "Indeed." I believe that I am a very competitive candidate for this position thanks to my

_____ **[d]** Sincerely,
Anthony Wong

_____ **[e]**
• Excellent proficiency in English
• Great passion for travel, and
• Business studies and experiences.

_____ **[f]** Please see my attached resume for additional information on my qualifications and experience.

_____ **[g]**
• Strong interpersonal skills and adaptability, and a detail-oriented personality
• Demonstrated organization and time management skills in launching Taiwanese Evening, an event that promoted Taiwanese culture, food, and music
• Successful experience leading my university department's graphic arts team.

_____ **[h]** Other key strengths that I possess for success in this position include the following:

Assignment ⇒ 寫下你的求職信

記住：

☑ 使用聯繫窗口的姓名（Dear Mr./Ms. ...）。

☑ 第一段，提及 1. 欲應徵之工作、2. 從何得知招聘資訊，以及 3. 針對該工作你最亮眼的三項技能，並使用徵才廣告中的關鍵字。

☑ 第二段，舉出 2～3 個印證上述技能的具體例子，並添加其他強項。

☑ 第三段，使用條列式寫法（名詞片語）列出所具備之其他資格 / 能力。

☑ 第四段，欲知更多資訊請參閱附件。

☑ 第五段，感謝審閱者並表達希望與之會面。

在你和招募人員之間的求職互動中，有五種不同類型的 follow-up emails（跟進電子郵件）。

第一種是寫在面試之前，假如發送履歷或職缺詢問信後皆未收到招募人員的任何消息，建議寫一封 follow-up email 確認對方是否收到了應徵資料；另外還有四種則寫於面試之後。

追蹤後續進度

第一種 follow-up email 與求職信非常類似。注意，第一段簡短即可，第二段詢問是否收到資料，第三段是求職信第二段和第三段的簡潔版。請看以下對照範例：

Cover Letter vs. follow-up email

Anthony's Cover Letter	Anthony's follow-up email
Dear Ms. Chan, This letter is to express my strong interest in the Market Associate position at Expedium posted on the website "Indeed." I believe that I am a very competitive candidate for this position thanks to my • Excellent proficiency in English • Great passion for travel, and • Business studies and experiences. After years of studying English by myself and in school and completing my bachelor's degree in foreign languages and literature, I received a TOEIC score of 980 out of 990, which is considered native-like ability, or C2 according to the CEFR.	From: awong@gmail.com To: expedium@travelservices.com Date: 23.02.2022 Subject: Follow up on my application for the market associate position Dear Ms. Chan, I am writing in connection with the market associate position at Expedium recently advertised on the website "Indeed." I submitted my resume and Cover Letter earlier this month for the above position. To date, I have not heard back from your office. I would like to confirm receipt of my application and reiterate my interest in the job.

I was an exchange student in Germany for one year, and I traveled to 15 countries in Europe during my free time and developed a strong interest in travelling and the tourism industry. After I returned to Taiwan, I decided to improve my business knowledge and business communication skills, so I enrolled in the six-month intensive Post-bachelor's Program in International Trade from the Taiwan External Trade Development Council's Institute of International Trade. This increased my knowledge of international trade processes and key terms and concepts, and also gave me the chance to undertake marketing projects, sales presentations, and negotiations.

Other key strengths that I possess for success in this position include the following:

- Strong interpersonal skills and adaptability, and a detail-oriented personality
- Demonstrated organization and time management skills in launching Taiwanese Evening, an event that promoted Taiwanese culture, food, and music
- Successful experience leading my university department's graphic arts team.

Please see my attached resume for additional information on my qualifications and experience.

Thank you for your time and consideration. I look forward to speaking with you about this employment opportunity. I can be reached anytime via the contact information above.

Sincerely,
Anthony Wong

I am very interested in working at Expedium and I believe my skills and experience would be a very good match for this position. As I mentioned in my original application, I am familiar with international trade process key terms and concepts, highly proficient in business English skills, and passionate about travelling and the tourism industry. Moreover, I have the following additional qualifications:

- Outstanding interpersonal skills, detail-oriented personality, and strong adaptability
- Demonstrated organization and time management skills in launching Taiwanese Evening, and event that promoted Taiwanese culture, food, and music
- Successful experience leading my university department's graphic arts team

If necessary, I would be glad to resend my application materials or to provide any further information you might need regarding my candidacy. I can be reached via this email address or the telephone number below.

Thank you again for your consideration and I look forward to hearing from you.

Sincerely yours,
Anthony Wong

Address: No. 10-5, Aly. 80, Guanter Ln., Pingtung, Taiwan
Mobile: 0975666129
Email: awong@gmail.com
tw.linkedin.com/in/antwong/

寄件者：awong@gmail.com
收件者：expedium@travelservices.com
日　　期：23.02.2022
主　　旨：追蹤行銷助理職位應徵後續

詹女士您好：

我是為了最近在 "Indeed" 網站上宣傳的 Expedium 行銷助理職位相關事宜來信。

本月初，我為了上述職位提交了履歷和求職信，而到目前為止，尚未收到貴辦公室的回覆。我想確認是否有收到我的應徵資料，並重申我對此職位的興趣。

我對在 Expedium 工作極感興趣，我相信我的技能和經驗非常適合此職位。正如我在原本的資料中提到的，我深諳國際貿易流程的關鍵術語和概念、精通商務英語，並且對旅行和旅遊業充滿熱情。此外，我還具備下列強項：

- 非凡的人際溝通能力、注重細節的個性和強大的適應能力
- 在發起推廣台灣文化、美食和音樂的「台灣之夜」活動中表現出的組織和時間管理能力
- 領導大學系上平面藝術團隊的成功經驗

如有必要，我很樂意重新發送我的應徵文件，或提供任何您可能需要的、有關我的候選資格之進一步資料。歡迎透過此電子郵件地址或下面的電話號碼與我聯繫。

再次感謝您的考慮，靜候佳音。

安東尼・黃
敬上

地址：台灣屏東廣德巷 80 弄 10-5 號
手機：0975666129
電子郵件：awong@gmail.com
tw.linkedin.com/in/antwong/

✎ Assignment ➡ 寫下你的 follow-up email

記住：

☑ 表明對什麼工作感興趣。

☑ 提及何時曾發送應徵資料，並詢問是否有收到。

☑ 重申對該職位的興趣和主要資格／能力。

☑ 告知如有必要願意重新發送資料。

☑ 感謝對方的時間。

　　其他四種電子郵件是寫於進行面試甚至面試前的電話聯絡之後。如下所示，功能及情況雖然各有不同，但不變的是讀起來都必須非常真誠和專業。

1. 感謝面試機會或電話聯繫。

　　超過五分之一的招募人員表示，如果他們沒有收到感謝信（thank-you note），他們就不太可能僱用那個人。信中可提及面試過程中一些有趣的細節，甚至補充你認為你當時沒有回答好的問題。

Pro Tip

面試時記得向面試官索取名片，並在面試後 24 小時內寫 email 向他們發送感謝信。

加分訣竅：也寫一封感謝信給接待你的人——他／她收到信會很感激的，甚至可能會向面試官美言幾句。

2. 雖然未獲錄取，但仍然感謝對方的寶貴時間。

　　即使你收到了遺憾的消息，仍然要保持禮貌和專業的態度以給人留下好印象。誰知道，說不定將來有一天你可能又會回到該公司再進行另一次面試，屆時他們可能會記得你的禮貌回應。

3. 感謝錄取，願接受該工作機會。

　　在這封 email 中，字裡行間應流露出你對即將做出貢獻充滿熱情，並提及該職位的一些細節和商定的就職日期。

4. 感謝錄取，但予以婉拒。

　　這是一封很難下筆的 email，因為你有責任給予該公司一個不接受工作機會的充分理由。畢竟，他們花時間面試不只一位求職者而最終選擇了你，因此為何婉拒必須深思熟慮再提出。盡量避免直接或缺乏說服力的原因，例如薪水太低、家人生病或計畫出國唸書等。

以下是可用於此四種情況的模板。**方框內粗體標示的字句**替換一下便可派上用場。

Exercise ⇒ 將四種 follow-up email 的類型與模板配對（答案見 **P.274**）

a. Thank you for the interview	b. No job offer
c. Job offer, I accept	d. Job offer, but I can't accept

1. Email follow-up type: _____

From:	awong@gmail.com
To:	expedium@travelservices.com
Date:	23.02.2022
Subject:	Anthony Wong – Reply to job offer

Dear Ms. Chan,

Thank you for your **[telephone call] [this morning]** regarding the **[market associate]** position at **[Expedium]**.

I would like to express my sincere gratitude for offering me the opportunity to work at **[Expedium]**.

Unfortunately, I will not be accepting the position as I **[already decided to take a position at another company two days ago since it appears to be a very good match for my current professional goals.]** It was a tough decision for me, and I hope you can understand.

Once again, thank you very much for the offer. I am sorry that I am unable to accept at the present time. However, should my circumstances change, I will certainly contact you again.

I wish you all the best in finding a suitable candidate for the position.

Best regards,
Anthony Wong

2. Email follow-up type: _____

From:	awong@gmail.com
To:	expedium@travelservices.com
Date:	23.02.2022
Subject:	Anthony Wong - Thank you for your time yesterday

Dear Ms. Chan,

I am writing regarding the interview I had with you **[yesterday]** for the position of **[market associate]**.

It was very enjoyable to talk with you about the position. The job seems to be **[a very good match]** for my skills and interests. The **[collaborative team and the fun, fast-changing and challenging culture]** that you described strongly confirmed my desire to work with you.

In addition to my enthusiasm, I will bring to the position **[strong business English communication skills, proactive attitude, and strong organization and time management skills]**.

I appreciate very much the time you took to interview me. I am very interested in working for you and I look forward to hearing from you regarding this position.

Sincerely yours,
Anthony Wong

3. Email follow-up type: _____

From:	awong@gmail.com
To:	expedium@travelservices.com
Date:	23.02.2022
Subject:	Anthony Wong – thank you for your time

Dear Ms. Chan,

Thank you for your **[telephone call] [this morning]** regarding the **[market associate]** position at **[Expedium]**.

I was disappointed to learn I did not get the job, but I would like to express my thanks for the professionalism showed to me during the interview process.

I would also like to reiterate my interest in working for **[Expedium]**, and if the position or similar one becomes available, please keep me in mind.

Thank you again for all your time and consideration.

Best regards,
Anthony Wong

4. Email follow-up type: _____

From:	awong@gmail.com
To:	expedium@travelservices.com
Date:	23.02.2022
Subject:	Anthony Wong - Job offer acceptance

Dear Ms. Chan,

Thank you for your **[telephone call] [yesterday]** regarding the **[market associate]** position at **[Expedium]**.

As discussed on the phone, I am very pleased to accept the position and I would like to thank you again for the opportunity. I am eager to make a positive contribution to the company and work with everyone on the **[Expedium]** team.

As agreed, my starting salary will be **[NTD 35,000]**. The package also includes **[labor health insurance, a three-week paid vacation in the first year, and reimbursements for leisure travel each year ($250-$750USD, depending on tenure)]**.

Once again, thank you for this opportunity and I look forward to starting employment with you on **[July 1, 20XX]**. If there is any additional information or paperwork you need from me prior to then, please let me know.

Best regards,
Anthony Wong

Assignment ➡ 試寫四種面試後 follow-up email

Thank you for the interview

_____

_____

_____

_____

_____

_____

_____

No job offer

_____

_____

_____

_____

_____

_____

_____

Job offer, accept

Job offer, cannot accept

Figure [26]: Recognized recommended allowance approve permit photo by rawpixel.com – Freepik.com

10

推薦信 Letters of Reference

邀請推薦人為你美言幾句使你與眾不同並提升優勢。

The Reference Letter is the kind of helping hand that can set you apart and give you an advantage.

關鍵

Key point

雖然企業徵才到了後期階段，招募人員才會審核推薦資料，但往往這部分是決定面試候選名單的關鍵考量因素。

學習藍圖

Plan

· 請求撰寫推薦信
· 邀請推薦 3 步驟
· 推薦信應載內容

Insight 洞見 ▶

在應徵工作或創建 LinkedIn 個人檔案時，推薦信是展示你的優勢，並使你看起來更值得信賴的重要方式。如果你是一個工作經驗不多或成就很少的應屆畢業生，尤其如此。

如何選定該向誰請求推薦？對象通常是你的主管或老師，但也可能是同事、朋友或家人。Indeed.com（2021 [29]）建議了幾個相當實用的標準，有助於選出能夠為你增色的推薦人：

- 此人不僅僅是專業上的聯絡人，更是你的良師益友。
- 此人幫助你度過了困難時期，並且看著你蛻變成更強大的人。
- 此人是一個特別優秀或具說服力的寫手，能夠輕鬆地寫出一封推薦信。
- 此人熟悉你所應徵的組織，或該組織熟知該位人士。
- 此人能夠談論你的優缺點，從而幫助你提升競爭力。

推薦人的姓名、職位和聯繫資訊寫於履歷底部。推薦信可以附件形式添加至 LinkedIn 檔案中的「個人簡介（About）」部分並設為「精選（Featured）」，甚至也可直接就在 LinkedIn 系統上請求推薦。邀請推薦人為你美言幾句能夠使你與眾不同並提升優勢。

🗨 Dialog

A: I've finished my resume, and LinkedIn profile, but I don't have much experience. Is there anything else I can do to strengthen my profile or resume?

B: Yes. You can add letters of reference or recommendation.

A: But I already listed references on my resume.

B: But those references mean that the recruiter has to contact them personally to hear their recommendation for you.

A: So, I should ask them for a Reference Letter?

B: Yes, this would make it easier for the recruiter. Also, you can add this type of reference to your LinkedIn Profile if the referee is also on LinkedIn.

A: Well, I don't think my math teacher or Bartissa supervisor are on LinkedIn.

B: Then you will need to contact them by email. But before you do that, you need to consider three things.

A：我已經把履歷和 LinkedIn 檔案都填寫完了，但我沒有太多經驗。我還能做些什麼來補強？

B：有的。妳可以添加推薦信。

A：我已經在履歷上列出了推薦人。

B：那些推薦人資料意味著招募人員必須親自聯繫他們，以聽取他們對妳的推薦。

A：那我應該向他們請求推薦信是嗎？

B：是的，這樣對招募人員來說比較簡單。此外，如果推薦人也有 LinkedIn 帳戶，也可以在上面直接把他們加到你的 LinkedIn 檔案裡。

A：嗯，我覺得我的數學老師或 Bartissa 主管應該不在 LinkedIn 上。

B：那妳就用 email 聯繫他們。不過，在這麼做之前，妳需要考慮三件事。

邀請推薦 3 步驟 ▼

Step 1：回顧以前的老師、雇主

第一步是想想你從前的雇主、老師或任何符合上頁所描述的人，其中是否有誰

- 曾與你保持良好關係？
- 可談談你的成就或與你正在尋找之工作相關的正面特質？

你可以詢問他們是否願意成為你的推薦人，並讓他們知道需要評論哪些方面。

讓我們看一下 Peter 的例子。Peter 過去曾於一所商業培訓機構學習，欲向其講師 Manuel 請求撰寫推薦信。

Step 2：聯繫對方並提出邀請

如果 Peter 想透過 LinkedIn 發出邀請，LinkedIn 上有一個預設的請求推薦訊息模板可用，但不建議直接毫無修改就傳送，這種請求訊息最好加以客製化，讓推薦人盡可能輕鬆地為你寫推薦信。

Example 1	Example 2
Dear Manuel, You were a wonderful mentor and coach, and one of the best instructors I have ever had. Could you please write me a recommendation that describes my strengths in your classes? I'd really appreciate your recommendation to validate my skills and experience. Best regards, Peter	Dear Manuel, You were a wonderful mentor and coach, and one of the best instructors I have ever had. **Your courses on sales and marketing, and the role plays you conducted have really helped raise my confidence and preparation for a career in sales.** **I am currently applying to IT companies like Dell, Asus, and Razer for a variety of sales positions.** Could you please write me a recommendation that describes my sales and negotiation abilities as you witnessed in your role plays and my class performance in general? I'd really appreciate your recommendation to validate my skills and experience. Best regards, Peter

Step 3：準備草稿

　　第三個步驟是在詢問推薦人的意願之前，先準備推薦信草稿。為什麼？因為常見的推薦人選，例如以前的師長或主管，極有可能會要求你擬一份初稿，原因也許是：

1. 他們很忙。
2. 他們對你的認識可能不夠或不太記得你，以至於無法寫出具體細節。
3. 他們知道你更清楚什麼與你的求職目標最相關。

接下來就是困難的部分了——為自己寫一封推薦信。

▣ Dialog

A: So, how should I ask for a Reference Letter?

B: That's not too hard, but you have to be ready to write it yourself first.

A: Really?! Is that normal?

B: Actually, it is. Very often, your teacher or supervisor is very busy and most importantly, may not remember the kind of details necessary for a good Reference Letter for the type of position you are applying for.

A: That makes sense, but I'll feel awkward praising myself.

B: I know, but you need to get used to it. You have to consistently do this throughout your job application process. Remember: you need to know your strengths, know that they are of value to the company, and make them clear to the recruiter.

A: I guess, but it still feels weird for me to write my own Reference Letter for my supervisor.

B: Don't worry, they will appreciate it and it will help them to agree to doing it. Another benefit is that if you get reference letters, you can include these PDFs in your LinkedIn Profile Featured section for everyone to see.

A: All right. So, how do I write my own Letter of Reference?

> **A：**所以，我應該怎麼請別人幫我寫推薦信？
>
> **B：**不會很難，但妳必須準備好自己先寫。
>
> **A：**真的嗎？！一般都這樣嗎？
>
> **B：**事實上，確實如此。很多時候，妳的老師或主管非常忙碌，最重要的是，關於妳要應徵的職位類型，一封有效的推薦信所應包含的細節，他們可能也不記得了。
>
> **A：**有道理，但我真的不好意思自誇。
>
> **B：**我懂，但妳要習慣。在整個求職過程中，從頭到尾妳都一直得要這麼做。記住，妳要了解自己的優勢，知道什麼對公司有價值，並向招募人員展示出來。
>
> **A：**我還是覺得幫主管寫自己的推薦信怪怪的。
>
> **B：**別想太多，他們會感激妳這樣做的，而且這也有助於讓他們同意幫妳寫推薦信。另一個好處是，假如妳收到推薦信，妳可以把那些 PDF 檔案也加到妳的 LinkedIn 檔案的「精選」欄位中讓所有人查看。
>
> **A：**了解。那麼，我該如何寫自己的推薦信？

　　爲使推薦信發揮效用，其內容須強而有力。這就是爲什麼你需要找到一位可自信地表揚你，並對你正在尋找之工作相關特定領域的資格發表評論的推薦人。

　　一封能夠爲求職者加分的推薦信應符合下列五個條件：

1. 說明信函目的。
2. 提及推薦人與被推薦人的關係。
3. 堅定而有說服力。
4. 包含推薦人知道的、記得的、關於被推薦人可加以評論之具體細節。
5. 與被推薦人正應徵之工作有關。

　　若你在向從前講師或雇主請求撰寫推薦信時附上一份寫得很好又合情合理的草稿，他們同意協助推薦的機會就會大大提高。

　　我們回頭看看 Peter 的例子。他可以再多想想他在 Manuel 的課堂上曾表現出哪些優點，比方說在課堂上他如何展示組織、溝通和解決問題等能力之經驗，並突顯與其欲投身之銷售領域相關的人格特質，例如團隊合作精神、親和力與人際溝通技巧等。

　　在一番構思並將草稿寫於單獨的文件之後，Peter 將以下電子郵件／訊息發送給了Manuel。

Ch
10

推薦信範本：請求撰寫（客製化並附草稿）

Dear Manuel,

... [same as Example 2 above] ... I know you are very busy, so I already wrote a first draft for you to consider. Please feel free to change anything and add your voice and tone. Best wishes, Peter.

Draft:

Peter is a quick thinking and empathetic problem solver with excellent communication skills. As an instructor for business English, sales, and negotiation courses at the International Trade Institute, I had the opportunity to observe Peter prepare and effectively conduct sales and negotiation role plays.

He is diligent and was always thoroughly prepared for my classes. Peter is able to talk with anyone and has the rare ability to identify prospects and diagnose their needs while quickly building a good rapport. From his interactions with his classmates, I noticed he is also a natural leader and very good at facilitating discussion and chairing meetings. He will undoubtedly be a valuable addition to any sales team.

親愛的 Manuel，

（前略，同第 229 頁範例 2）想必您一定很忙碌，所以我已經寫好了一份草稿供你參考。您可任意更改任何內容並添加您的意見。Peter 敬上。

草稿：

Peter 是一個思維敏捷、有同理心的問題解決者，並具備出類拔萃的溝通技巧。身為一名外貿協會培訓中心商務英語、銷售與談判課程的講師，我有機會觀察 Peter 在銷售和談判角色扮演中從準備到有效進行的過程。

Peter 個性勤奮，總是為我的課程做好充分的準備。他能夠與任何人交談，並且具有在快速建立良好關係的同時分辨出潛在客戶並了解其需求的罕見能力。從他與同學的互動中，我注意到他也是一個天生的領導者，十分善於促進討論和主持會議。毫無疑問地，他將成為任何銷售團隊的生力軍。

有了這份草稿，Peter 為 Manuel 完成了大部分工作，讓他很容易理解推薦的重點應放在什麼地方。

以下有助於 Peter 應徵業務類工作的推薦要點屬於何種加分資訊？（可複選）

a. strong and convincing
b. specific details that the referee knows
c. related to the job

Peter's reference

_____ 1. Peter is a quick thinking and empathetic problem solver with excellent communication skills.

_____ 2. As an instructor for business English, sales, and negotiation courses at the International Trade Institute, I had the opportunity to observe Peter prepare and effectively conduct sales and negotiation role plays.

_____ 3. He is diligent and was always thoroughly prepared for my classes.

_____ 4. Peter is able to talk with anyone and has the rare ability to identify prospects and diagnose their needs while building a personable relationship.

_____ 5. From his interactions with his classmates, I noticed he is also a natural leader and very good at facilitating discussion and chairing meetings.

_____ 6. He will undoubtedly be a valuable addition to any sales team.

Ch
10

　　透過此練習，你會發現每個句子至少包含了三分之二種類的資訊，而且它們有一個共通點──讀起來都「堅定而有說服力」。這個簡短的版本正適合於 LinkedIn 上使用，而假如需要更正式的推薦信，則可參考以下的模板。

💬 Dialog

A: I'm not sure if I should ask my math teacher or coffee shop supervisor for a Reference Letter. What do you think?

B: Well, from what you told me, I think your coffee shop supervisor is the better choice because he can comment on your real work experience and also your good customer service attitude. That relates directly to the sales job you want to apply for.

A: OK. Do you have any examples for me to follow?

B: Yes, I have one for a teacher or professor and another for an employer.

A: I'll focus on the employer one and write a draft to show you.

> **A：** 我不確定是否應該向我的數學老師或咖啡館主管請求推薦信。你覺得呢？
>
> **B：** 嗯，從妳告訴我的情況來看，我認為咖啡館主管比較合適，因為他可以評論妳的真實工作經歷，以及妳良好的客服態度。這與妳要應徵的銷售工作是有直接關聯的。
>
> **A：** OK。你有什麼例子可以讓我參考嗎？
>
> **B：** 有，我有一個是要給老師或教授的版本，另一個是給雇主的。
>
> **A：** 我會以雇主版為主，寫一份草稿給你看。

模板：教授／講師推薦信

Referee name
Referee title
Referee organization
Referee phone number
Referee email
Date

To Whom it May Concern, / Dear **[Name of Employer or Graduate School Committee]**,

I am very pleased / It is my great pleasure to write a letter of recommendation for **[full name of student]**. I highly recommend **[student name]** to your organization, especially for a position related to **[field, e.g. sales]**.

I have known **[student name]** for the past **[number of months, semesters, years]** as **[he/she]** has taken the following courses that I teach:

- **[list courses, give brief description of content of course]**
- **[list courses, give brief description of content of course]**
- **[list courses, give brief description of content of course]**.

As **[his/her]** professor, I have had an opportunity to observe **[his/her]** participation and interaction in class and to evaluate **[name of student]**'s knowledge of the subject. **[He/she]** was an outstanding student. **[Student name]** demonstrated not only **[his/her]** work ethic, follow-through, and teamwork, but also that **[he/she]** can accomplish tasks in an efficient and timely manner.

[Give one or two specific examples of the student's performance. It is also a good idea to mention relationships with other students and activities outside of class. It would be useful to highlight any areas in which he or she improved and developed certain abilities.]

I am confident that **[student name]** has the ability to successfully deal with any challenge that **[he/she]** meets. **[His/her]** **[three above-mentioned key traits (e.g. patience, teaching ability, and strong computer programming skill)]**, prepare **[him/her]** to make a valuable contribution to **[company/ organization/school/program]**. I have no hesitation endorsing **[student name]** to become a member of your team at **[company/organization /school/program]**.

Sincerely,
[referee name]

推薦人姓名
推薦人職稱
推薦人工作機構
推薦人電話號碼
推薦人電子郵件
日期

敬啓者／親愛的〔欲應徵職位之雇主姓名或研究所委員會〕：

很高興為〔**學生全名**〕寫此推薦信。容我向貴公司／組織強烈推薦〔**學生姓名**〕，特別是針對與〔**領域（例如銷售）**〕相關的職位。

我認識〔**學生姓名**〕已經〔**月數、學期數、年數**〕了，因為〔**他／她**〕曾經上過我所教授的下列課程：

- 〔**列出課程，簡要說明課程內容**〕
- 〔**列出課程，簡要說明課程內容**〕
- 〔**列出課程，簡要說明課程內容**〕

作為〔**他的／她的**〕教授，我有機會觀察〔**他／她**〕在課堂上的參與和互動，並評估〔**學生姓名**〕對該學科的了解。〔**他／她**〕是一名優秀的學生。〔**學生姓名**〕不僅展示了〔**他的／她的**〕職業道德、堅持不懈的態度和團隊合作精神，還展示了〔**他／她**〕能夠高效、及時地完成任務。

〔**舉一兩個該學生表現的具體例子。建議提及他／她與其他學生的關係，以及課外活動。突顯他／她改進和發展某些能力的任何領域也會很有用。**〕

我相信〔**學生姓名**〕有能力成功應對〔**他／她**〕所遇到的任何挑戰。〔**他的／她的**〕〔**上述三個關鍵特質（例如耐心、教學能力、強大的電腦程式設計技能等）**〕，讓〔**他／她**〕能夠為〔**公司／組織／學校／專案**〕做出寶貴的貢獻。我毫不猶豫地支持〔**學生姓名**〕成為〔**公司／組織／學校／專案**〕團隊的一員。

誠摯地，
〔**推薦人姓名**〕

如果需要更長、更正式的推薦信，Peter 可以這樣寫。

推薦信範本：教授／講師

Manuel Hernandez, PhD
Instructor
International Trade Institute
02-1234-5678
mhernandez@iti.org
October 15, 2022

Dear Hiring Manager or Sales Manager,

It is my great pleasure to write a letter of recommendation for Peter Chen. I highly recommend Peter to your organization, especially for a position related to sales and marketing.

I have known Peter for over one1 year as he has taken the following courses that I teach here at the International Trade Institute:

- **Sales Skills**
- **Negotiation Strategies**
- **Business English.**

As his instructor, I have had an opportunity to observe his participation and interaction in class and to evaluate Peter's knowledge of the above subjects. He was an outstanding student. Peter demonstrated not only that he is responsible and works very well on a team, but also that he can accomplish tasks in an efficient and timely manner.

I was especially impressed with his ability to empathetically and carefully identify a prospect's needs in our sales role plays, which he then used as the basis for his persuasive sales presentations. This is something I teach and get all students to practice, but Peter picked up on this very quickly, almost naturally. He is quick -thinking and has a very good ability to interact and socialize with people. I remember that he organized a few outside of class social activities and her his classmates all seemed to genuinely like him. His confidence and presentation skills noticeably improved in my courses, as his presentations became more clearly structured and more fluent.

I am confident that Peter has the ability to successfully deal with any challenge that he meets. In particular, his empathy for others, fast-learning ability, and strong communication skills have prepared him to make a valuable contribution to any sales and marketing team. I have no hesitation endorsing Peter to become a member of your team at your company.

Sincerely,
Manuel Hernandez, PhD

Manuel Hernandez 博士
TAITRA 外貿協會培訓中心講師
02-1234-5678
mhernandez@iti.org
2022 年 10 月 15 日

敬愛的招募經理或業務經理：

很高興為 Peter Chen 寫此推薦信。容我向貴公司強烈推薦 Peter，特別是針對與銷售和行銷相關的職位。

我認識 Peter 已經一年多了，因為他曾經上過我在外貿協會培訓中心教授的下列課程：

- 銷售技巧
- 談判策略
- 商務英語

作為他的講師，我有機會觀察他在課堂上的參與和互動，並評估 Peter 對上述科目的了解。他是一名優秀的學生。Peter 不僅展示了他有責任心，於團隊中表現良好，還展示了他能夠高效、及時地完成任務。

他在我們的銷售角色扮演活動中所展現的善解人意，以及細心察覺潛在客戶需求的能力，特別令我印象深刻；此後他也以此能力作為基礎發揮至他極具說服力的業務簡報。這是我教給所有學生並讓所有學生練習的技能，Peter 很快就學會了這一點，彷彿是天性一般。他思維敏捷，具有很好的與人互動和社交的能力。我記得他組織了一些課外的社交活動，他的同學們都相當喜歡他。他的自信和表達技巧在我的課程中大幅提升，簡報結構愈來愈清晰與流暢。

我相信 Peter 有能力成功應對他所遇到的任何挑戰。尤其以他對他人的同理心、快速的學習能力和強大的溝通能力，讓他能夠為任何銷售和行銷團隊做出寶貴貢獻。我毫不猶豫地支持 Peter 成為貴公司團隊的一員。

誠摯地，
Manuel Hernandez 博士

如果 Peter 找到以前的雇主，他的推薦信模板則如下頁所示。

模板：雇主推薦信

Referee name
Referee title
Referee organization
Referee phone number
Referee email
Date

To Whom it May Concern, / Dear **[Name of Employer or Graduate School Committee]**,

Confirm dates, job title(s), capacity, and salary and benefits details if required/ appropriate.

Confirm that the person's performance and attitude was (at all times) satisfactory or exceeded expectations or standards.

Optional: Brief details of the person's responsibilities

Optional: Brief details of their qualifications (education, skills, experiences) and characteristics (personality)

Optional (but reassuring for reader): State that you would willingly re-employ the person if the opportunity arose

Optional: Offer to provide more information if required

Yours sincerely,
[referee name]

推薦人姓名
推薦人職稱
推薦人工作機構
推薦人電話號碼
推薦人電子郵件
日期

敬啓者／親愛的〔欲應徵職位之雇主姓名或研究所委員會〕：

如需要／適當，證實被推薦人在前公司的工作期間、職稱、能力、薪資與福利詳情。

肯定被推薦人的表現和態度（始終）令人滿意或超出預期／標準。

可寫可不寫：被推薦人的職責簡要說明。

可寫可不寫：被推薦人的資格（教育、技能、經驗）和個性的簡要說明。

可寫可不寫（但有助於審閱者消除疑慮）：表明如果有機會，自己願意重新僱用被推薦人。

可寫可不寫：如需要，可提供更多資訊。

誠摯地，
〔推薦人姓名〕

推薦信範本：雇主

Luisa Hsia
Sales Manager
Octoprime Technologies
02-1234-6789
lhsia@octoprime.com
October 5, 2021

To whom it may concern,

I confirm that Peter Chen was employed as a sales executive with this company from July 23, 2018 to August 4, 2021, and was paid an annual salary of US$31,000 plus commission and quarterly quota bonuses. His job as Sales Executive carries the following responsibilities

- **meeting with clients virtually or during sales visits**
- **demonstrating and presenting products**
- **developing new business**
- **maintaining accurate records**
- **attending trade exhibitions, conferences, and meetings**
- **reviewing sales performance**
- **negotiating contracts and packages.**

Peter is skilled in meeting clients, building a rapport with them, and delivering professional and customized product presentations. He is very reliable, likeable, quick-thinking, and able to speak four languages.

I was saddened when Peter left our company, but he was able to get a promotion opportunity elsewhere that would have taken him a few more years to get at our company. I was happy for him about personally when he took this opportunity, but I would happily re-employ Peter if he came back. Peter was a valuable member of our sales team who consistently achieved good results and surpassed expectations.

Please feel free to let me know if I can be of any further assistance.

Yours sincerely,
Luisa Hsia

Luisa Hsia
Octoprime 科技業務經理
02-1234-6789
lhsia@octoprime.com
2021 年 10 月 5 日

敬啓者：

我證實 2018 年 7 月 23 日至 2021 年 8 月 4 日期間，Peter Chen 曾受僱於本公司擔任業務主管，年薪 31,000 美元，外加佣金和季配額獎金，其作為業務主管的職責包括：

- 透過線上或實地拜訪與客戶會面
- 展示產品與做簡報
- 開發新業務
- 確切管理記錄
- 參加貿易展覽、大小會議
- 審查銷售業績
- 協商合約和薪酬待遇

Peter 擅長與客戶會面並與其建立融洽關係，以及提供專業的客製化產品簡報。他非常可靠、討喜、思維敏捷，並且能夠說四種語言。

當 Peter 離開我們公司時，我感到相當難過，但是這樣他能夠在其他地方獲得晉升機會，若在敝公司的話則還需要多花幾年時間。因此，當他決定接受此機會時，我個人為他感到很高興，假如他有意回來，我會很樂意重新僱用 Peter。Peter 是我們銷售團隊的重要成員，他始終都能達到很棒的成績並往往超出我們所預期。

如果我能夠提供任何進一步的協助，請隨時聯繫我。

誠摯地，
Luisa Hsia

📝 Dialog

A: I've finished the reference letter I'll send to my boss at Bartissa coffee. Here it is.

B: Let's see. It's OK, but not as strong as it should be. Are you confident you did a good job at serving customers with a good attitude?

A: Absolutely. I loved that part of the job.

B: If that's true, then you need to emphasize this and make it sound strong and convincing. And let's add a few more details. I made some changes. What do you think?

A: Wow. It sounds much stronger ... but I feel a bit embarrassed to send it to Mr. Tsao.

B: Don't be. He will either make it stronger or tone it down if it's too strong. But if you have a good relationship with him and you did a good job, you should be more confident in sounding strong and convincing and adding details related to the sales positions you are applying for.

> **A**：我已經寫好要寄給我在 Bartissa 咖啡館的老闆的推薦信了。在這裡。
>
> **B**：讓我看看。寫得是不錯，但缺乏它應該有的力道。妳有沒有信心自己以前都是用良好的態度為顧客服務？
>
> **A**：當然。我愛那份工作的那一部分。
>
> **B**：如果是真的，那妳就要強調這一點，讓它讀起來有力道。我們再添加一些細節吧。我做了一些修改。妳覺得怎麼樣？
>
> **A**：哇。讀起來變得有力許多……但是要把它寄給曹先生，我有點不好意思。
>
> **B**：不用感到不好意思。他看了之後會再進一步強調，或者，假如強度太超過了，他也會修改得比較柔和。不過如果妳和他的關係很好，而且妳確實做得很好，妳應該更有信心，字裡行間要堅定、有說服力，然後添加一些與妳應徵的業務職位相關的細節。

Before and After：來自雇主的推薦信

Before	After

Before

Chien-Ming Tsao
Store Manager
Bartissa Coffee
02-2340-6789
cmtsao@gmail.com
October 5, 2022

To whom it may concern,

I confirm that Jellabie Dai was employed as a server and barista with this store from June 2020 to September 2022. Her job as server and barista included the following responsibilities

- **Greet customers when entering or leaving the store**
- **Serve customers and make coffee**
- **Manage transactions with customers using cash register**
- **Resolve customer complaints**
- **Track transactions on balance sheets and report any discrepancies**
- **Maintain clean and tidy checkout areas.**

Jellabie got along with our customers to deliver warm and friendly service and was able to handle customer complaints. She was good at tracking cashier transactions and rarely had any discrepancies on her balance sheets.

I know that Jellabie has other plans and that is why she left Bartissa. But I would re-employ Jellabie if she came back. She was a good worker and good team player. I think She she woulb would be a good addition to any sales and customer service team.

After

Chien-Ming Tsao
Store Manager
Bartissa Coffee
02-2340-6789
cmtsao@gmail.com
October 5, 2022

To whom it may concern,

I confirm that Jellabie Dai was employed as a server and barista with this store from June 2020 to September 2022. Her job as server and barista included the following responsibilities

- **Greet customers when entering or leaving the store**
- **Serve customers with a pleasant attitude**
- **Build rapport with customers with the aim of making them become loyal return customers**
- **Manage transactions with customers using cash register**
- **Resolve customer complaints**
- **Track transactions on balance sheets and report any discrepancies**
- **Maintain clean and tidy checkout areas.**

Jellabie has excellent interpersonal skills and was always able to build rapport with clients and deliver cheerful and enthusiastic service. She is quick-thinking and was good at handling customer complaints. She was detail-oriented and very careful tracking cashier transactions, which means meant she rarely had any discrepancies on her balance sheets.

Staff come and go in the coffee shop business, but I was sad to see Jellabie leave. I know that many of our customers enjoyed her warm service and miss her too, so I would happily re-employ Jellabie if she ever came back. Jellabie's work performance and attitude always surpassed expectations and I have no doubt she would contribute greatly to any company and team in roles like customer service or sales where excellent people skills are required.

Please feel free to let me know if I can be of any further assistance.

Yours sincerely,
Chien-Ming Tsao

曹建明
Bartissa 咖啡館經理
02-2340-6789
cmtsao@gmail.com
2022 年 10 月 5 日

敬啓者：

我證實 2020 年 6 月至 2022 年 9 月期間，Jellabie Dai 曾於本店擔任侍者和咖啡師，其作為侍者和咖啡師的職責包括：

- 招呼顧客進店與離店
- 服務顧客和沖煮咖啡
- 使用收銀機管理顧客交易
- 解決顧客投訴問題
- 在收支報表上追蹤交易並報告任何差異
- 保持收銀台乾淨整潔

Jellabie 與我們的顧客相處融洽，提供熱情友好的服務，並且有能力處理客訴。她擅長追蹤收銀機的每筆交易，她值班的收支報表上很少出現任何差異。

我知道 Jellabie 有其他職涯計畫，也就是她離開 Bartissa 的原因。但如果她有意回來，我會重新僱用她。Jellabie 是一名優秀的員工和團隊合作者。我認為她會是任何銷售和客服團隊的生力軍。

如果我能夠提供任何進一步的幫助，請隨時聯繫我。

誠摯地，
曹建明

Please feel free to let me know if I can be of any further assistance.

Yours sincerely,
Chien-Ming Tsao

曹建明
Bartissa 咖啡館經理
02-2340-6789
cmtsao@gmail.com
2022 年 10 月 5 日

敬啓者：

我證實 2020 年 6 月至 2022 年 9 月期間，Jellabie Dai 曾於本店擔任侍者和咖啡師，其作為侍者和咖啡師的職責包括：

- 招呼顧客進店與離店
- 以愉快的態度服務顧客
- 與顧客建立融洽關係以使他們成為忠實的回頭客
- 使用收銀機管理顧客交易
- 解決顧客投訴問題
- 在收支報表上追蹤交易並報告任何差異
- 保持收銀台乾淨整潔

Jellabie 具有出色的人際溝通能力，總是能夠與顧客打好關係，並提供愉快和熱情的服務。她思維敏捷，善於處理客訴。她注重細節，鉅細靡遺地追蹤收銀機的每筆交易，這意味著她值班時的收支報表上很少出現任何差異。

咖啡館的工作人員來來去去，但看到 Jellabie 離開，我感到非常難過。我知道我們的許多顧客都很喜歡她熱情的服務也很想念她，所以如果她回來，我會很樂意重新僱用她。Jellabie 的工作表現和態度總是超出預期，我毫不懷疑她會為任何需要強大人際交往能力的公司和團隊做出一番貢獻，例如客服或銷售的職位。

如果我能夠提供任何進一步的幫助，請隨時聯繫我。

誠摯地，
曹建明

簡而言之，本章的重點即附上推薦信，這將使你和你的履歷更具可信度。此外，記得客製化推薦請求訊息並提供草稿，讓幫你推薦的人更方便。本章所介紹的範本和模板可協助你快速編寫有效的推薦信，完成之後別忘了將其添加至 LinkedIn 上的「精選（Featured）」欄位。

當你和你的老師／教授或前雇主一起盡心完成推薦信函時，它將能創造最大的成功機會——鎖定你正在尋找的工作，並給審閱的招募人員留下深刻印象。

Assignment ➡ 試寫推薦信：教授／講師或雇主

記住：

☑ 提及推薦人和求職者的姓名和彼此關係，以及所應徵的職位。

☑ 以具體例子突顯求職者的相關資格／能力。

☑ 強力推薦求職者，為其背書。

List of Figures

References

Introduction

[1] Glassdoor Team (2015, January 20). 50 HR & Recruiting Stats That Make You Think. https://www.glassdoor.com/employers/blog/50-hr-recruiting-stats-make-think/ [accessed 2022-07-25]

[2] CareerBuilder (2019, June 10). THESE 5 SIMPLE MISTAKES COULD BE COSTING YOU THE JOB. https://www.careerbuilder.com/advice/these-5-simple-mistakes-could-be-costing-you-the-job [accessed 2022-07-25]

[3] Jobvite (2016). Jobvite Recruiter Nation Report 2016. https://www.jobvite.com/jobvite-recruiter-nation-report-2016/ [accessed 2022-07-25]

[4] CareerExplorer.com

[5] Gallup (2017). Gallup State of the American Workplace Report 2017. https://www.gallup.com/workplace/238085/state-american-workplace-report-2017.aspx [accessed 2022-07-25]

[6] Seaman, A. (2020, August 3). How to find a winning job search strategy? https://www.linkedin.com/pulse/how-find-winning-job-search-strategy-andrew-seaman-/?trackingId=%2Bw1kGVTdTGit%2FbG6kPFuaQ%3D%3D [accessed 2022-07-25]

[7] TheLadders (2022, May 23). Computers reading resumes & your job search in 2022. https://www.theladders.com/career-advice/computers-reading-resumes-and-your-job-search-in-2020 [accessed 2022-07-25]

[8] CareerBuilder (2018, August 9). More Than Half of Employers Have Found Content on Social Media That Caused Them NOT to Hire a Candidate, According to Recent CareerBuilder Survey. https://press.careerbuilder.com/2018-08-09-More-Than-Half-of-Employers-Have-Found-Content-on-Social-Media-That-Caused-Them-NOT-to-Hire-a-Candidate-According-to-Recent-CareerBuilder-Survey [accessed 2022-07-25]

Chapter 1

[1] Glassdoor Team (2015, January 20). 50 HR & Recruiting Stats That Make You Think. https://www.glassdoor.com/employers/blog/50-hr-recruiting-stats-make-think/ [accessed 2022-07-25]

[9] Turczynski, B. (2022, April 22). 2022 HR Statistics: Job Search, Hiring, Recruiting & Interviews. https://zety.com/blog/hr-statistics#:~:text=On%20average%2C%20each%20corporate%20job,one%20will%20get%20the%20job [accessed 2022-07-27]

[4] CareerExplorer.com

[3] Jobvite (2016). Jobvite Recruiter Nation Report 2016. https://www.jobvite.com/jobvite-recruiter-nation-report-2016/ [accessed 2022-07-25]

[10] Pew Research Center (2016, October 6). The State of American Jobs. https://www.pewresearch.org/social-trends/2016/10/06/the-state-of-american-jobs/ [accessed 2022-07-27]

Chapter 2

[11] CareerBuilder (2014, April 10). Overwhelming Majority of Companies Say Soft Skills Are Just as Important as Hard Skills, According to a New CareerBuilder Survey. https://press.careerbuilder. com/2014-04-10-Overwhelming-Majority-of-Companies-Say-Soft-Skills-Are-Just-as-Important-as-Hard-Skills-According-to-a-New-CareerBuilder-Survey [accessed 2022-07-26]

[12] Wonderlic. (2016). Hard Facts About Soft Skills An actionable review of employer perspectives, expectations and recommendations. http://docs.wixstatic.com/ugd/cceaf9_ec9ed750296142f18efdd4 9f4930f6d3.pdf [accessed 2022-07-26]

[13] CareerBuilder (2016, September 22). CareerBuilder's Annual Survey Reveals The Most Outrageous Resume Mistakes Employers Have Found. https://press.careerbuilder.com/2016-09-21-CareerBuilders-Annual-Survey-Reveals-The-Most-Outrageous-Resume-Mistakes-Employers-Have-Found [accessed 2022-07-26]

[14] Lainez, A. (2021, April 14). How to Tell if You Need to Invest in a Professionally Written Resume? [Cites TheLadders study for this statistic] https://www.linkedin.com/pulse/how-tell-you-need-invest-professionally-written-resume-anda-lainez/ [accessed 2022-07-26]

Chapter 4

[15] TheLadders (2018). Eye-Tracking Study. https://www.theladders.com/static/images/basicSite/pdfs/ TheLadders-EyeTracking-StudyC2.pdf [accessed 2022-07-26]

[16] Tomaszewski, M. (2022, November 15). The 3 Best Resume Formats to Use in 2022 (Examples). https:// zety.com/blog/resume-formats [accessed 2022-11-27]

Chapter 5

[17] Lutov, S. (2021, May 3). 4 Surprising Factors That Influence Hiring Decisions. https://liverecruiter. com/2021/05/03/4-surprising-factors-that-influence-hiring-decisions [CareerBuilder report cited in this article; couldn't locate it on the net, though] [accessed 2022-07-26]

Chapter 6

[3] Jobvite (2016). Jobvite Recruiter Nation Report 2016. https://www.jobvite.com/jobvite-recruiter-nation-report-2016/ [accessed 2022-07-25]

[8] CareerBuilder (2018, August 9). More Than Half of Employers Have Found Content on Social Media That Caused Them NOT to Hire a Candidate, According to Recent CareerBuilder Survey. https://press. careerbuilder.com/2018-08-09-More-Than-Half-of-Employers-Have-Found-Content-on-Social-Media-That-Caused-Them-NOT-to-Hire-a-Candidate-According-to-Recent-CareerBuilder-Survey [accessed 2022-07-25]

[9] Turczynski, B. (2022, April 22). 2022 HR Statistics: Job Search, Hiring, Recruiting & Interviews. https:// zety.com/blog/hr-statistics#:~:text=On%20average%2C%20each%20corporate%20job,one%20 will%20get%20the%20job [accessed 2022-07-27]

[18] LinkedIn (no date). https://news.linkedin.com/about-us#Statistics [accessed 2022-07-26]

[19] Career Attraction Team (no date). HOW MANY LINKEDIN CONNECTIONS DO YOU REALLY NEED? https://careerattraction.com/many-linkedin-connections-really-need/ [accessed 2022-07-26]

Chapter 7

[20] Alexis, M. (2021). Marketing on LinkedIn (LinkedIn training video). https://www.LinkedIn.com/learning/marketing-on-LinkedIn-2021 [accessed 2022-07-27]

[21] Kim, L. (2021, November 22). How to Write the Perfect LinkedIn Connection Request? https://www.wordstream.com/blog/ws/2016/01/18/linkedin-connection-requests [accessed 2022-07-27]

[22] Alexis, M. (2021, July 14). 6 Message Templates for LinkedIn Connection Request Success. https://www.linkedin.com/pulse/6-message-templates-linkedin-connection-request-success-/?trackingId=3HW5C78RFxgrYzeTWIJUGw%3D%3D [accessed 2022-07-27]

[23] Bliss, R. (2019, December 19). The Art Of The Comment On LinkedIn. https://www.linkedin.com/pulse/art-comment-linkedin-richard-bliss/ [accessed 2022-07-27]

[24] Morgan, H. (2019, April 10). How To Post Engaging Comments on LinkedIn? https://careersherpa.net/how-to-post-engaging-comments-on-LinkedIn/ [accessed 2022-07-27]

[25] mann-co. (2018, June 19). 6 Types of Comments to Leave on LinkedIn. https://mann-co.com/6-types-comments-leave-LinkedIn [accessed 2022-07-27]

[26] Career Attraction Team (no date). HOW TO USE SMART COMMENTING TO GET NOTICED ON LINKEDIN? https://careerattraction.com/use-smart-commenting-get-noticed-LinkedIn/ [accessed 2022-07-27]

Chapter 8

[27] Indeed Editorial Team (2021, September 15). How To Make a Video Job Application in 6 Steps? https://www.indeed.com/career-advice/interviewing/how-to-make-video-job-application [accessed 2022-07-27]

Chapter 9

[2] CareerBuilder (2019, June 10). THESE 5 SIMPLE MISTAKES COULD BE COSTING YOU THE JOB. https://www.careerbuilder.com/advice/these-5-simple-mistakes-could-be-costing-you-the-job [accessed 2022-07-25]

[28] Indeed Editorial Team (2021, February 27). How to Write a Job Inquiry Letter? (With Examples) https://www.indeed.com/career-advice/finding-a-job/how-to-write-a-job-inquiry-letter [accessed 2022-07-27]

Chapter 10

[29] Indeed Editorial Team (2021, February 23). When Do Employers Call References? Everything You Need To Know to Get the Job. https://www.indeed.com/career-advice/finding-a-job/when-do-employers-call-references [accessed 2022-07-27]

Jellabie's job application samples

履歷範本：描述引以自豪的三項成功經歷

- I led the university debate team to 2 national championships (winning second place both times) because of my skills in presentations, interpersonal communication, analysis, and leadership.

- I won awards for excellent academic performance in high school and college due to my independence, diligence and quick learning ability.

- I achieved a TOEIC score of 790 as a result of my passion for learning languages and cultures as well as years of effort reading English news and watching English movies and TV shows.

履歷範本：個人簡介（**Profile**）

Jellabie Dai

0955-5555

jellabie@school.edu

123 Chung Cheung Road,

New Taipei City

PROFILE

- Led university debate team to 2 national championships
- Strong interpersonal communication, analysis, and leadership skills
- Won awards for excellent academic performance in high school and college
- Responsible, independent, diligent, and a quick learner
- Achieved a 790 TOEIC score with passion for learning languages and cultures

履歷範本：一般通用

Jellabie (Yi-ran) Dai

0955-555-555   jellabie@school.edu

123 Chung Cheung Road, New Taipei City

OBJECTIVE: SALES SPECIALIST

PROFILE
- Led university debate team for 2 years and won 2 national awards
- Enthusiastic leader and team player with superior interpersonal and communication skills
- Creative, analytical thinker and quick learner with well-rounded knowledge in science, engineering, business, sociology, literature, and art
- Able to work independently and take risks; always ready to accept challenges and respond to changes

EDUCATION
- BA, Economics, *Banciao University*, New Taipei City — *2019–2022*
- Leader of university Debate Team; organized training about debate procedures and skills, led the team to 2 national championships — *2020–2021*
- Won award for excellent academic performance — *2020*

Jingmei Girls High School, Taipei — *2016–2019*
- Won award for excellent academic performance — *2018, 2019*

EXPERIENCE
Intern, Epoch Foundation in Taiwan, Taipei — *Mar 2022–present*
- Assisted communication between governmental, academic, and commercial sectors
- Managed cases, received guests, researched/summarized/translated information

Server, Bartissa Coffee Shop, Banciao, New Taipei City — *2020–2022*
- Opened and closed store, handled all sales, built customer relationships

SKILLS & ACHIEVEMENTS
- Languages: Native speaker of Chinese (Mandarin and Taiwanese); fluent in English (TOEIC 790; 2020)

REFERENCES
Mr. Chien-Ming Tsao, Bartissa Store Manager, cmtsao@gmail.com

Dr. Mei-hua Wang, Banciao University Professor of Economics, meihua2233@gmail.com

Jellabie (Yi-ran) Dai

0955-555-555   jellabie@school.edu

123 Chung Cheung Road, New Taipei City

OBJECTIVE: IBMM SALES SPECIALIST

PROFILE

- University graduate with passion for sales and persuasion, and strong interest in selling/promoting information system products
- Superior interpersonal, communication, and presentation skills: Led debate team for 2 years and won 2 national awards
- Goal oriented and an ability to work under pressure
- Aggressive, self-motivated, fast-learning team player who is also able to work independently
- Creative analytical thinker

EDUCATION

Banciao University, New Taipei City   *2019–2022*

Bachelor of Arts, Economics

- Leader of university Debate Team; organized training about debate procedures and skills, led the team to 2 national championships   *2020–2021*
- Developed strong leadership and interpersonal communication skills
- Won award for excellent academic performance

Jingmei Girls High School, Taipei   *2016–2019*

- Won awards for excellent academic performance

EXPERIENCE

Intern, Epoch Foundation in Taiwan, Taipei   *Mar 2022–pres*

- Assisted communication between governmental, academic and commercial sectors
- Managed cases, received guests, researched/summarized/translated information

Server, Bartissa Coffee Shop, Banciao, New Taipei City   *2020–2022*

- Opened and closed store, handled total sales, built customer relationships

SKILLS & ACHIEVEMENTS

- Languages: Native speaker of Chinese (Mandarin and Taiwanese); fluent in English (TOEIC 790; 2020)
- Led university debate team to 2 national competitions (2020–2021)

REFERENCES

Mr. Chien-Ming Tsao, Bartissa Store Manager, cmtsao@gmail.com

Dr. Mei-hua Wang, Banciao University Professor of Economics, meihua2233@gmail.com

LinkedIn 範本：Headline, About, and Experience

Headline
Seeking a job in Sales | Excellent team player with superior interpersonal and communication skills | Led university debate team to 2 national championships

About
I joined the debate team in university because I enjoyed analyzing ideas. Two national championships later, I became fascinated with interpersonal communication and the ability to persuade people. This interest continued when I worked at Bartissa in customer service to develop customer relationships that helped with customer loyalty.

With my experiences as the debate team leader, team player and customer service at Bartissa coffee, I learned how important it is to listen to others and make useful suggestions and contributions. I love working on a team and doing my part to be useful and help the team be successful.

I am now looking for a job in sales to put my strengths and passions to work. In a sales or sales assistant position, I can offer

- Diligence and aggressive learning to understand and promote products
- Passion for working with people on a team and also for building customer relationships
- Strong listening and presentation skills in English and Chinese to build relationships with customers.

If this sounds interesting, please connect with me. I'd love to have the opportunity to learn how I can contribute to your company.

Experience
As debate team leader for 2 years, I developed strong interpersonal communication, presentation, and leadership skills. As leader, my goal was to enter the national debate championships, so I organized frequent training and practice sessions with my teammates and teachers. As a result, we competed in the national championships two years in a row and came in second place both times.

As a barista and server, I improved my customer service skills and learned how to build rapport with customers to encourage them to become loyal customers. I also managed transactions with customers at the cash register and tracked transactions and balance sheets.

自介影片腳本範例

Hi, my name is Jellabie Dai.

I have a degree in Economics and strong interest in business.

I also have a passion for researching, presenting, and collaborating.

I think this started in university when I joined the debate team. Two national championships later, I became fascinated with interpersonal communication and the ability to persuade people.

This interest continued when I worked at Bartissa in customer service. I loved to develop customer relationships and customer loyalty.

I love working on a team and doing my part to be useful and help the team be successful.

I am now looking for a job in sales where I can use my strengths to aggressively research and promote products and to use my communication and presentation skills in English and Chinese to build customer rapport.

If this sounds interesting, please connect with me. I'd love to have the opportunity to learn how I can contribute to your company.

(154 words, about 60 secs)

職缺詢問信範本

Jellabie (Yi-ran) Dai

jellabie@school.edu   0955-555-555   tw.linkedin.com/in/jellabiedai/

As a recent graduate in economics and an ecofriendly tech enthusiast, I am eager to find a position in an innovative and green company. I recently discovered your company on LinkedIn and have read about your products and really admire your creativity and corporate values of reducing waste, reusing materials, and making your products repairable. I am highly motivated and hardworking, and I would love to be part of your sales or customer service team if a position opens.

From my experiences in customer service at a coffee shop, I learned the importance of interpersonal communication skills and I enjoyed making an effort to remember people's names and orders to increase customer loyalty. I developed my research and persuasive presentation skills in university when I was leader of the debate club. We went to the national championships twice and we came in second both times. My degree in economics gives me a solid understanding of business and with my high English proficiency (TOEIC 790), I am ready to start a career in international sales or customer service. I look forward to using my strengths and experiences to contribute to an excellent company like GreenTexx.

I hope we can set up a time to meet to discuss how my qualifications can be a benefit to your company. If you have any questions regarding my skills, please call or email me at the contacts listed at the top of the letter. Thank you so much for reviewing my resume. I look forward to hearing from you.

求職信範本

Jellabie (Yi-ran) Dai

jellabie@school.edu 0955-555-555 tw.linkedin.com/in/jellabiedai/

May 22, 2022
Michael Tan
IBMM
4F, 7 Song-Jen Rd.,
Taipei City, Taiwan, 11044

Dear Mr. Tan,

This letter is to express my interest in the sales Specialist position at IBMM posted on your website. I believe that I am a very competitive candidate for this position thanks to my

- Passion for sales and IT products
- Strong interpersonal and persuasive communication skills, and
- Goal-oriented personality and ability to work under pressure both independently and on a team.

My experience in customer service at a coffee shop taught me how to build customer relationships and create more loyal customers. I made an effort to remember customer names and preferred orders, which allowed me to anticipate their order and ask them about it even before they spoke. I think customers appreciate this personalized service. I also developed strong analytic and communication skills when I was the leader of the debate club in university. I organized several trainings and worked closely with my teammates to prepare for debates and competitions. Through our teamwork and effort, we went to the national championships twice and came in second place both times.

Other key strengths that I possess for success in this position include the following:
- A bachelor's degree in Economics
- An aggressive and learning attitude
- Very good English proficiency (TOEIC 790)
- Strong research skills
- A responsible and detail-oriented personality.

Please see my attached resume for additional information on my qualifications and experience.

Thank you for your time and consideration. I look forward to speaking with you about this employment opportunity. I can be reached anytime at the contact information above.

Sincerely,
Jellabie (Yi-ran) Dai

jellabie@school.edu
0955-555-555
123 Chung Cheung Road, New Taipei City

推薦信範本：來自雇主

Chien-Ming Tsao
Store Manager
Bartissa Coffee
02-2340-6789
cmtsao@gmail.com
October 5, 2022

To whom it may concern,

I confirm that Jellabie Dai was employed as a server and barista with this store from June 2020 to September 2022. Her job as server and barista included the following responsibilities

- **Greet customers when entering or leaving the store**
- **Serve customers with a pleasant attitude**
- **Build rapport with customers with the aim of making them become loyal return customers**
- **Manage transactions with customers using cash register**
- **Resolve customer complaints**
- **Track transactions on balance sheets and report any discrepancies**
- **Maintain clean and tidy checkout areas.**

Jellabie has excellent interpersonal skills and was always able to build rapport with clients and deliver cheerful and enthusiastic service. She is quick-thinking and was good at handling customer complaints. She was detail-oriented and very careful tracking cashier transactions, which means meant she rarely had any discrepancies on her balance sheets.

Staff come and go in the coffee shop business, but I was sad to see Jellabie leave. I know that many of our customers enjoyed her warm service and miss her too, so I would happily re-employ Jellabie if she ever came back. Jellabie's work performance and attitude always surpassed expectations and I have no doubt she would contribute greatly to any company and team in roles like customer service or sales where excellent people skills are required.

Please feel free to let me know if I can be of any further assistance.

Yours sincerely,
Chien-Ming Tsao

Answers to Exercises

P.41

Answers ➡ 1. a　2. a　3. b　4. a　5. a

1. 她在高中時期不需要去補習班是**由於**她自律的學習習慣。
2. 很多人未在履歷上強調自己的優勢，**所以**他們得不到工作面試機會。
3. 他無法晉升為國際銷售經理**歸咎於**他那 650 分的多益低分。
4. **由於**那些錯別字和打字失誤，招募人員把她的履歷扔進了垃圾桶。
5. **因為**她有很強的協作和領導能力，她的銷售團隊的業績總是超越目標。

P.51

Answers ➡ 1. a　2. d　3. b　4. c、d　5. b　6. c

1. 為什麼沒有句子（主詞＋動詞）？
   a. 閱讀起來更快更方便　b. 寫作者偷懶
2. 條列項目中可看到哪些資訊？
   a. 技巧和能力　b. 經驗　c. 個性　**d. 以上皆是**
3. 條列式文法的三種類型為下列何者：
   a. (1) 主詞＋動詞　(2) 動詞過去式　(3) 形容詞＋名詞
   b. (1) 動詞過去式　(2) 形容詞＋名詞　(3) Able（能夠）to＋動詞原形
4. Peter 使用了哪兩種文法類型來描述技巧和能力？
   a. 主詞＋動詞　b. 動詞過去式　**c. 形容詞＋名詞**　**d. Able（能夠）to＋動詞原形**
5. Peter 使用了什麼文法來描述工作經驗？
   a. 主詞＋動詞　**b. 動詞過去式**　c. 形容詞＋名詞　d. Able（能夠）to＋動詞原形
6. Peter 使用了什麼文法來描述個性？
   a. 主詞＋動詞　b. 動詞過去式　**c. 形容詞（或形容詞＋名詞）**　d. Able（能夠）to＋動詞原形

P.54

Answers ➡ 1. c　2. e　3. a　4. b　5. f　6. d

- 大學畢業並擁有國際貿易證照
- 對商業管理與分析有**強烈的興趣**
- 能夠**服務客戶與解決**他們的問題
- 積極進取、**熱情**、學習快速，在壓力下工作表現良好的團隊合作者
- 具**流利的**商務電郵通訊和**簡報**能力

陳彼得

台灣桃園大學街 123 號   0934 987 654   peterchen@gmail.com

1. 應徵職務
製藥公司的行銷助理職位

2. 個人簡介
- 擁有理學學士學位的高中科學家教老師
- 曾為學生迎新活動設計宣傳海報和影片
- 能夠使用 Photoshop 編輯照片，使用 Adobe Premier 製作社群媒體影片，以及使用 StreamYard 做直播活動
- 曾任學生迎新活動總召和小隊長訓練員
- 主動積極的團隊領導者和團隊合作者，具出色的溝通技巧

3. 教育背景
桃園市桃園大學   *2015–2019*
理學學士，生物學

4. 工作經驗
桃園大學學生住宿顧問   *2018 年 3 月至今*
- 目前為住宿學生提供學術和個人諮詢
- 曾參與多樣化的意識和領導力訓練

5. 志工經驗
桃園市立中學   *2016 年至今*
- 曾輔導 10 ～ 11 年級學生科學和數學，協助徬徨的城市學生制定了學習計畫
- 曾指導迎新活動（3 年）   *2015 年、2016 年、2017 年 8 月*
- 曾獲邀參加同儕領導、團隊建立和多元文化責任感工作坊；負責訓練小隊長
- 曾任迎新活動總召並負責宣傳
- 曾使用 Photoshop 設計傳單和海報

6. 技能與成就
諳 Adobe Premier 和 Da Vinci Resolve 影片編輯、Photoshop
擁有 MS Excel 和 PowerPoint 證照（精通）
英語能力佳（多益 820 分）

7. 推薦人
李奇鳴教授（台中大學生物系），Licc@ut.edu.tw

P.69

Answers ⬇

1. Jellabie 在尋找什麼工作？
   Sales specialist（業務專員）

2. 她是否能夠和別人好好共事？你如何得知？
   是。從 **Yes. "... team player with superior interpersonal and communication skills"** 這句話得知。

3. 她會成為公司的好員工嗎？
   會。由 **"Enthusiastic ... team player with superior interpersonal and communication skills"; "quick learner", "Able to work independently and take risks; always ready to accept challenges and respond to changes"** 可知，她擁有許多理想新進員工特質。

4. 她是個善於思考的人嗎？
   是。由 **"Creative, analytical thinker and quick learner"** 可知。

5. 她是否可能擅長克服困難？你如何得知？
   是。從 **"Able to work independently and take risks; always ready to accept challenges and respond to changes"** 這句話得知。

P.83

Answers ➡ 答案皆為 NO。

1. 是否有足夠的空白以便掃描？
2. 名字是否足夠清楚？
3. 是否提到了應徵職務？
4. 聯絡方式是否足夠簡潔？
5. 是否包含個人簡介部分？
6. 是否有清晰可見的日期？
7. 是否有項目符號可加快閱讀速度？
8. 是否有具體的細節和數據？

K 陳

地址：111 台灣台北市士林區大東路 51 號 2F
電話：0975299869　電子郵件：kenny83@gmail.com

教育和培訓
銘傳大學，台北，台灣
金融學系學士
重點科目：財務報表分析、投資、金融市場、風險管理、國際金融管理
- 曾成功分析「全球能源市場於國際經濟暨台灣經濟之影響」並做出專題簡報
- 對企業管理和分析有濃厚的興趣
- 能夠使用電腦應用程式進行研究
- 曾和一個團隊合作，並於北部金融盃排球比賽中獲勝

工作經驗
國泰世華商業銀行，台北

實習生，銀行櫃員
- 作為銀行櫃員實習生表現良好
- 曾提供優質服務以建立良好關係並解決問題
- 積極進取、充滿熱忱、學習能力強，能夠獨立工作以學習標準作業流程

銘傳大學，台北
英語導師
- 曾輔導並增強學生的英語技能
- 曾設計一份調查問卷，並和學生一起成功採訪了士林夜市的遊客

語言能力
國語、台語、英語

P.85

Answers ➜ 答案皆為正確無誤。

1. 更容易掃描
2. 提供更多資訊
3. 最重要的訊息置於前 1/3
4. 有更多的數據和具說服力的細節

肯尼 TJ 陳

kenny83@gmail.com   0975299869
111 台灣台北市士林區大東路 51 號 2F

應徵職務：摩根大通分析師

個人簡介
- 大學畢業並擁有國際貿易證照
- 對企業管理和分析有濃厚的興趣
- 能夠有效地服務客戶並解決他們的問題
- 積極進取、熱情、學習能力強，具團隊合作精神，在壓力下工作表現良好
- 商務英語流利，善口語溝通與簡報

教育和培訓
TAITRA 外貿協會培訓中心，台北，台灣   1/2022–6/2022
學士後國際貿易專班（600 多個小時）
重點科目：財務報表分析、經濟學、會計學、談判、商務英語、簡報
- 曾研究分析遊戲產業市場及相關公司財務報表
- 培養了強大的英語商務簡報與溝通技巧

銘傳大學，台北，台灣   2018–2021
金融學系學士
重點科目：財務報表分析、投資、金融市場、風險管理、國際金融管理

- 曾分析「全球能源市場於國際經濟暨台灣經濟之影響」並做出成功的專題簡報
- 對企業管理和分析有濃厚的興趣
- 能夠利用 SAS、Excel 和其他應用程式進行研究

活動
- 曾與部門團隊合作，在金融盃排球比賽中奪冠
- 曾參加 IEFA（國際經濟、金融暨會計研討會）和 CSBF（兩岸金融研討會）

工作經驗
國泰世華商業銀行，台北　　　　　　　　　　　　　　　　　　3/2021–6/2021
實習生，銀行櫃員
- 曾完成 500 小時的實習後擔任銀行櫃員
- 曾提供優質服務以建立良好關係並解決問題
- 積極進取、熱情、學習能力強，能夠獨立工作以學習標準作業流程

銘傳大學，台北　　　　　　　　　　　　　　　　　　　　　　2018–2020
英語導師
- 曾輔導並增強學生的英語技能
- 曾設計一份遊客調查問卷，並和學生一起在士林夜市採訪了 45 名遊客以練習英語

語言能力
國語、台語、英語（TOEIC 770）

P.87
Answers ➡ 1. h　　2. b　　3. e　　4. j　　5. f　　6. k　　7. a　　8. d　　9. g　　10. i　　11. c

安東尼・黃
tw.linkedin.com/in/antwong/　　0975666129　　awong@gmail.com
台灣屏東廣德巷 80 弄 10-5 號

應徵職務：EXPEDIUM 行銷助理

資歷摘要

- 大學畢業並擁有國際貿易證照
- 學習能力強、注重細節與團隊合作精神，在壓力下工作表現良好
- 具優異的商務簡報、談判與會議英語能力
- **1.　精通　** 繪圖程式和線上旅遊服務
- 對推廣 Expedium 產品有濃厚的興趣，且對旅行充滿熱情；曾到訪超過 **2.　35 個國家　**

教育和培訓

TAITRA 外貿協會培訓中心，台北，台灣　　　　　　　　　　　　　　2018
擁有學士後國際貿易證照
- 重點科目：商務談判、簡報、行銷、社群銷售、影片編輯、資訊圖表設計、LinkedIn 文案

國立中山大學，高雄，台灣　　　　　　　　　　　　　　　　　　2013–2017
外國語文學系學士

累計 GPA：**3. _____3.96_____**

- 榮譽：國立中山大學傑出學生獎　　　　　　　　　　2014、2015

志工經歷和活動
_____

交換學生　　　　　　　　　　　　　　　2016 年 9 月至 2017 年 8 月
紐倫堡應用技術大學，德國

- 曾成功籌畫、發起及行銷台灣之夜活動，將台灣文化、美食和音樂推廣給超過 **4. _____60 名參加者_____**
- 在新環境中迅速成長並積極學習德語
- 熟悉旅遊 app 和網站，**5. _____例如 Expedium、Airbnb、Booking.com 等_____**
- 對旅行和旅遊業產生了濃厚的興趣

平面藝術總監　　　　　　　　　　　　　　　　　　2014–2016
DFLL 學生會，高雄，台灣

- 曾監督 **6. _____4 名美編_____** 的小組
- 曾與團隊成員和其他部門的學生合作
- 曾高效成功地組織 **7. _____10 個活動_____**，包括 100 多人的聯合聖誕派對和 **8. _____80 多位高中生_____** 的英語營
- 曾創建 Facebook 粉絲專頁並設計了 **9. _____邀請函、海報、衣服和道具_____** 以宣傳活動

技巧與能力
_____

Canva、Adobe Illustrator、Photoshop—**10. _____進階的_____** 熟練程度
國語—母語，英語—接近母語的熟練程度（**11. _____TOEIC 980_____**；CEFR C2），德語—中級（德國紐倫堡一年交換生），韓語—中級

P.105
Answers
Management
Ad #1
oversee large, complex projects
directing and evaluating project vision and strategy
project completion and team management
managing client communication, allocating resources
maintaining team productivity and morale in high-pressure situations
2–4 years of managerial experience
ability to manage multidisciplinary projects with 10+ people
Ad #2
Manage the Professional Services team to execute on and complete the deliverables called out in the Statement of Work
Demonstrated management, leadership, communication, motivational and influencing skills
proven record of managing software/hardware system integration projects/programs
feel comfortable in a leadership role in a matrix management environment

Communication
Ad #2
Work with the prospective professional services customer to define the scope of work and provide it to the customer for approval
Manage the client relationship
able to effectively communicate verbally and written with individual contributors, management, executive staff, as well as with the customer

Technical
Ad #1
understand the business environment and work product
evaluate technical specifications
defining and driving project deliverables
facilitating development and operations project teams
defining, creating, and maintaining a project plan
IT expertise
Ad #2
Identify the external resources to develop a detailed Statement of Work
thorough understanding of the software development process

Other
Ad #1
Bachelor's degree in management, engineering, computer science, business or similar field
4+ years in professional services or consulting

廣告 1：高級 IT 專案經理	廣告 2：專案經理
本職務必須能夠監督大型、複雜的專案，控管並理解業務環境與產品，以及評估技術規格。 主要職責包括指導和評估專案願景和策略，對專案完成與團隊管理負責，定義和推動專案可交付成果，以及協助開發與維護團隊。 本職務將負責定義、創建和維運專案計畫，管理日常客戶溝通，分配資源，以及在高壓情況下維持團隊生產力和士氣。 意者須具 IT 專業知識，並擁有管理、工程、電腦、商業或類似領域的學士學位，4 年以上的專業服務或諮詢工作資歷，2～4 年的管理經驗，以及管理 10 人以上多重領域專案的能力。	本公司專業服務團隊開放一個專案經理的職缺。 職責： • 與潛在的專業服務客戶一起定義工作範圍，並將之提供給客戶批准。 • 判定具必要技能的外部及內部資源，以制定詳細的工作說明書。 • 管理專業服務團隊以執行並完成工作說明書中列出的可交付成果。管理客戶關係。 條件： • 具管理、領導、溝通、激勵和影響力的實務能力。 • 必須對軟體開發程序有透徹的了解，從系統（軟硬體）的角度尤佳。 • 必須有管理軟硬體系統整合專案的實務紀錄。 • 習慣於矩陣式管理環境中擔任領導角色。 • 必須能夠和個人貢獻者、管理階層、執行人員以及客戶進行有效的口頭與書面溝通。 • 致力於對品質的承諾。 • 具診斷核心問題和協調能力的問題解決者。

P.119

Answers ⬇

1. c（有較多具體的細節，使用較簡短的片語）

2. a（有較多資訊、細節和成就）

3. c（包含有趣的細節和令人難忘的金句：「致力於用藝術和科技提升我們的社會」）

1. 原本的寫法：

我透過數據分析、視覺輔助工具和資訊圖表幫助公司以創新的方式進行網路行銷。我能夠幫助公司擴大市場。

a. 幫助公司做網路行銷｜能夠分析數據並製作視覺輔助工具和資訊圖表。

b. 具數據分析和數據視覺化技能的網路行銷專員。

c. 創新的數位行銷專員｜Google 和 Facebook 分析｜使用 R 語言進行數據視覺化

2. 原本的寫法：

我是一個熱情且有愛心的人，正尋求改變的機會。同時我做事也非常有條理和注重細節，盡力使一切都變得更好。

a. 對市場行銷和公關充滿熱情｜曾任 smart pitch 獲勝影片的主講人｜曾代表大學參加模擬聯合國｜強大的組織能力｜注重細節

b. 熱情且有愛心的人，正尋求公關界有所變化的工作機會｜強大的組織能力｜注重細節的個性

c. 對市場行銷和公關充滿熱情｜強大的組織能力｜注重細節

3. 原本的寫法：

數位行銷專員｜事業發展專家｜表演藝術家

a. 尋求事業發展界的工作機會｜用藝術和科技做出改變｜數位行銷專員｜表演藝術家

b. 事業發展專家｜對藝術和科技充滿熱情｜數位行銷專員｜表演藝術家

c. 有抱負的事業發展專家｜致力於用藝術和科技提升我們的社會｜數位行銷專員｜舞者｜編舞家

P.133

Answers ⬇

1. b [n and n]　　**2. a [v-ed, v-ed, and v-ed]**　　**3. a [adj and adj]**　　**4. a [V-O or V-O]**

5. c lacks parallelism; d has good parallelism

6. I make it my mission to get to know my clients, to understand their needs, and to provide top-notch service.

1. 下列何者為並列句？

a. 要精通網站設計，應擅長 JavaScript 並知道如何使用 SEO。

b. 要精通網站設計，應擅長 JavaScript 和 SEO。

2. 下列何者為並列句？

a. 所有產品都必須經過測試、批准和仔細包裝。

b. 所有產品都必須經過測試、批准，而且我們也應仔細包裝它們。

3. 下列何者為並列句？

a. 這個 app 不僅昂貴且不可靠。

b. 這個 app 不僅昂貴，而且它也不可靠。

4. 下列何者為並列句？
   a. 你要不就主持會議，要不就做會議紀錄。
   b. 你可以主持會議或者做會議紀錄。
5. 以下段落中哪個句子缺乏平行結構？（c）哪個句子有好的平行結構？（d）
   a. Amelia Earhart 曾經說過：「一次善舉，四面八方生根發芽，長出新樹。」
   b. 作為一間小型乾洗和裁縫店的老闆，我信奉這句格言。
   c. 我將認識客戶、了解他們的需求，以及提供一流的服務視為自己的任務。
   d. 無論是清洗最喜愛的服裝、剪裁婚紗，還是在背包上縫製客訂布章，我都以極快速的時間内提供最佳
   服務而感到自豪，同時始終以善為宗旨。
   e. 當小生意未開店營業時，你會發現我總是和丈夫及兩個可愛的孩子一起在探索世界。
6. 請用平行結構改寫下面這個句子。 Hint 使用三個並列的不定詞＋受詞（to+V-O）片語。
   I make it my mission to get to know my clients, to understand their needs, and to provide top-
   notch service.

P.141
Answers ➤ 1. a   2. a   3. c   4. b   5. d
a. 現在簡單式   b. 現在進行式   c. 過去式   d. 現在完成式   e. 未來式

P.143
Answers ➤ 1. a   2. b   3. b   4. b   5. a   6. b   7. a   8. a   9. b   10. b   11. a   12. a
 1. 從開始工作以來，他就一直是這家公司的員工。
 2. 他在會議上介紹的行銷點子並不是很吸引人。
 3. 我們的業務正在迅速擴張，我們正在招募許多新人。
 4. 2009 年到 2012 年 Richardson 先生曾在該公司工作三年。
 5. 預計幾天後抵達的訪客需要我們幫忙尋找一家好的飯店。
 6. 我已閱讀您的申請並將其發送給經理審核。
 7. 我們的會議太多以至於沒有足夠的時間專注於我們的主要工作任務。
    Note 在相當少的情況下 b 也可以是正確的。
 8. 上週的資格考試很簡單。（不像）前兩次的不及格率為 30%。
 9. 明天下午我需要帶我女兒去看醫生，所以我沒辦法出席會議。
10. John 曾四次獲得年度員工獎。
11. 當我在唸大學時，我創辦了自己的公司。
12. 在我以前的工作中，我帶領了一個由六名銷售人員組成的團隊。

P.154

Answers ➡ **[A]** a. 123　　b. 3　　c. 4　　d. 5

　　　　　　 [B] a. 123　　b. 3　　c. 3　　d. 4　　e. 5

[A]　嗨 Gyllis，你的文章中有很多關於 ELT 銷售技巧的好建議。非常感謝你這篇富教育性的文章，我學到了很多東西。我也在這個產業，希望我們可以建立關係。祝週末愉快，Antony

[B]　Jaime 您好，我剛剛完成了您在 LinkedIn 上的精彩課程！您真是一位了不起的演講者，我光是從觀察您如何組織和呈現觀點中就獲益良多。您給的建議很棒，讓我做了很多筆記，甚至激發了更多的靈感 :) 我很希望與您建立關係，以便將來我可以向您學習更多。祝您有愉快的一天！– Pete

P.159

Answers ➡ **[A]** 1. b　　2. c　　3. f　　4. d　　5. e　　6. a

　　　　　　 [B] 1. c　　2. e　　3. a　　4. d　　5. b　　6. f

[A]　嗨，Fabrize！

　　很高興在上週的馬德里 NLP 會議上見到你。關於你講解你如何利用機器學習來改善你的遊戲化行銷，我覺得十分感興趣。希望我們能聯繫上。我期待著關注你的工作，同時獲得更多的學習！

　　祝好，

　　Alphie

[B]　Haruki 您好，

　　我注意到您是大阪地區的招募人員。我想聯繫您以討論是否有合作的可能性。我是一名擁有 15 年資歷的自由文案寫手，現正尋找新的機會。我想知道我是否適合您目前任何的職缺。

　　希望能夠盡快與您聊聊，

　　Ruru

P.166

Answers ➡ 1. f　　2. c　　3. e　　4. d　　5. a　　6. b

1. 我是否可以留下一個資源的連結？我認為它與主題相關，可以為您的讀者增加價值。

2. @Arvind，我注意到 En-Tai 說了一些與你的問題有關的事情…… @En-Tai，你能回答 @Arvind 關於……的問題嗎？

3. 嗨，Jon。如果你不介意，或許我可以幫助回答你的問題。……

4. 這篇文章太棒了，Arvind。我想知道你是否考慮過把 ＿＿＿＿＿＿ 納入，因為它似乎與目前的主題相關。

5. 你提到了 ＿＿＿＿＿＿。這是一個很好的觀點，而我知道它非常正確，因為我記得我曾碰過 ＿＿＿＿＿＿ 的實例。

6. 我認為你的貼文很有趣且深具洞見。我要分享到我的動態消息。

P.182

修改後的版本是 B。它增加了更多的細節，將句子和想法串聯得更流暢，並且聽起來更口語化。

版本 A	版本 B
我的名字是婕拉比‧戴。	嗨，我的名字是婕拉比‧戴。
我擁有經濟學學位，因此我對商業產生了興趣。	我擁有經濟學學位，並且對商業有濃厚的興趣。
我喜歡做研究並發表，以及與人合作。	我也熱衷於研究、發表和合作。
大學時，我加入了辯論隊，我們闖進了兩次全國錦標賽。	我想是從大學期間我加入辯論隊開始的吧。兩次全國錦標賽之後，我開始著迷於人際溝通和說服他人的能力。
我開始對人際溝通與說服他人的能力感興趣。	
我曾在 Bartissa 工作，擔任服務生和咖啡師為顧客提供服務。我也是一名收銀員，負責追蹤銷售與現金收支平衡。	當我在 Bartissa 從事客服工作時，這個興趣仍然持續著。我熱愛與顧客打好關係以發展顧客忠誠度。
我喜歡在團隊中工作，並盡我所能幫助團隊成功。	我喜歡在團隊中工作，並盡我所能幫助團隊成功。
現正尋找一份銷售工作，讓我可以利用自己的強項積極研究和推廣產品，並善用我優異的英語聽力和表達能力（多益 790 分）以及中文能力來與顧客建立融洽關係。	我現在正在尋找一份銷售工作，讓我可以利用自己的強項積極研究和推廣產品，以及善用我的中英文溝通和表達技巧來與顧客建立融洽關係。
謝謝您。	看到這裡如果你對我感到有興趣，請與我聯繫。我很希望有機會學習如何為貴公司貢獻一份心力。

P.187

1. **Which** 　2. **But**（但是）　3. **Also/and**（而且）　4. **Therefore**（所以）
5. **During my university studies**（在我大學就讀期間）　6. **Chance**（機會）
7. **Teamwork**（團隊合作）　8. **Desire**（強烈希望）　9. **Learn more about**（學習更多）
10. **Participate in**（參與）　11. **Further enhance**（進一步提升）　12. **Like**（像是）

Tip 左欄是正式的書面英文，通常較長且較不常用；右欄是非正式的口語英文，通常較短且使用頻率較高。

Answers ⊕

1. a) Ecofriendly tech enthusiast

b) Discovered company on LinkedIn – admires products and corporate values

2. 以上皆是

3. sales or customer service

4. (3, 1, 5, 2, 4)

5. b

1. Jellabie 與該公司的兩個連結是什麼？

(a) 環保科技愛好者

(b) 在 LinkedIn 上搜尋到該公司──欣賞其產品和企業價值

2. 她具備哪些資格？在相關敘述前打勾。

以上皆是（經濟系畢業生、環保科技愛好者、個性主動積極、工作勤奮、欲從事客服或業務工作）

3. 她對什麼職位感興趣？

業務或客服

4. 她列出的五個技能的順序是什麼？在技能敘述前寫上數字。

3 表達技巧

1 提升客服品質和顧客忠誠度的人際溝通技巧

5 英語能力

2 研究能力

4 經濟學和商業知識

5. 為什麼 Jellabie 要將技能依序列出？

a. 沒有理由

b. 最重要的技能優先列出

c. 最重要的技能壓軸列出

P.206

Answers ➡ **Paragraph 1: (3,2,1)**   **Paragraph 2: (2,1,4,3)**   **Paragraph 3: (2,1,3)**

> Dear Mr. Chow,
>
> With a degree in Foreign Languages and Literature and certificate in International Trade and passion for travel, I am eager to find a position in the travel industry. I have used your service several times on my travels in Europe and admire your first-class technology and marketing. I would love to be part of your team in either sales, marketing or customer service.
>
> I have a TOEIC score of 980 out of 990, which is considered nativelike, or C2 according to the CEFR. During my Bachelor's Degree in Foreign Languages and Literature, I was then an exchange student in Germany where I improved my German (Intermediate, CEFR A2-B1) and traveled to 15 countries in Europe. These travel experiences convinced me to choose a

career in the tourism industry. To improve my business knowledge and communication skills, I enrolled in a 6-month intensive Post-bachelor's program in International Trade where I completed several marketing projects, sales presentations and negotiations. In this program, I was able to use my strong interpersonal skills and a detail-oriented personality as well as skills in image and video editing that I developed in college.

I hope we can set up a time to meet to discuss how my qualifications can contribute to your company. If you have any questions regarding my skills, please call or email me at the contact information at the top of the letter. Thank you for your time to review my resume. I look forward to hearing from you.

Sincerely,
Anthony Wong

周先生您好：

擁有外國語言文學學位和國際貿易證照，以及對旅行的熱情，我熱切希望於旅遊業覓得一職。我在歐洲旅行時曾多次使用貴公司的服務，相當欣賞您們一流的科技和行銷。我很想成為貴團隊的一員，無論是業務、行銷或客服職位。

我的多益成績是 980 分（滿分 990 分），這是被認定為母語等級或根據 CEFR 的 C2 程度。在攻讀外國語言文學士學位期間，我曾經去德國當交換學生，在那裡我提升了我的德語（中級，CEFR A2-B1），並遊歷了歐洲的 15 個國家。這些旅行經歷讓我決定選擇旅遊業開創職涯。為加強商業知識和溝通技巧，我曾參加為期六個月的國際貿易學士後密集專班，並完成了幾個行銷專案、業務簡報和談判演練。在此專班，我得以發揮我強大的人際溝通能力和注重細節的個性，並運用我在大學培養的圖像與影片編輯技能。

希望我們可以安排時間會面討論我的能力如何為貴公司增色。若您對我的技能有任何疑問，請透過信件頂部的聯繫資訊來電或發電子郵件。感謝您撥冗審閱我的履歷。靜候佳音。

誠摯地
安東尼・黃

Dear Ms. Chan,

This letter is to express my strong interest in the Market Associate position at Expedium posted on the website "Indeed." I believe that I am a very competitive candidate for this position thanks to my

- Excellent proficiency in English
- Great passion for travel, and
- Business studies and experiences.

After years of studying English by myself and in school and completing my bachelor's degree in foreign languages and literature, I received a TOEIC score of 980 out of 990, which is considered native-like ability, or C2 according to the CEFR. I was an exchange student in Germany for one year, and I traveled to 15 countries in Europe during my free time and developed a strong interest in travelling and the tourism industry. After I returned to Taiwan, I decided to improve my business knowledge and business communication skills, so I enrolled in the six-month intensive Post-bachelor's Program in International Trade from the Taiwan External Trade Development Council's Institute of International Trade. This increased my knowledge of international trade processes and key terms and concepts, and also gave me the chance to undertake marketing projects, sales presentations, and negotiations.

Other key strengths that I possess for success in this position include the following:

- Strong interpersonal skills and adaptability, and a detail-oriented personality
- Demonstrated organization and time management skills in launching Taiwanese Evening, an event that promoted Taiwanese culture, food, and music
- Successful experience leading my university department's graphic arts team.

Please see my attached resume for additional information on my qualifications and experience.

Thank you for your time and consideration. I look forward to speaking with you about this employment opportunity. I can be reached anytime via the contact information above.

Sincerely,
Anthony Wong

敬愛的詹女士：

此信是為了表達我對 "Indeed" 網站上發布的 Expedium 行銷助理一職的強烈興趣。我相信針對此職位我是一個極具競爭力的候選人，這要歸功於我：

- 優異的英語能力
- 對旅行的熱情
- 企業相關的學經驗

經過自學和在學校修習了多年英語，並完成了外國語文學系學士學位後，我考取了 980 分的多益成績（滿分 990 分），這是被認定為母語等級或根據 CEFR 的 C2 程度。我曾經在德國做了一年的交換學生，並於閒暇時間遊歷了歐洲 15 個國家，因而對旅行和旅遊業產生了濃厚的興趣。回到台灣後，我決定提升自己的商業知識和商務溝通能力，於是報名參加了外貿協會培訓中心為期六個月的國際貿易學士後密集專班，這增加了我對國際貿易流程和關鍵術語與概念的了解，也讓我有機會實作行銷專案、業務簡報和談判演練。

讓我能夠勝任此職位的其他強項包括：

- 強大的人際溝通能力、適應能力和注重細節的個性
- 在發起推廣台灣文化、美食和音樂的「台灣之夜」活動中表現出的組織和時間管理能力
- 領導大學系上平面藝術團隊的成功經驗

關於我的資格與工作經驗，欲知更多資訊，請參閱隨附履歷。

感謝您的時間和考慮。期待與您討論此工作機會。歡迎透過上面的聯繫資訊隨時聯絡我。

安東尼・黃
敬上

P.221

Answers ➲ 1. d   2. a   3. b   4. c

1. 感謝錄取，但予以婉拒

寄件者：awong@gmail.com
收件者：expedium@travelservices.com
日　期：23.02.2022
主　旨：Anthony Wong 回覆工作機會

詹女士您好：

謝謝您〔今早〕就〔Expedium〕的〔行銷專員〕職位一事〔來電〕。

我衷心感謝您提供我在〔Expedium〕工作的機會。

可惜的是，我無法接受此職位，因為我〔兩天前已決定在另一家公司任職，因為該職務與我目前的職涯目標似乎十分吻合。〕這對我來說是一個艱難的決定，希望您能諒解。

再次非常感謝您錄取我。非常抱歉我目前無法接受貴公司的青睞。然而，假如情況有變，我一定會再次與您聯繫。

祝您順利找到該職位的最佳候選人。

安東尼·黃
敬上

2. 感謝面試機會

寄件者：awong@gmail.com
收件者：expedium@travelservices.com
日　期：23.02.2022
主　旨：Anthony Wong 感謝您昨日的寶貴時間

詹女士您好：

我是為了〔昨天〕與您就〔行銷專員〕一職所進行的面試來信。

與您談論此職位非常愉快。這份工作似乎與我的技能和興趣〔十分匹配〕。您描述的〔協作團隊及有趣、快速變化和具挑戰性的文化〕讓我更加確認了我想與您共事的願望。

除了熱情之外，我還將帶來〔優異的商務英語溝通能力、積極主動的態度、強大的組織和時間管理能力〕。

非常感謝您花時間與我面談。希望有機會在您旗下工作，靜候佳音。

安東尼·黃
敬上

3. 未獲錄取

寄件者：awong@gmail.com
收件者：expedium@travelservices.com
日　期：23.02.2022
主　旨：Anthony Wong 感謝您的寶貴時間

詹女士您好：

謝謝您〔今早〕就〔Expedium〕的〔行銷專員〕職位一事〔來電〕。

得知我沒有得到這份工作，我感到十分失望，但我還是要對面試過程中貴公司向我展示的專業精神表達謝意。

我想重申我對在〔Expedium〕工作的興趣，如果未來該職位開缺或有類似職缺，希望能將我列入考慮。

再次感謝您撥冗與我面談。

安東尼 · 黃
敬上

4. 感謝錄取，願接受該工作機會

寄件者：awong@gmail.com
收件者：expedium@travelservices.com
日　期：23.02.2022
主　旨：Anthony Wong 接受工作機會

詹女士您好：

謝謝您〔昨天〕就〔Expedium〕的〔行銷專員〕職位一事〔來電〕。

正如電話中我們所討論的，我很高興接受此職務，我想再次感謝您給我這個機會。我渴望為公司做出一番積極的貢獻，並與〔Expedium〕團隊的每個人一起打拚。

依照約定，我的起薪是〔NTD 35, 000〕，含〔勞健保、第一年為期三週的特休，以及每年休閒旅費報銷額度（$250–$750 美元，視任期而定）〕。

再次感謝您的青睞，期待自〔20XX 年 7 月 1 日〕起在您旗下工作。如果在此之前，您需要我提供任何其他資訊或書面資料，請不吝告知。

安東尼 · 黃
敬上

Answers ➡ **Example 2**

我相信 Manuel 會欣賞右欄的範本，因為 Peter 具體提出了針對其於銷售和談判方面的課堂表現，以及目前正在應徵的業務工作此二部分請他提供評語的建議。

範本 1	範本 2
親愛的 Manuel：	親愛的 Manuel：
您是一位傑出的教師，也是我遇到過的最好的指導者之一。 您能否幫我寫一份推薦信，描述我在您的課程中的優點？ 非常感謝您的推薦以驗證我的技能和經驗。 Peter 敬上	您是一位傑出的教師，也是我遇到過的最好的指導者之一。您的行銷課程與您所扮演的角色，確實幫助我強化了信心和從事銷售業的準備。 我目前正在向 Dell、Asus 和 Razer 等 IT 公司應徵業務職位。您能否幫我寫一份推薦信，描述從您的角度見證的我的銷售和談判能力，以及我在課堂上的整體表現？ 非常感謝您的推薦以驗證我的技能和經驗。 Peter 敬上

P.233

Answers ➡ 1. a, b   2. a, c   3. a, b, c   4. a, b, c   5. a, b, c   6. a, c

a. 堅定而有說服力 b. 推薦人知道的具體細節 c. 與 Peter 正應徵之工作有關

Notes

Notes

Notes

國家圖書館出版品預行編目（CIP）資料

數位英文履歷寫作指南：連結社群創新自我行銷力 /
　Nigel P. Daly作；李筱汝譯. -- 初版. -- 臺北市：波斯納
出版有限公司, 2023. 01
　　面；　公分
　ISBN 978-626-96356-9-6（平裝）

1. CST：英語　2. CST：履歷表　3. CST：寫作法

805.179　　　　　　　　　　　　　　　111017543

數位英文履歷寫作指南：
連結社群創新自我行銷力

作　　　者 / Nigel P. Daly
譯　　　者 / 李筱汝
執行編輯 / 游玉旻

出　　　版 / 波斯納出版有限公司
地　　　址 / 100 台北市館前路 26 號 6 樓
電　　　話 / (02) 2314-2525
傳　　　真 / (02) 2312-3535
客服專線 / (02) 2314-3535
客服信箱 / btservice@betamedia.com.tw
郵撥帳號 / 19493777
帳戶名稱 / 波斯納出版有限公司

總 經 銷 / 時報文化出版企業股份有限公司
地　　　址 / 桃園市龜山區萬壽路二段 351 號
電　　　話 / (02) 2306-6842

出版日期 / 2023 年 1 月初版一刷
定　　　價 / 420 元
I S B N / 978-626-96356-9-6

貝塔網址：www.betamedia.com.tw

喚醒你的英文語感！

Get a Feel for English !

喚醒你的英文語感 !

Get a Feel for English !